THE
BILLIONAIRES
THE
STEPBROTHERS

THE BILLIONAIRES THE STEPBROTHERS

CALISTA FOX

ST. MARTIN'S GRIFFIN

NEW YORK

THE BILLIONAIRES: THE STEPBROTHERS. Copyright © 2017 by Calista Fox. All rights reserved. Printed in the United States of America. For information, address St. Martin's Press, 175 Fifth Avenue, New York, N.Y. 10010.

www.stmartins.com

Designed by Omar Chapa

The Library of Congress Cataloging-in-Publication Data is available upon request.

ISBN 978-1-250-09644-9 (trade paperback)
ISBN 978-1-250-09645-6 (ebook)

Our books may be purchased in bulk for promotional, educational, or business use. Please contact your local bookseller or the Macmillan Corporate and Premium Sales Department at 1-800-221-7945, extension 5442, or by email at MacmillanSpecialMarkets@macmillan.com.

First Edition: December 2017

10 9 8 7 6 5 4 3 2 1

For Nikki
I miss you every day.

ACKNOWLEDGMENTS

As this series comes to a close, I'd like to once again thank my editor, Monique Patterson. I'm so thrilled you fell in love with the concept and characters, and the note you sent to me regarding this last book made me remember, during a very hectic and stressful time, why I love to write and how meaningful it is to me to touch someone else's life with a story from the heart.

Thanks, as always, to my agent, Sarah E. Younger, of the Nancy Yost Literary Agency.

I am always thinking of my family and friends when it comes to acknowledgments, because they are incredibly understanding of the demands on my time when I'm working on a series and I greatly appreciate that. I love you all.

For my readers—I truly hope you've enjoyed this rather unorthodox journey! I have met some wonderful fans through this series, and each and every email and social media post to tell me how much you love my billionaires stays with me in my heart. You are also much appreciated!

THE
BILLIONAIRES

THE
STEPBROTHERS

ONE

"I don't appreciate being stood up." Scarlet Drake dropped her small clutch on the table of a semi-circular booth tucked into a corner of the lounge in San Francisco's newly opened Crestmont Hotel in the Financial District, showcasing the Bay Bridge and glittery skyline through a wall of floor-to-ceiling windows. The man occupying the booth had agreed to meet with her two nights ago in Chicago and had never shown up. He'd never even checked into the suite that had been booked for him.

Now he slowly lifted his gaze from his iPhone and let it linger—mostly on her breasts.

Scarlet's agitation would have flared, except that Michael Vandenberg was hotter than hell. Rich as sin. A wolf of Wall Street, though he wasn't a stockbroker. He was a real estate mogul who also dominated the commodities market.

And was, quite possibly, a brilliant art thief.

Which made her pulse race a bit faster. Not exactly a sensible reaction, because she could very well be staring danger in the face. A face that boasted prominent angles that had her internal temperature rising in a heartbeat.

Jesus, why does he have to be so damn good-looking?

Scarlet bit back a lustful sigh. This evening—this meeting—was mission critical. Therefore, Michael Vandenberg's chiseled-to-perfection appearance needed to be the absolute last thing on her mind.

"You must be Miss Drake," he ventured, breaking into her errant thoughts.

She gave a slight nod, hoping to remain neutral, indifferent. Not so innately affected by him—all tall, dark, and devilishly handsome, with smoky gray-blue eyes and thick, lush obsidian hair.

"You are impressively persistent," he told her. "Tenacious, even."

His gaze unabashedly raked over her, from her sleek dark-auburn strands, along the curve-hugging one-shouldered red minidress she wore, to her five-inch black stilettos—and moved just as slowly back up.

Flashing a pearly grin that dripped wickedness, he added, "I'm flattered that you've followed me from coast to coast. Had you thought to email me a photo when you first contacted me for a meeting, I likely wouldn't have evaded you these past few months."

His tone was rich and sensual. The kind of arousing bedroom voice that would remain ingrained on her brain, to be called upon in the future when she indulged in midnight fantasies with her fancy seven-speed-plus-thrusting-action vibrator. The kind of intimate voice that seeped deep into a woman's soul. Made heat rush through her veins.

Scarlet tried to calm her raging pulse as she hitched her chin and said, "I'm not here for you to ogle, Mr. Vandenberg."

So why were her nipples tightening and her clit tingling?

Setting aside his phone, Vandenberg reached for his cocktail and took a sip. Scarlet slid into the booth, uninvited, and crossed her legs. The lounge was dimly lit, upscale, crawling with people. But there were plenty of nooks and crannies for privacy, this being one of them.

He told her, "You're much too beautiful to be an insurance fraud investigator."

"Thank you, though that sentiment won't make up for you ditching me in about ten different cities." It was impossible to contain her excitement. Despite the runaround she'd gotten from Vandenberg and his people, she'd remained in hot pursuit of him. And had *finally* caught up with him.

Admittedly, Scarlet loved the thrill of the chase. Her doggedness had paid off in spades tonight.

Yet she strove for a professional air as she inquired, "What were you expecting, anyway?"

His daring gaze eased over her again like a warm caress. He said, "Someone all buttoned up and stuffy, who looks like they work for the IRS."

She couldn't help but smile. "So I've disappointed you."

"Indeed. It'd be much easier to tell you to go the hell away if you looked like you were from the IRS."

"My apologies. Now . . . I have questions for you that—"

A server suddenly appeared at Scarlet's elbow and cleared her throat to announce her arrival, the intrusion cutting Scarlet off.

The young, attractive blonde smiled suggestively at Vandenberg as though Scarlet didn't even exist. "May I bring you another Bombay Sapphire martini, sir?"

"Certainly."

Several seconds ticked by before the other woman dragged her gaze from the handsome billionaire to ask Scarlet, with decidedly less enthusiasm, "And for you?"

"Grey Goose martini, extra olives."

"Excellent." Her eyes snapped back to Vandenberg. Scarlet resisted the urge to roll hers. The man did not lack for female attention; that was for damn sure.

"Put it on my tab," he amiably said.

"Of course, Mr. Vandenberg." The blonde gave him a flirty look and then flounced off.

He took note of the deliberate sway to her hips, but only briefly. Then his smoldering gaze was on Scarlet again. "Where were we, Miss Drake?"

"I have questions that—"

"Ah, yes. Right." He sat back in the seat and rested his arm along the top of the booth, his long, tapered fingers mere centimeters away from brushing against her skin. Bizarrely tempting her to slide a half inch his way to make physical contact.

Was that his intention? To distract Scarlet from her grilling? Perhaps that was how he'd gotten away with such a light interrogation and minimal testimony when the FBI had quizzed him. After all, the agent had been female, Scarlet had learned. Vandenberg had probably drawn her into his sticky web from the get-go and she'd taken his "Scout's honor" without a dubious thought.

Scarlet couldn't fault the agent. Even she felt the intrinsic pull. She tried to convince herself that it had little to do with the enigmatic man himself, was more likely the result of having gone so long without a quick romp to curb some hormonal tendencies.

Scarlet really did work too much.

But her seemingly never-ending dry spell needed to take a back burner to her investigation. Easily *would*, if Michael Vandenberg didn't spark all kinds of riotous emotions within her. So effortlessly. So quickly. And she had a feeling he sensed her ardent response to him, hence the reason he'd gone straight for the jugular, knowing exactly why she was interested in speaking with him and countering it by taking advantage of the instant and obvious sexual chemistry between them.

With a mischievous crook of his brow, he said, "You finally have me where you want me."

Hardly. But the two of them naked and tangled in rumpled

sheets was not a notion she could afford to entertain at the moment.

Regardless, a shiver cascaded down her spine and she squirmed uncomfortably in her seat.

His voice was still low and sexy as he added, "For a few minutes, anyway."

Scarlet's body betrayed her further. Her stomach fluttered and the throbbing between her legs radiated deep in her core.

This mysterious man possessed a magnetic, potent presence that kept her charged and breathless. She'd seen enough photos of him during her initial research phase to know he was gorgeous, broad shouldered, powerful. A force to be reckoned with in business . . . and, without doubt, pleasure.

She should have been well prepared for the full impact of him. But clearly was not.

Yes, Scarlet was a thrill seeker. One of the reasons she was so good at her job. But the sort of buzz that hummed through her because of Vandenberg's penetrating gaze was the most enticing thrill of all. Causing her usual tunnel-vision concentration to wane.

Eye on the ball, Scarlet.

Eye. On. The. Ball.

"So you'll answer my questions?" she asked.

"Singular—just one. After you answer mine."

A no-brainer.

"You want to know why I'm investigating a cold case," she mused.

"No." His smoky eyes held her captive. "I want to know if you always wear short, tight dresses when you confront potential criminals."

Not missing a beat, she told him, "Well, *potential* is the operative word here, correct? And besides, the venue warrants the attire."

"Hmm. Does it?" He leaned in and boldly rested his free hand on her bare thigh, while his arm remained draped along the back of the booth, keeping them in cozy proximity to each other. "This particular dress does everything to evoke a man's desire. Are you sure your plan isn't to seduce a confession out of me for a crime I didn't commit?"

"An arrogant assumption. And that's two questions," she said, her chest rising and falling faster than normal as her heart rate accelerated with the tantalizing sensation of his thumb absently sweeping over her skin.

"I figure I'm entitled," he told her. "You've placed dozens of calls to my office, trying to track me down. Why are you so fixated on an art collection that disappeared over five years ago? The statute of limitations for prosecution has run out."

"There's still time to file a civil suit."

"Only if you can prove the collection wasn't stolen and that my family fraudulently reported the theft to the insurance company."

The adrenaline pumped as they got down to business.

Well, *almost* down to business.

There was the matter of his palm on her thigh. This time, she was convinced it was on purpose, to sidetrack her.

It was too damn bad his gaze was so sizzling, his touch so electrifying.

But she had something much more important to focus on. And she needed him to back off so she could do her job.

She waited for the server to deliver their cocktails. Then Scarlet said, "I carry a gun, Mr. Vandenberg. I'm also a certified Krav Maga instructor. I can break your hand without even breaking a sweat. And what I can do to your balls will put you in traction for a week. You're playing a very risky game with me right now."

His wicked grin returned. "Feisty and fiery. You live up to the traits associated with your hair color and your name." He reached for his drink. Took a sip.

Despite her hands-off warning, she instantly missed the heat of flesh on flesh, his smooth, supple skin, the strength in his fingers. The nearness of him.

She groaned inwardly. Scarlet was typically a much more controlled person, solely engrossed in her work as an independent investigator. She had a stellar reputation in the insurance industry and a phenomenal success rate. She'd recovered numerous stolen items that in most cases helped companies to recover erroneous claims paid to clients—and send thieves to jail.

But her attention was definitely divided this evening.

So, too, was Vandenberg's. Only he seemed a tad annoyed by the new development as three men in suits walked into the lounge.

He took another long drink from his glass before telling Scarlet, "I'd love to continue sitting here with you, staring into those beautiful green eyes of yours—"

"This isn't a date, Mr. Vandenberg."

"However, my associates have just arrived," he said, ignoring her comment. "I have a dinner meeting."

"It's a little late for dinner."

"I'm sure I can persuade the kitchen to whip something up. I'd invite you to join us, but we're plotting our next big coup."

"Of course you are."

"So what do you want to know, Miss Drake? Aside from the obvious—did I do it? To which I vehemently reply *no*. I did not steal eighteen million dollars' worth of artwork."

"I wouldn't expect you to simply say yes. What I want is for you to tell me what you were doing at eleven o'clock that night, which is the point of time identified by the FBI that the collection was reported as missing from the mansion."

"I already gave my alibi to the FBI. Nearly six years ago."

"I'm asking you to provide it to me. Tonight."

She held his now-steely gaze, not cowering in the least. Though her heart continued with its staccato beat and she wondered if he could hear the erratic cadence.

Vandenberg leaned close again, his palm flattening once more on her thigh.

Her breath caught—over the searing touch *and* his audaciousness.

In a deep, measured tone, he murmured, "My father and his new wife were throwing a party on the south lawn of their Hamptons estate. At eleven that evening, I was in the guesthouse with a wildly passionate brunette and a luscious Scandinavian blonde, both of whom were enjoying multiple orgasms while, unbeknownst to me, someone was robbing the gallery."

One corner of the rogue's mouth lifted. He moved away from Scarlet and scooted out of the booth. Snatched his black suit jacket that lay neatly across the top and slipped into the garment.

"I didn't have anything to do with the theft. Stop chasing your own tail, Miss Drake."

He turned away, but Scarlet didn't give up. She asked, "What about the five mil that was deposited into one of your accounts right around the time the insurance company released a check on the claim? That wasn't your cut of the heist?"

Vandenberg glanced at her over his shoulder, his expression an ominous one. She'd struck a nerve. He slowly faced her, lifted his cocktail from the table, and drained the glass. Seemingly refraining from slamming it back down, he set the crystal tumbler aside and told her, "It was an inheritance, Miss Drake. And I'd appreciate it if you kept that pretty nose of yours out of my finances."

She mustered a polite tone—somehow keeping a provocative one at bay as her body burned—and said, "Not until I discover exactly what happened to those paintings, where they are today, and whether your family falsified the claim."

"That's a very risky game for *you* to play, Miss Drake." He gave her a pointed look. Then stalked off.

Leaving exhilaration and a hint of foreboding thrumming in her veins.

An oh-so-scintillating combination for an adrenaline junkie such as herself.

And equally dangerous . . .

Michael couldn't get the feisty redhead out of his mind, despite how brief and rapid-fire their encounter had been. Even as his chief operating officer, chief general counsel, and chief financial officer discussed the various impediments inherent to the multibillion-dollar deal he was *this close* to signing, Michael continued to peer into the lounge, toward that dark corner where he'd left Scarlet Drake.

He couldn't actually see her from his spot in the empty dining room, but he could envision her sipping her martini, sliding the toothpick into her tempting mouth, and sucking off a fat olive.

His groin tightened at the thought of her sucking *him* off.

Damn, she was sexy. Drop-dead gorgeous, with long, sculpted legs and a curvy hourglass figure. She'd sent his pulse into the red zone with her beautiful face, shimmering emerald irises, and those full, plump, crimson-colored lips he desperately wanted to feel wrapped around his cock.

He hadn't been kidding when he'd told her that if he'd known what she looked like, how sultry and sassy she was, he wouldn't have led Scarlet on a wild-goose chase. He hadn't wanted to deal with her at all when he'd learned she was an insurance fraud investigator— and had known instinctively the exact case she was probing into.

But he really didn't give a damn now about her profession or her cause. Now all that registered was her silky skin, the soft hitches of her breath, and the tremors along her spine when he touched her.

The woman had him hot and bothered—from the moment

he'd glanced up from his phone and found her standing defiantly in front of his table. He wanted her, plain and simple.

And Michael Vandenberg was a man who always got what he wanted.

So while his COO, CGC, and CFO hashed out details of this next investment, debated contract terms and conditions, and each gave their two cents' worth on the pros and cons of the latest acquisition, Michael let all the background noise and advice simmer in his head as he typed out an e-mail message to his personal butler at the Crestmont and shot it off, wondering if Scarlet Drake would take the bait he'd intrepidly offered. . . .

TWO

Scarlet had just walked into her hotel room at the St. Francis and was slipping off her high heels when there was a soft knock on the door.

"Delivery for Miss Drake," came a male voice from the other side.

At nearly twelve o'clock at night?

She frowned. But her inquisitive nature couldn't resist. She peered through the peephole to find a uniformed employee patiently waiting for her—cap, gloves, name tag, and all. Official looking enough, yet she kept her purse in hand, where her 9mm was concealed, as she pulled back the security latch, flipped the lock, and opened the door.

"My apologies for disturbing you," he said. "The front desk alerted me that you'd arrived back at the hotel." He handed over a formal white envelope and added, "This is for you. Have a nice evening."

He turned to go, but she hastily said, "Wait." And tucked the packet under her arm so that she could retrieve a tip from her clutch.

"Thank you, but that's not necessary," the deliveryman told her

as she fished out the cash. "The gratuity has been taken care of."
He whirled around in his polished shoes and marched down the
hallway toward the bank of elevators.

Scarlet closed the door and engaged the dead bolt. She set her
handbag on the entryway table and then eyed the envelope with
her name elegantly scrawled across it in thick black ink.

Excitement rippled through her over a secret missive as the
clock inched toward midnight.

Her love of intrigue was genetic. Her grandmother, who'd raised
her in the wine country of River Cross, California, after Scarlet's
parents had died, was an international bestselling mystery writer.
Scarlet's parents had been super-sleuths themselves, her father for
a global law firm and her mother for a private investigator here in
San Fran.

She missed them dearly but was grateful for the traits they'd
passed on to her and felt equally blessed to have had her gran look
after her.

Scarlet crossed to the desk, where she'd spied a silver-plated
letter opener when she'd unpacked her clothes earlier. She'd had to
make a reservation at the St. Francis overlooking Union Square,
rather than the Crestmont—where Vandenberg was residing this
evening—because that particular hotel was booked several months
in advance, amidst its grand opening. And she did not possess the
same influence as the real estate tycoon to score a room.

Though Scarlet's home in River Cross was little more than an
hour away, she'd planned to stay in the city, not knowing how late
it would be if she eventually met up with the elusive Michael Vandenberg or whether she'd need to hop on another plane to try to
catch him elsewhere.

One of her best friends, wine heiress Jewel Catalano, had gotten her assistant at Catalano Enterprises to strike up a conversation with Vandenberg's assistant, and that had gone a long way in
aiding Scarlet's attempt to pin down precisely where Vandenberg

was supposed to be tonight and when, so that she could finally say she'd had a successful trip chasing the shadowy man who fascinated her beyond all belief.

And who would land her a hefty bonus if she could prove he had, indeed, pilfered the paintings from his father's estate—or served as an accomplice to the larceny. All verifying that the claim submitted years ago had been under fraudulent terms.

Her excitement escalated as she slid the tip of the opener behind the flap and then extracted a note card in heavy stock that had one short line of text centered in the middle, in the same script and glossy ink that matched the front of the packet.

Let's make it a date. Michael

Flames instantly blazed over her skin.

Okay, perhaps she was a bit *too* attracted to him. Definitely a bad thing in all capacities.

The man was so very far out of her league—a woman who hadn't had sex in longer than she cared to admit. Not to mention, he was well out of her tax bracket. By *a lot*.

And then there was that tedious little matter of her suspecting he was the mastermind behind a crime that had never been solved. Not a single piece from that entire missing collection had ever hit an auction house or black market or was listed as a private sale.

So if the artwork had never been fenced, the thief or thieves wouldn't have gained monetarily beyond that insurance check, or a portion thereof, for felonious services rendered.

Which led Scarlet to believe that the expensive collection was still being enjoyed by the owners who'd also pocketed the claim money. Those paintings had to be on display, under lock and key, somewhere on the Vandenberg estate. She was convinced of it.

Scarlet's gut told her Michael might be involved in the scam because of the coincidental timing of the deposit into one of his accounts. And the fact that his father, Mitcham Vandenberg, was a notorious miser.

From what she'd gleaned with the help of her research-hound other BFF, Bayli Styles, Michael had required substantial capital for his first major investment at the age of twenty-four. His father had not provided it. But the five million had conveniently appeared in Michael's account precisely when he'd needed it the most—and that cash flow had helped to launch his career and his own personal empire.

It was all a cut-and-dried scenario in her mind . . . *if* she could just get a glimpse inside the Vandenberg estate or discern where else that collection might be stashed. The FBI had closed the case with no solid leads. The insurance company had settled.

But the voice of reason in Scarlet's head told her that two and two had already been put together. And now it was just a matter of producing proof that her conspiracy theory was dead on the money. Literally.

Getting closer to Michael Vandenberg was her key to unraveling this case.

So while it went against her better judgment to fall down this new rabbit hole he was digging—again, because Scarlet was much too taken by his dark, rakish looks and seductive voice—she was willing to play along. It just might yield more clues for her to investigate, more pieces of the puzzle to help her see the big picture and solve this mystery.

As she contemplated this, the landline on the desk rang.

She snatched the receiver and said, "This is Scarlet Drake."

"Good evening, Miss Drake. This is the valet. A car has just arrived for you."

Her stomach flipped in sheer titillation, mostly related to the golden nugget she'd managed to crack open because she hadn't given up after numerous failed attempts to confront Vandenberg.

THE BILLIONAIRES: THE STEPBROTHERS   15

She said, "I'll be right down." She hung up the phone and hurried to the closet.

The prospect of a clandestine evening had her pulling out a black long-sleeved dress with a reasonable hemline. She paired it with knee-high black leather boots and a trench coat. She pulled the sash tight at her waist and then slipped her cell, ID, pepper spray, and AMEX card into a slim purse that she draped across her torso.

After securing her weapon in the safe, she left her room and found the driver waiting for her under the porte cochere.

He greeted her as he opened the door of the town car.

"Thank you." Scarlet slid into the backseat, feeling a heady rush from the covert turn of events. When the driver climbed behind the wheel, Scarlet asked, "Where are we going?"

He provided an address that she sent to both Jewel and Bayli via text. She might be an eager beaver when it came to a mysterious meet-up, but she also knew to take precautionary measures.

She would concede that it wasn't the smartest thing to get personally involved with Michael Vandenberg. But as she'd contended earlier, one of her best strategies was to get close enough to him that she could find a way into the mansion and snoop around.

And this just might be her foot in the door.

God, her juices were flowing as things heated up!

She could barely sit still in her seat as the car traversed the city, up and down the hilly terrain to the edge of North Beach, not far from where Scarlet and the girls had rented their first flat when they'd started at San Francisco State University together ten years ago.

Scarlet loved this part of the city. A silvery-gray haze rolled over the wharf and ribboned through the tall buildings. The soulful sounds of foghorns drifted from the bay. The clanging of the bell on the Powell-Mason cable car echoed down the corridor of restaurants and bars, and the sidewalks were riddled with late-night diners and partygoers. The energetic vibe mixed with the scent of garlic and created an inviting, invigorating ambience.

When they reached their destination, the car double-parked alongside a brick building. The driver opened Scarlet's door again.

He told her, "Downstairs." Then he drove off, likely per Vandenberg's instructions.

Scarlet stared at the building she recognized, with steps leading up to the entry. It was a nightclub. But she'd never known of there being an establishment downstairs. In fact . . . she couldn't even find the downstairs.

Her gaze roved the brick wall. No railing or steps to access an underground unit.

She strolled around the corner and continued down the alley, keeping her mind clear to listen for noises surrounding her, any footsteps that might follow.

Her pulse picked up as she walked farther along the narrow passage. Yet there was still no magical portal.

Her extreme curiosity gave way to frustration that Vandenberg had given her the slip again.

He wasn't helping her to buy into his self-proclaimed innocence.

Scarlet was just about to turn around and head back to the corner where she could catch a cab to the St. Francis when she spotted a shiny black door. It was at street level, so that didn't seem right. But what the hell?

She walked toward it, slid back the latch, and yanked the heavy metal slab open. A hard-driving beat suddenly filled the alley. She stepped inside and closed the door behind her. There was a single bare bulb blazing in the tapered entryway, which led to a black wrought-iron spiral staircase descending into the bowels of the facility.

Scarlet shot off another text to her friends, to give her exact location.

She then made her way down to a lower level with maybe a ten-foot ceiling and a long stainless-steel bar that was lined with patrons and shots of tequila. Sapphire and silver strobe lights bounced off the tables and stools. The music was loud with a quick tempo and reverberated within her.

A petite chestnut-haired twentysomething greeted her. "May I take your coat?" she asked over the wail of electric guitars and animated conversations, offering Scarlet a claim ticket.

She divested herself of the trench coat but kept her purse strapped across her body and tucked the perforated piece of paper inside.

Scanning the throng of people, she searched for Michael, knowing he'd stand out even in a dense crowd. But she didn't catch sight of him as she wove through the conglomeration, heading toward the bar. She wedged herself between a burly sort and a lean-muscled guy and further surveyed the scene.

The inner sanctum gave way to a break in the wall so that the club flowed into a larger space, mostly occupied by an enormous dance floor that was edged by tables, sofas, and chairs.

This back portion spanned two stories, with black iron catwalks suspended from chains overhead. The walkways were fused together in a crisscross shape, creating a huge X above the dance floor, and several women in skimpy lingerie and high heels gyrated and whirled about to the music, *Coyote Ugly* style. Voluminous tresses flew about as their heads whipped this way and that. It was like walking onto a 1980s MTV video set. Or being front row at a rock 'n' roll Victoria's Secret show.

"Buy you a drink?" the burly one asked Scarlet.

"Thanks, but I'll get my own." She caught the attention of the bartender and ordered a martini. "Dirty it up, will you?"

"You got it."

While he made her cocktail, Scarlet's gaze returned to the dance floor. Then she eyed the perimeter, finally catching a tall, wide shadow on the move. He stealthily worked his way through the crowd toward her, shifting out of the inky fringes so that the flashes of light fell on him.

Scarlet's heart nearly stopped.

This was not a version of Michael Vandenberg she'd ever expected to see.

He'd ditched the designer suit and neatly styled hair. Instead, he was dressed all in black—leather jacket, V-necked T-shirt, jeans, and boots. His short onyx hair was tousled, sticking on end in places.

The breath escaped her body in one long stream.

Hell-o, Big Bad Wolf.

An ultra-sexy, riveting Big Bad Wolf.

And that did not bode well for her.

Scarlet vaguely heard the bartender serve her her drink and tell her how much she owed. She barely heard anything beyond the thumping of her heart.

Her nipples were instantly hard again. Her panties damp.

And Michael hadn't even reached her yet.

He did, however, stare directly at her, his gaze locking with hers. Heat blazed in his eyes and a cocky expression crossed his captivating face . . . she gaped.

Warning signals went off in the back of her head, a million red flags unfurling and catching a stiff breeze.

He was a double threat—wildly arousing *and* quite possibly a villain.

Not exactly the type of man a smart woman would be creaming over at midnight in a nondescript club she didn't even know the name of.

As he approached her, he extracted folded bills from his front pocket and peeled off a fifty. He reached around her, his gaze unwavering, and slapped the cash on the bar. "For the lady's drink. And I'll have a Bombay Sapphire martini."

"Right away, Mr. Vandenberg."

"So you're a regular?" Scarlet asked him, shocked her words didn't slide from her mouth on a pool of drool.

"You've surpassed your allotted questions, Miss Drake."

"I'm not interrogating you at the moment," she told him. "I thought this was a date."

He gave her another roguish grin. "Nice to see you can take off your investigator's hat for the evening." His lids dipped a tad, as did his voice. "Hope that's not all you're willing to take off."

Her inner walls clenched. But she teasingly said, "Don't push your luck. And you may as well call me Scarlet. Or I will start quizzing you about the art collection."

He stared deeper into her eyes, his raw intensity searing her insides, turning her blood molten. "I promise I didn't steal those paintings. I want you to believe me."

She debated this for several suspended seconds. Considering who he was—affluent and powerful—she told him, "You don't care if I believe you or not. Like you said, you can't be prosecuted at this point. And if you lost a civil suit, compensatory damages would be chump change to you. Had you been caught red-handed before you'd made your own fortune that would have been a different story. But it's currently not a detrimental situation to you financially. Just a hit to your reputation if you actually are guilty."

"My reputation would survive. I don't see Martha Stewart's empire crumbling. So why pursue an investigation?"

"It's the principle of the matter."

His grin widened. "Gorgeous and ethical. You'll completely do me in." He winked. "Drink your martini." His head inclined toward the bar.

Scarlet tore her gaze from his and reached for her glass just as the bartender delivered Michael's cocktail. He and Scarlet clinked rims and she sipped.

Then she asked, "Seriously, how does everyone know who you are? I'm sure they don't *all* read the *Wall Street Journal*."

"I'm the new landlord here. I closed on the building last week."

"Figures," she murmured into her martini. Then said, "I didn't even know this place existed. Took a while to find the entrance."

"That's on purpose, I'm told. A bit secretive for a more exclusive clientele."

"I'm sure you enjoy the eye candy." She hitched her chin toward the catwalks.

His gaze didn't follow. "I'm more interested in what's standing in front of me."

Despite his attention being on her, he must have caught a movement in his peripheral vision, because he gently shifted her toward the wall a second before someone bumped into the burly guy and sent his drink sloshing over the side.

"Oh!" Scarlet would have been wearing his cocktail and perhaps hers as well if Michael hadn't carefully pressed her up against the bricks, her backside absorbing the cold stone, her front flaming as he crowded her, his body shielding hers.

"Thanks for the save," she said, breathless.

"Just trying to spare the dress."

"I think we're safe now." She hoped he'd take the hint and step away.

Conversely . . . Christ, it felt good to have him so close to her again. His strength and magnetism rolled off him in waves, engulfing her. She inhaled his heated, masculine scent, and if she leaned in just an inch she could sweep her lips and tongue along his throat, taste his skin, feel his muscles bunch all around her.

"You're devouring me with that hypnotic gaze of yours," he whispered against her temple, making her skin tingle.

She shouldn't have heard him above the din, but she'd tuned everything else out.

His hand was on her hip where he'd gripped her to move her out of the way of the collision. The other held his glass. She still had her drink in hand as well—and decided that was probably a good thing—or she'd be sliding her palms under his shirt and exploring all those corrugated grooves and rigid sinew she knew she'd find.

Her fingers burned to touch him.

Scarlet mentally shook her head. Sipped her martini in hopes of cooling her insides. Didn't work. She was still teeming with anticipation of what Michael Vandenberg really had in store for her this evening.

Because instinct told her it wasn't just cocktails and casual flirtation.

Sure enough, he took her glass and set it on the bar, along with his. Then he twined their fingers and gave a tug.

"Come on. Let's dance."

Her heart fluttered. Her brow crooked. "You dance?"

"Why not?" He led her out onto the packed floor. Pulled her into his arms as the music slowed to a less head-banging beat, morphing into a more manageable one so that they could move together.

Their bodies melded, her breasts nestling below his pecs and his thigh wedging between her legs. Scarlet stared up at him as the zings ricocheted through her.

With her insides instantly going haywire, it was a wonder she could latch on to a sane thought, let alone speak.

Somehow, she found the ability to ask, "Are you just doing this in hopes of getting me to back off the case?"

He held her even tighter, tucking her more firmly against him.

His erection rubbed along her hip and he muttered in her ear, "Does it feel like I'm just doing this so you'll back off?"

Her free hand curled around the nape of his neck while her fingers remained tangled with his, their hands resting against his chest.

A tinge of vulnerability crept in on Scarlet. She'd spent so much of her life following her gut instincts, getting her high from solving puzzles, that she'd had neither the time nor the inclination to pursue romantic relationships.

More than that, she'd never really met men worthy of a career derailment. Perhaps it'd always been the skeptic in her that made her automatically assume there was a personal agenda being pushed, a shady angle that would somehow be to her detriment. She was suspicious by nature—went with the territory given her ancestry—and that made her wary of deceit and betrayal.

Therefore, she did not typically engage in endeavors such as this that would leave her wide open for epic emotional failure. She'd been shattered once before, with her parents' deaths. No need for a repeat performance or additional heartache.

But she couldn't deny she was mesmerized by Michael's compelling gray-blue eyes and the sensual sway of his hips. The possessiveness of his embrace. The way they fit so perfectly together. The way they moved as one, as though they'd been doing this forever, were meant to be this glued to each other.

There were professional lines Scarlet didn't cross as a rule. But she was dying to know more about this man beyond what Bayli's research had unearthed. Therefore, Scarlet was willing to cave to some of her inquisitiveness. Just a little.

She said, "So I already know you graduated from Princeton, which makes it understandable how you have such keen business sense. But I'm confused as to where the commodities knack comes from."

"My great-great-grandfather owned one of the largest sugar plantations in Hawaii. The significance of commodities, including the importance of buying and selling them, was passed down to me."

She gave a slight nod. "I did discover a deed in Oahu belonging to M. Vandenberg. I figured it was in your father's possession."

"No, that's my personal holding, also passed down to me. Though I sold off a portion of the plantation when I first inherited it. That's how I ended up with the five million you mentioned earlier."

"And why did you keep the rest of the land? I hardly take you for a harvester of cane sugar."

"Actually, the history and the current state of affairs related to sugar production and exportation is tumultuous. With past strangleholds in Hawaii and strict governmental policies, there are a lot of constraints and complex variables that affect the economy and the labor force, even here on the mainland as it pertains to sugar manufacturing and importation. The majority of plantations on the islands have closed; mine's on the cusp. I have different plans for the acreage, still in soft commodities since I have future contracts at stake in the exchange market."

"Can't be easy keeping track of all of your investments."

He chuckled. "I have people who do that for me."

Scarlet gave this some thought, then said, "I don't believe you'd rely too heavily on them. You seem to be the type who keeps his finger on the pulse of his business."

"And business is really the last thing I want to discuss this evening." His impish expression held her spellbound. "I'm finding this current twist of fate much more fascinating."

His hand at the small of her back inched lower until he palmed an ass cheek. With the dance floor as crowded as it was, she knew no one took note. He squeezed roughly and it sent a wicked thrill through her.

"You're big on taking liberties, aren't you?" she asked.

"Can't help it. You're irresistible." He pressed his thigh more firmly between her legs. Used his hand on her butt to grind her apex against his flexed muscles.

Good Lord, he'd been right. This was a risky game to play.

His warm breath teased strands of her hair as he said, "You smell damn good. Feel even better."

His words . . . his touch . . . his thigh rubbing her sex . . . Christ, it took him mere minutes to send her into sensory overload.

He murmured, "I'm dying to know how you taste."

She stifled a moan. Not that anyone would hear it. Except for Michael.

Risky barreled headfirst into *lethal*.

She really had no idea who she was dealing with. Was caught up in and conflicted by the burning desire to interrogate and the forbidden need to let him weave his web, ensnare her.

With her mouth so damn close to his throat and that pulsating point at its base, all she had to do was lift her chin and her lips would graze his skin.

Her heart thundered at the notion and the beats pounded in her ears.

Somehow, she found the good sense to say, "This really shouldn't be happening."

"I'm not a criminal, Scarlet," he all but growled in agitation. "Yes, I can be ruthless. Cutthroat when it comes to business transactions. But I'm *not* a thief."

His body tensed and there was an odd shift in the air between them. That rawness that had exuded from him at the Crestmont when she'd pressed him about the money she'd suspected was his cut of the insurance check returned in a flash.

And goddamn it, the angst and virility radiating from him was a huge turn-on.

But even more than that . . . The conviction in his tone and in his eyes called to her gut instincts again.

The problem was, she *wanted* to believe him.

Scarlet wanted to trust in his solemn, though slightly tormented, gaze.

It wasn't just her coming at him with suspicions of his involvement in the theft that had him oozing the need to convince her of his innocence. It was something else. Something far beyond her comprehension . . . Something that ran much deeper and made her think of that ominous look that had crossed his face when she'd mentioned the inheritance in the lounge.

There was something about the sugar plantation, his line of grandfathers, the money . . . ? She had no idea. But her curiosity soared like never before.

She said, "Maybe you're not a thief. But you do have secrets. A lot of them. I can read it on your face, see it in your eyes. And your defense mechanisms are meant to keep me from learning them. So again . . . Is there really something going on here—between us— or is all this physical interaction just your way of throwing me off the investigative trail?"

THREE

It should annoy him that she was so point-blank.

It didn't.

Something about Scarlet Drake thrilled Michael in a way he couldn't remember ever experiencing. She was intuitive and inquisitive. Downright candid and blunt. Brazen.

It was refreshing. Sexy. Stimulating.

Even if she did push his buttons.

He wasn't used to a full-court press—from anyone. He had billions in the bank that he'd worked his ass off for, and his professional reputation was hard-earned and well warranted.

He didn't like being questioned or second-guessed.

Somehow, he couldn't bring himself to mind in this instance. The beautiful investigator constantly challenging him made him even harder.

Michael said, "I can't fake an erection. Answers that question."

"Then your intention really is to make me come on your leg."

"I got you that excited?"

"You already know that answer." Looking a bit out of sorts, she said, "I need the ladies' room." She whirled around and started to march off but returned to him two seconds later. "How did you find me at the St. Francis, anyway?"

"How'd you find me at the Crestmont?" he countered.

"By making a hell of a lot of phone calls."

"Well, there you go. I have a hell of a lot of people willing to do that for *me*." He flashed another grin. Then added, "Bathroom's down the side hall, toward the back, on the right."

"Thank you." She spun around again and threaded her way through the mass of people.

Michael's full attention was fixated on Scarlet's enticing backside and the small, tight ass he wanted to fuck.

He wondered if she was as spirited and adventuresome in the bedroom as she was out of it. Decided that was likely the case. And followed her.

Propping a shoulder against a jutting wall from the supply closet on the opposite side of the restrooms, in a dimly lit corner, he folded his arms over his chest and crossed his booted ankles, waiting for her.

When Scarlet caught sight of him minutes later and joined him, she had a curious look on her face. She asked, "Afraid I'd get lost?"

"Not in the least. I suspect you have no trouble at all finding your way around."

"It took a little wandering about and a leap of faith to locate the entrance to this place. Why so covert about our date?"

"Adds an element of intrigue. I get the feeling you like it that way."

"I do get a rush from it."

"Hmph." He reached for her hand again and tugged her closer to him. His head bent to hers and he murmured, "Let's see what else you get a rush from."

His lips slid over her glossy ones, which tasted faintly of

vanilla and vodka. His groin tightened, his cock straining the zipper of his jeans. He snaked his arm around her and hauled her up against him just as his mouth sealed to hers. To hell with the few people coming and going in this area.

Her lips parted and his tongue swept inside to tangle with hers, sending fire roaring through his veins. Her body melded to his again, in complete surrender, and Michael took what she offered, deepening the kiss, intensifying it, silently telling her how hot he was for her.

Dancing with Scarlet had been an alluring temptation unto itself, with her breasts pressed to his chest and her sensational body rubbing against his. Add a scorching kiss to the scenario and he was quickly losing his mind for her.

The immediate and intense chemistry that had sparked between them when she'd appeared at his table at the lounge earlier had reignited when she'd been grinding along his leg. Now he felt a five-alarm rager building within him, and Michael yearned to do something about it.

Breaking the kiss, he led her across the hall and unhooked the chain blocking the access to the stairwell and the restricted area above for the catwalks. He gestured for her to precede him as he secured the chain behind them. At the top of the steps was an alcove shrouded by walls, though the sapphire lights reflected on the outskirts so that he caught the intermittent glimpses of Scarlet in the flickering illumination.

He backed her against a wall and kissed her. Her arms wound around his neck, the fingers of one hand plowing through his hair. Her body writhed, all her enticing curves and arousing femininity teasing his senses. This woman was a drug and he was instantly addicted.

He had one hand on her hip and the other skated up her bare thigh, from the top of her boot to the hem of her skirt. His fingers slipped behind the material and grazed the triangle of her satin thong. Her drenched thong.

Lightning exploded in his head.

He ripped his mouth from hers. "Fuck," he ground out. His fingers stroked her pussy lips through the soaked satin. "You're so fucking wet," he whispered in her ear.

"How can that possibly be a surprise?" she said on a broken breath.

"Scarlet." His testosterone shot through the roof. His heart hammered in his chest. "I have to make you come."

She let out a sexy moan over the clamor of the music and the throng below them. If one of the catwalk dancers ventured to the edge of their stage, he and Scarlet might be discovered. But he'd already noted the women in lingerie's pattern and they generally stuck to the midsections, where they were better viewed by the audience.

Even if anyone could catch a glimpse at this secluded spot, they'd only see the shadow Michael created with his back to them. Scarlet was well concealed by his larger frame. So he didn't give another thought to not having absolute privacy. Just fell into the fated moment and let his rampant desire for her take over.

He whisked aside the material at her apex and his fingertips brushed over her moist folds.

Her body jolted at the intimate contact. "Jesus," she muttered. And tightened her hold on his strands of hair.

Michael stroked slowly at first, then circled her clit, the knot of nerves swelling under his touch. His mouth crashed over hers once more and he engaged her in another blazing lip-lock as two fingers sank into her and he pumped assertively, the heel of his hand rubbing against her clit.

He absorbed the tremors running through her. Determined to get her off. *Needing* to get her off. His fingers were coated with her cream and he stroked more fervently, until she tore her mouth from his and gasped.

"Oh, God." Her nails dug into his nape. Her tremors turned into quaking.

"You're so damn close."

So damn fast.

"*Yes.*"

He quickened his pace, his fingers plunging deep, until he found *the* spot. And worked her feverishly.

"Michael." Her head fell back; her eyelids fluttered closed. "Right there. Oh, God, yes. Just like that . . ."

He took the opportunity presented and his lips and tongue skated up the long column of her neck. In the far recesses of his mind, he cataloged every catch of her breath, the sweet taste of her, the smell of her, the feel of her. The stimulating sound of her throaty moans.

He pumped a bit faster. The heel of his hand massaged her clit a bit harder. He sensed the moment she was about to come undone and nipped at her skin, just below her ear. Then murmured, "Lose it for me, baby."

Her inner muscles clenched his fingers. She cried out.

"Oh, yeah," he said on a low groan, everything inside him pulling so tight it was a wonder he didn't erupt right along with her.

Her pussy milked his fingers as she rode out the orgasm, clinging to him, her breaths mere whimpers of ecstasy.

"You're driving me wild," he told her.

When the quaking of her body eased into a mild tremble, he withdrew from her. Stepped away to get a grip on himself. His back pressed to the wall opposite her and he watched the blue and silver strobes reflect against her flushed skin as she fought for longer, steadier streams of air.

That she'd been so damn wet for him before he'd even touched her and had come so quickly made him even harder. Made him want to shove her skirt up and drive deep into her.

She seemed to know it. Closed the gap between them. As she stared up at him with lust in her eyes, her hands slipped under the hem of his shirt. Her fingers traced the grooves of his abdomen before her palms flattened against his solid muscles and slid upward to his chest.

Michael clasped her hips and lowered his head, drawing her into another sizzling kiss.

Her hands skimmed down his stomach again and around to his back, exploring liberally, getting him hotter, then splaying over his shoulder blades. He cupped her ass cheeks, kneading them as he rubbed his erection against her mound.

Christ, he needed to be inside her. And it wasn't just to sate his own voracious sexual appetite. He desperately wanted to set her off again, with his cock thrusting into her until she fell apart and screamed his name as she came.

He wasn't sure he'd ever wanted a woman so badly, so urgently.

So when her palms slid away from his shoulders and her fingers toyed with the silver buckle on his belt, it took all the restraint Michael possessed to cover her hands with his to stop her.

Every fiber of his being burned to let her unfasten his jeans, to coax her to her knees in front of him and allow him to fuck her mouth, to have her swallow him down, drain him, quell the throbbing—the aching—between his legs and low in his gut.

But even that wouldn't be enough. And he knew it.

Breaking their kiss, he told her, "Not here."

He twined his fingers with hers and led her downstairs. She willingly followed, not even asking where they were going.

"Where's your claim ticket?" His voice was gruff with the need clawing at him, shredding him from the inside out.

With her free hand, she retrieved the slip of paper from her purse and gave it to him. He collected her coat and helped her into it. He tipped the check girl and then guided Scarlet out of the club. They walked the alley in silence and rounded the corner of the building. Took only a few steps before they reached the car waiting for him, provided by the Crestmont.

The driver was on the ball, catching sight of Michael in the rearview mirror and jumping out of the vehicle to open the back door just as Michael and his date reached it.

Scarlet eased onto the leather seat and Michael slipped in beside her.

He couldn't quite decipher what the hell had come over him—from the moment he'd met her. It wasn't in his nature to take a woman back to his hotel room. If he had an itch that needed to be scratched, he'd go to her place. Keep things casual, allow for a convenient, no muss–no fuss exit when they'd both had their fill.

But he wasn't looking for a fast fuck and quick escape this time. Otherwise, he would have used his dick instead of his fingers when he'd had the sexy investigator pinned to the wall.

Unfortunately, it was damn near impossible to keep his hands off her. As the car left the curb, his palm slid over her bare thigh, his fingers grazing the inner portion.

The side of his hand glided along her folds through her panties. She coiled her arm with his, her breasts pressing to his biceps. She wriggled on the seat next to him. Her breathing turned thin and raspy. She nuzzled her face in the crook of his neck, but he heard her murmur, "I need to come again."

"Soon."

"Now."

His cock still throbbed in wild beats. His balls pulled tight. It'd behoove him to adjust himself, but he didn't move. Scarlet was tangled up in him and used her hand on top of his to force him to rub her clit with more pressure as she apparently tried to keep her writhing inconspicuous. But they were riding in a fully loaded extended town car with a privacy window, so Michael didn't worry too much about discretion.

He told her, "I want you naked, beneath me."

She moaned. "I don't know what the hell you're doing to me, but it feels damn good. All of it."

"I'm just getting started. Wait until my head is between your legs."

Her eyelids drifted shut. "Oh, God."

He bit back a triumphant grin. Said, "I'm dying to eat your pussy. Taste you on my tongue. Make you beg for more."

"Michael," she said on a velvety breath. "I'm going to—"

"It makes you hot, doesn't it? Knowing what I want to do to you? Knowing what I'm *going* to do to you?"

"Yes."

"I'm going to fuck you hard," he whispered in her ear. "Are you ready for that?"

Her eyes snapped open and she stared at him, a bit dazedly. "*Yes.*"

"Are you on the pill?"

She nodded.

"And—"

"I haven't been with anyone in over two years."

His jaw clenched. That was a damn shame considering how passionate she was. Conversely . . . It was advantageous for Michael.

"I've been tested. And, Scarlet"—his breath rustled strands of her auburn hair as he told her, "I want to come inside you."

Then he kissed her. Fiercely. Felt the shiver run through her.

He stroked that swollen pearl between her legs a bit more forcefully.

Her inner thighs squeezed their clasped hands.

She jerked her mouth away and buried her face against his neck again.

"Oh, God," she squeaked out, obviously trying to quiet herself. "Michael. Oh, Christ."

Her teeth sank into his skin, stifling her cry as she came. Her body vibrated against his, her panties even wetter than before. Making him insanely hard.

All he had to do was palm his cock through his jeans and he knew he'd explode.

It was damn tempting. Because she had him clinging to the ledge, dangling by his fingertips.

His head fell back against the top of the seat and he stared up at the ceiling of the car, fighting for just enough composure to keep it together a few minutes more, hating that they weren't in his hotel suite already. He swallowed down a lump of desire and willed some control when all he really wanted to do was haul her into his lap so that she straddled him and let her ride his dick until they both let go and gave in to the free fall of a powerful release.

He still had one hand pressed to her apex and he raked the other through his hair. Wished his heart weren't slamming against his ribs.

Her lips smoothed over the spot on his throat where she'd bitten him. She hadn't drawn blood, but he was damn certain there were teeth indentations in his flesh. He didn't care about that. What mattered was that he could make her come so hard she nearly took a chunk out of him. And he hadn't even gotten serious yet.

The car reached the hotel and a valet opened the door. Michael stepped out, uncomfortable as hell and tugging Scarlet along with him. She kept herself glued to him, a little unstable on her tall boot heels. He knew it wasn't from the martini. And gloated inwardly over how he'd completely unraveled her.

Though he couldn't be too cocky. She was doing the same to him.

They walked through the lobby, mostly empty this time of night. Entering an elevator, Michael inserted his electronic key into the slot above the panel of buttons and hit PH for the pent-house.

They traveled in silence up to the top floor, but the air between them, surrounding them, was sexually charged, crackling with anticipation. It felt like an eternity before the elevator came to a halt. He grabbed his card key and headed for the double doors of his room, Scarlet keeping pace with his brisk stride.

Once inside the penthouse, he tossed the key on the table in the center of the foyer and pulled her farther into the suite, pri-marily cast in shadows, aside from the dim glow of strategically placed security lights and the wall of windows with the drapes swept away to reveal the San Francisco skyline, featuring the land-mark Transamerica Pyramid.

He shrugged out of his leather jacket and left it on a sofa. Then he hastily untied the sash at her waist and divested her of her coat. His fingers curled around the material of her skirt, just below her hips, and he yanked the dress up and over her head, adding it to the mounting pile of clothing.

His jaw worked rigorously as he took in the sight of her in a red satin and black lace bra, matching panties, and the sexy-as-sin thigh-high boots.

There wasn't a woman on the catwalk back at the club who could hold a candle to her. Scarlet Drake was perfection in his eyes.

Michael would have taken a moment to thank his lucky stars that this gorgeous creature was single and standing in the middle of his living room, but he couldn't keep his hands off her that long.

As his mouth crashed over hers, his arm slipped around her and he unfastened her bra with the pinching of his finger and thumb. Still kissing her, he whisked the lingerie away and then cupped her breasts, every one of his nerve endings igniting as he caressed the full, firm mounds and brushed the pads of his thumbs over her puckered nipples.

She gripped his biceps and held on as he backed her against the oversized desk. His hands left her breasts and he grabbed her about the waist to hoist her up so she sat on the mahogany surface.

He caught the sides of her skimpy thong in the crook of his index fingers and stripped the material away as she lifted slightly to facilitate the undressing. He left her boots on.

His forearms hooked the backs of her knees and he spread her legs wide, with both heels planted on the desk. She flattened her palms against the surface at her hips. Licked her lips and gave him a provocative look.

"You know I want you," she said. Stirring his emotions as much as she ratcheted his lust.

Michael's fingertips glided along her pussy lips. "You know what *I* want first."

He sank to his knees and blew a breath over her glistening flesh.

She let out a small cry.

He held her thighs open as his tongue slowly, lightly, caressed her tight, highly tempting pink parts. Sampling her. Teasing her.

She threaded her fingers through his hair again. "This is about to get out of control, isn't it?"

"Yes." Though he was fairly certain it already had. He'd purposely evaded her for months. Then he'd taken one look at her and he'd *had* to have her.

At the moment, however, he was solely dedicated to pleasuring her with his mouth.

He spread her folds with his thumbs and his tongue fluttered over her clit. Her hips jerked as she gasped.

"Michael," she said on a sharp moan. "It's been forever since anyone's done this to me."

"You taste so damn good," he muttered. Then continued flickering his tongue against the little pearl.

Her inner thighs quivered. Her breathy pants of air filled the otherwise quiet room.

Michael alternated his technique from the flitting to a long lapping motion to the flitting. He could feel the ribbons of excitement race through her, sensed her restlessness as she clutched thick locks of his hair.

He tugged on her folds with his lips, making her whimper.

"That feels incredible," she told him. "Everything you do feels so incredible."

"Wait'll I fuck you." He toyed with her further by circling her opening with the tip of his tongue before penetrating the narrow canal.

"Michael!" Her hips rose off the desk. "Oh, God. You're going to make me come again."

That was certainly the plan. He went back to licking the swollen knot of nerves as he eased one finger inside her. She pressed herself more firmly to his mouth, her pelvis undulating with his rhythm. He worked in a second finger and pumped vigorously. She was dripping wet, her cream coating his tongue and his fingers.

He was rock-hard and wasn't quite sure how he was going to survive a few more minutes of not being buried in her warm, slick depths. But he was still a man on a mission.

His mouth left her pussy and trailed upward, over her belly to her breasts as he stood. His tongue curled around a beaded center. He continued massaging her inner walls with a steady, purposeful pace, the pad of his thumb rubbing her clit at the same time.

He drew her nipple into his mouth, his teeth gently scraping.

"Yes," she said. "I love that. Suck my nipples."

He paid the other one the same attention.

"Oh, yes. Oh, God, yes."

Michael was caught between the torment of being so damn close to exploding and the erotic pleasure of pushing her higher.

Enjoying her body. Thriving on the way she responded to him, the trembling that besieged her and the scarcity of her breath.

She'd come even harder this time. He'd make sure of it.

He kissed her passionately. Stroked faster. Then broke the kiss and returned to her nipple with a stronger suctioning.

"Michael!" she called out. Her inner muscles clenched at his fingers as she climaxed. Clenching so damn tight, making him crazed because he wanted it to be his cock her pussy contracted around.

He didn't withdraw from her as her hips continued to roll and she stole the last vestiges of orgasm.

Michael left feathery kisses along the tops of her breasts, across her collarbone, up her neck.

"Think I've died and gone to heaven," she whispered.

"Not yet. I'm not done with you."

"There won't be anything left of me when you are."

He kissed her, then said, "I think you can handle it."

"Then don't hold back."

His gaze locked with hers. "I don't intend to."

FOUR

Scarlet's insides blazed brighter. She was already incinerating from the hotter-than-hell man staring so deeply into her eyes and the sensational orgasms he'd given her. Michael's hunky body between her legs made every inch of her sizzle even more.

She released the strands of his hair that she'd probably yanked on too firmly when she'd come, but he didn't seem to mind. She fisted the material at his nape and pulled, dragging his shirt over his head, breaking their eye contact for only a brief second. Tossing aside the garment, she ran both hands along his sinewy forearms and up to his bulging biceps. He was magnificently built, all sculpted muscles and smooth, tanned skin.

Her hands continued to roam, up to his broad shoulders, then down the front of him. He had a solid, well-defined pectoral ledge that her fingers grazed, her nails gently rasping his small, pebbled nipples.

His teeth ground. She was testing his restraint. She could see it in his smoldering gaze. Could feel it in the intensity that radiated from him.

She kept up her exploration, loving the way his body tensed as her fingertips skimmed his cut abs, heading south. When she reached the buckle on his belt, he let out a harsh grunt that was additional confirmation she was pushing him right to the edge.

Exhilaration trilled down her spine. Her pussy ached in anticipation of being filled and stretched by him. She felt the moisture ooze from her opening along her cleft. No one had ever made her so wet.

She deftly unfastened him and shoved his briefs and jeans over his hips. She tore her gaze from Michael's and it landed on his cock. Thick and wide and mouthwatering.

The sudden desire to suck him to completion gripped her. She wanted his shaft against her tongue, his tip stroking the back of her throat before he lost it and came in her mouth.

But the desperate need to have him deep inside her overrode the fantasy. Her fingers encircled his base and she pumped slowly. Hunger flashed in his smoky eyes.

She told him, "Photos in the *Wall Street Journal* don't capture your animal magnetism. That can only fully be experienced in person."

His lips brushed over hers and he murmured, "Then let me give you the full, in-person experience."

Her stomach flipped. "Thank you for not making me beg."

He pried her fingers from his dick. "You almost have *me* begging."

Michael's blatant, engaging look sent liquid fire through her. He pressed her legs wider apart with his palms on her inner thighs and his thick shaft glided along her folds, back and forth. Taunting her. He eased slightly back and his tip rubbed against her clit. He leaned into her and his cock slid along her slick flesh, his balls grazing her cleft and anus.

The man was a master at building the sexual tension and intensifying the dark cravings he'd sparked from the onset.

"Okay, now I'm begging," she said in a strained tone. "You want to be inside me, don't you?"

"Ah, fuck, yes."

He curved his arm under one of her bent legs and lifted it off the desk, slinging her boot-clad calf over his shoulder as he leaned close to her again and his cockhead penetrated her, sending high-voltage bolts through her body.

"Oh, God!" Her head flew back on her shoulders.

"Don't squeeze," Michael hissed out. "I already know how tight you are. And I'm two seconds away from ending this party if you're any tighter."

She tried to relax her inner muscles. But they involuntarily sought something that had been elusive for so very, very long. Too damn long.

As much as she wanted to plead with Michael to stop playing and get down to business, she could see he was hanging on by a thin thread. She'd gotten him all worked up at the club, had felt his erection the entire time. So she had no doubt the scorching sensations were about to burst wide open for him as much as for her.

Scarlet laid back against the desk, sprawling across it. Raising her arms over her head, she clasped the far edge.

"Now that's a hell of a sight," he said. And thrust into her, pushing all the air from her lungs on a wild scream.

He didn't give her even a moment to assimilate to his girth, stretching her taut. His hips bucked and he fucked her assertively. Exactly what she wanted. *But good Lord . . .* He was huge inside her and plunging deep, fast. Jarring her body, making her grip the ledge more firmly.

He slid his free arm under her at her lower back and her spine bowed so that her head and shoulders were the only part of her touching the glass top as her ass lifted off the surface and her other leg wrapped around his waist.

"Yes," she sobbed. "Oh, God, yes. Michael!" He pounded into her and it was everything she needed. Everything she'd longed for as her best friends were hooking up with amazingly satisfying men and all Scarlet had was her work.

She'd ached for this sort of fulfillment—the dirtier the better at this point, because her hormones were raging. More than ever since she'd met Michael.

He seemed to innately know how to please her, how to rock her to the core of her being.

The way he angled her hips into his thrusts allowed him to push farther into her. So incredibly deep. His pelvis both ground and pumped, so he was stimulating every bit of her pussy, inside and out. His heat surrounded her. His muscles brushed against her flushed skin, keeping her fully connected to him. Scarlet was about to crash head-on into another earth-shattering orgasm.

"Christ, you're exciting to watch as I fuck you," he told her.

As sensational as it felt to have him take her with such abandon, she needed to come again. It was too fiery and too intense to hold on to.

"Fuck me," she insisted. "Harder. Oh, God, Michael. Fuck my pussy. Make me come."

Her fingers uncoiled from the ledge. One of her palms flattened on the desk at her hip. The other gripped his forearm as it was locked around her leg that was draped over his shoulder. She used the leverage to pull him closer to her, rolled her hips with his enticing erratic movements, and felt all the insanity and electricity arcing between them and humming through her coalesce and erupt.

She cried his name as the orgasm slammed into her. Little white and gold orbs burst behind her closed lids. Every fiber of her being ignited. And just when she thought she couldn't lose herself any further in the moment, he thrust into her once more, his body convulsed, and then she felt his hot seed flood her pussy.

"Yes!" she shrieked. "That is so good!"

"Scarlet!" He pushed as far as he could, his cock buried to

the hilt. "Oh, fuck!" Violent shudders rocked him. His breath came in heavy pulls, every exhale caressing the inner swells of her breasts.

Scarlet kept her eyes closed, knowing they'd just dance crazily in their sockets if she opened them anyway. She fought for more than just razor-thin slices of air. She'd never been so winded before. Nor had her body ever tingled so vibrantly. From her nose to her toes and every erogenous zone in between.

She was still buzzing from the release when Michael straightened and took her by the hand. He gently hauled her up. He withdrew from her and, with a little shifting, had her legs and arms coiled around him. She was limp and boneless, but he held her tightly and carried her across the vast penthouse to his master suite. Balancing her with one hand, he yanked back the covers in the large bed and set her there. Then he worked the zipper of one boot and removed it, rolled down her black stocking, and repeated the process with the other.

"Damn sexy," he said. "You in the boots. You out of the boots."

His gaze roved her naked body and she didn't miss that his cock twitched.

"Get comfortable," he told her.

Not in a million years would she have expected Michael Vandenberg to assume she'd stay over or invite her to do so. She didn't take him for the type to embrace afterglow cuddling. And maybe he wasn't, so she scooted to the opposite side of the mattress while he ducked into the bathroom to tidy up.

When he joined her, he said, "We like the same side." He climbed in behind her and she moved to accommodate him. "Don't go too far." His arms wound around her as he spooned her.

Scarlet's heart skipped a beat. She wasn't used to the wild and wicked sex; that was a given. But this soft and tender affection from the Wolf of Wall Street?

What the fuck? flashed in her head.

He held her tightly, possessively. His body curled around hers, another perfect fit.

He said, "I hadn't realized I needed a jump start until I laid eyes on you earlier this evening. I am forever a fan of your persistence."

Something twisted inside of Scarlet. Not necessarily in a bad way. She wiggled slightly so that he gave way to her and she turned to face him.

"Michael." She gazed at him with little more than the flicker of the lights from the unadorned windows to faintly illuminate his steely features. "If you tell me again that you're innocent, I'll believe you."

She worked off intuition, after all. And it was speaking loud and clear to her.

But she had to hear him say the words at this moment, at this point in time. Following the highly charged evening they'd had and the way he was so in tune to her needs, to her desires . . . She felt a connection she'd never experienced before—and trusted it heart and soul.

She just needed to hear the conviction in his tone.

He swept away strands of hair from her temple and told her, "I assure you I was exactly where I said I was when the collection was stolen. And I wouldn't have benefited from plotting or participating in the robbery. The paintings were bought by my father, yes. But they were gifted to my stepmother. A belated wedding present, because he waited until he had all the pieces before he gave them to her. So that insurance check was handed directly to her."

Scarlet's brow knitted. "It was made out to him."

"Yes, because he was the one to purchase the collection and pay the premium on it. The money was transferred into her account. Hers to do with what she pleased."

Scarlet's mind whirled. "Did she buy new artwork?"

"No. She claimed the paintings my father had selected for her originally meant too much for her to randomly go out and replace them."

"She started taking art history classes at NYU after she married your father, Michael. There'd be nothing random about her selections—"

"It's sentimentality that holds her back. How do you substitute a gift that was so thoughtfully assembled for you?"

Scarlet considered this. He had a point, of course. Yet . . . "I looked into her finances, too. Her net worth didn't improve, individually. Of course, she's linked to your father's fortune, but where'd the insurance money go?"

Michael placed a finger over her lips. "Scarlet. You can talk about this until the sun comes up. I can't help you. I'm sorry. I don't know what happened to that collection. And to be damn honest with you, I don't give a rip. Do you understand?"

"Were you jealous he'd given her such an expensive gift?" she asked around his finger. "Or that the family fortune paid for it—at about the same time your father had refused to subsidize your first business venture?"

Michael's hand fell away. "My father insisted that whatever I did with my future from the time I turned sixteen was completely up to me. There was no access to a trust fund—not until I'm forty. *Forty*, Scarlet. So, yes, I had to figure out how to pay for Princeton. I had to figure out how to fund my enterprises. With no one's help. No, I wasn't jealous. I was too busy being resourceful."

"But the five mil—"

"A saving grace, without doubt. It came after I'd graduated, with a student loan hanging over my head. That sugar plantation I inherited helped me to invest in my future. I'm grateful for it and that I was able to sell off a small portion. But make no mistake, Scarlet. That money did *not* come from criminal activity."

He stared at her.

Scarlet could clearly see there was more to his story. A difficult push and pull between him and his father. Including a gauntlet thrown down by the senior Vandenberg indicating Michael had to work his way up the food chain in order to prove himself worthy of a chunk of the family pie?

She said, "I certainly don't discount everything you've done to become the successful entrepreneur you are today. You're a self-made man—"

"Let's not take that notion *too* far," he contended. "I was born with a silver spoon in my mouth. No hiding or disguising it. I just wasn't handed everything on the proverbial platter that's anticipated to follow. I did have to work for the things I wanted. Yet I obviously had advantages as well."

With a soft smile, she said, "Big of you to admit all that. And I'm not trying to accuse you of anything. I'm trying to understand who you are. I already admire what I've learned to date. It's just that I have a job to do, you know?"

"Yeah, I know." He kissed her, then added, "My advice, however, is that you look outside the mansion walls for your culprit, not within them."

Scarlet gave a slow nod. "There are theories."

"I've heard them."

"Not mine."

"Whatever happened that night isn't my responsibility or concern. Do I feel bad Karina's paintings were stolen?" He gave a noncommittal shrug of his shoulder. "I don't know. She came into my life at a difficult time, when I was still dealing with my mother's death and the terms of my trust fund. We didn't hit it off. Worse, she insinuated a son my age into the household. I wasn't ready for that. Not at first. So I was emotionally detached."

"Just one more question," Scarlet ventured, sensing she was losing him to an angst that related to family matters, not art theft. "Do you still feel that way about her?"

Michael let out a long breath. Rolled onto his back. Though he brought Scarlet with him so she was tucked under his arm, against his hard body.

As his fingers absently twirled her long strands, he said, "I have a complicated relationship with my family. The turmoil dates back to childhood, so it's not exactly Karina's fault. I didn't agree with how quickly my father could get over one wife in favor of a new one."

Scarlet knew that Lindsay Vandenberg, Michael's mother, was a cancer patient who'd died of pneumonia. She also knew that Mitcham had married Karina the same year he'd buried Lindsay. Naturally, that made Scarlet wonder if Karina had been waiting in the wings, and for how long. Had she and Mitcham secretly been involved prior to Lindsay's illnesses? Or maybe not so secretly—had Michael known about it?

Did any of this matter?

Scarlet wasn't sure.

So for the moment, she dropped the topic. She needed to process the entire interaction with him this evening and everything she'd discerned thus far.

Her hand splayed over his chest and her fingertips lightly stroked his warm, smooth skin. She said, "Thank you for tolerating my inquiry. I'm not trying to be invasive. I have a mind that doesn't really shut down. Hard as I try. It can be a bit of a curse sometimes. I require constant mental stimulation. Puzzles provide that."

"Scarlet . . ." He sighed. "I haven't been avoiding you because I have something to hide. I have a hectic schedule. I travel every week. I have meeting after meeting. Every day. Well into the night. I created this world, this reality, for myself, but it can also be a double-edged sword. I have to pick and choose who I give my time to." He was quiet for a few moments, then told her, "I'll confess that you being so damn striking and wearing that skintight red dress this evening nabbed my attention. Yet it was so much more beyond your appearance that held it. You get me hot, yes. Especially in that black mini and the boots you changed into. But you also intrigue me. Fascinate me. Whatever. It's impossible to deny."

Her lips pressed to that tempting indentation at the base of his throat. Then she gazed at him. "It's no longer a criminal case, Michael. I still have to follow every lead, though. Help the insurance company recoup any monies if that's appropriate."

His body stiffened. Scarlet continued to stare into his eyes.

In a tight voice, Michael explained, "The thing about Vandenbergs is that they don't like people digging into their business. It's sort of a centuries-old entitlement thing. We tend to think we're above reproach. So of course we find anyone who's purposely searching for the chinks in our armor to be . . . offensive."

"I get what you're saying." It was a veiled warning. But one she could live with. So much so, she slipped a leg over his hunky body and straddled him. She placed her palms on his chest, and as her sex slowly glided against his rapidly thickening erection she said, "But despite my poking and prodding, I don't think you find me the least bit offensive."

Michael's large hands clasped her hips. He shifted just so. Sank into her, blissfully filling her. And said, "Not in the least."

FIVE

Scarlet woke to the delicate aroma of a rose. The bed was still warm and cozy, though she knew she slept alone in it.

She opened her eyes and smiled at the red bloom resting on Michael's pillow. He was still in the penthouse; she could hear him in the bathroom, talking on his cell while he shaved and moussed and did whatever the hell else he did to look so mind-bogglingly gorgeous.

A silvery haze loomed over the bay and wrapped around the skyscrapers like a thick blanket. A light mist splattered itty-bitty droplets against the enormous windowpanes. The drizzle would eventually dissipate once the fog burned off.

Scarlet had always loved the moody morning weather. It was sultry and provocative with a personality all its own.

She spared a glance at the clock on the nightstand. Six a.m. Time to get a move-on and find new leads for her case.

Before she even had a chance to throw back the covers and gather up her boots. Michael emerged from the bathroom and swooped in, sitting on the edge of the mattress.

He said, "You're either a light sleeper or an early riser by nature."

"Both," she told him. "My grandmother's one of the crazies

who thinks the crack of dawn is the absolute best part of the day. And she's usually bustling about, brewing the world's strongest coffee, so you have no choice but to wake up. She's typically always on the phone or the computer, too. I could never help but eavesdrop. Her work captivates me."

"Who, exactly, is your grandmother?"

"L. C. Seymour."

He chuckled. "You're shitting me."

"Nope."

"All right then. That's impressive. *New York Times* bestselling mystery author. Her books make blockbuster movies."

"Yes. And her mind is more hyperactive than mine."

"Who would have thought that possible?" He winked. Then kissed her.

Scarlet would have melted, except that she had a plan to stick to. She gently shoved Michael aside and leapt to her feet. "I have to go. You clearly have work to do and I've got mine as well."

"Hey, hey." He reached for her hand and pulled, forcing her to return to the bed. "Settle in. Checkout's not until three. Order room service and enjoy the views over mimosas."

"Oh, sure. So you can call me a slacker."

He grinned. "You've sufficiently proven that that is not the case. Now . . . I unfortunately have a flight to catch."

"New York or one of your exotic locales?"

"New York. I have a board meeting to attend. Otherwise, I'd get naked with you again and share the mimosas afterward."

Her fingertips grazed his silk tie. "Yes, it is a shame that you're all buttoned up."

"With a car waiting to take me to the airport."

She softly kissed his lips and whispered against them, "Thanks for not completely shutting me out."

"And what about the hot sex?"

"Makes me a fan of persistence, too."

He laughed quietly. His hand cupped the side of her face and he kissed her, long and leisurely, despite his comment about having a car waiting for him. The kiss went on and on, heating her insides. Making her long for the naked scenario, darn it.

When he eventually dragged his mouth away, he said, "Gotta go. I'll call you." He kissed the tip of her nose, then slipped from the bed, grabbing his jacket from the suit rack in the corner before disappearing out the door.

Scarlet fell against the mound of pillows and let out a lusty sigh. The man was all kinds of sexy. And she was ridiculously turned on by him. With just a kiss. Well, a kiss and the reminder of everything he'd done to her the night before.

He wasn't just an amazing lover; he also stirred emotions within her. Perhaps it was because of his strained family relations. Not to mention his mother's death, which clearly weighed heavy in his heart. Scarlet could commiserate.

There was also the addition of a new brother, sprung on Michael out of the blue. During the volatile teenaged years, no less. And of course the issue of his father being so controlling couldn't be discounted. Mitcham had refused to grant Michael access to the Vandenberg empire—wouldn't for another decade.

Not that Michael needed that capital now. He was set for several lifetimes. But it was probably the principle of the matter that rubbed him raw. Chances were very good he'd had tons of expectations heaped on him from birth. High expectations. Maybe even some unrealistic ones, given his surname and a reputation to be upheld. What must it have been like to grow up in a mansion with such a dominant force of nature as a father, who likely placed restrictions and perimeters around that childhood?

To follow all the rules and then discover it was basically for naught—because all you were left with when it came time to spread your wings was the Vandenberg name. And nothing to back it up.

His father telling Michael when he was sixteen that he'd have to pay for his own college education—and, again, likely expecting him to attend an Ivy League school—offered Michael the opportunity to research and apply for scholarships, certainly. Save money from after-school and summer jobs. But, Jesus. Princeton couldn't come cheap.

All of Scarlet's speculation was healthy for the brain, but really, she was more interested in the layers beneath Michael Vandenberg's impeccably tailored CEO-by-day and devilishly handsome bad-boy-by-night persona. She wanted to dissect him, pick him apart. Get to the core of who he was and what he really sought in the grand scheme of things. Greater success than his father as some sort of fuck-you to Mitcham for being a hard-ass? Or did Michael seek approval? A less tenuous bond with his parents . . . and some peace from his mother's passing?

With Scarlet's curiosity shifting into high gear, she knew there was no point in attempting to sleep. Luckily, with Bayli in New York and the East Coast being three hours ahead of the West it was a respectable hour to ring her friend.

So Scarlet left the cozy comfort of the bed, snatched the luxurious midnight-blue robe on the bench at the foot of the mattress, which Michael had thoughtfully laid out for her, and padded barefoot into the living room to retrieve her phone from her purse.

"Well, hello there, sunshine," came Bayli's cheerful voice when she connected Scarlet's Skype call.

"You are way too chipper, my friend," Scarlet grumbled. "I haven't even had coffee yet."

"And oh, my God," Bayli suddenly gasped. "You have some serious sex hair going on! *Where* are you and *who* is he?"

Scarlet couldn't fight the smile. "I'm currently in the penthouse of the new Crestmont in San Fran." She panned the camera over the elegantly appointed living room and the sweeping views of the bay and the Financial District.

Bayli whistled under her breath. "Stellar."

"Yes, well, it gets better," Scarlet told her. "After I finally made contact with my elusive wraith, and then later hooked up with him at the club, we came here."

"That's Michael Vandenberg's penthouse suite?" Bayli's eyes popped. "Holy Moses. You . . . and him. Oh. My. God."

"Might as well add Jesus, Mary, and Joseph to that sentiment. Because I was singing some praises last night."

Bayli's radiant smile filled the screen. "You wicked, wicked woman!"

"'Bout time. Good grief. It should be a crime to go as long as I have without sex. Great sex. Mind-blowing, core-shaking sex, to be exact."

"Ooohh, the best kind. But . . . uh . . . speaking of crimes, girlfriend . . . you just slept with a person of interest in a case you're working."

"Yeah, there is that." Scarlet wandered the vast room and located the in-suite iPad that featured touch-of-a-button butler service. She shot off a note to the designated attendant, requesting a pot of coffee and a bagel with cream cheese. As she scooped up her clothing that was strewn about, she told Bayli, "I will confess to a lapse in morals. In my defense, however . . ." She blew out a long breath. "He was worth every unraveled scruple. And then some."

"Wow. Coming from you, that's saying something. What's going on with you two?"

"I have no idea, honestly. Just that last night was sensational and I wouldn't be opposed to a repeat performance. But he's on his way back to New York. And I need fresh clues to pursue."

"Well, you're in luck there, too," Bayli excitedly said. "The official FBI report has finally arrived—so much more conclusive than the vague snapshot provided by the insurance company. I printed a hard copy and FedExed it to you."

"Knowing you the way I do, you've read it from cover to cover already."

"Twice."

Scarlet laughed. "Naturally. So, what exactly was Michael's entire statement?"

"Let me pull up the PDF." A few moments ticked by; then she gave the alibi verbatim. Nothing different from what Michael had told Scarlet, just a bit more detailed, including the names of the women he'd been pleasuring while someone was ripping off his stepmother's art collection.

Which reminded Scarlet that Michael had mentioned his stepbrother last night. "Tell me more about Sam Reed."

"Total enigma. Same age as Michael, thirty. Also went to Princeton. He studied architecture. Never joined a firm, though. A year after the paintings went missing, he was in a car accident with his fiancée. Very tragic story. They were returning to the Hamptons estate from a local charity function when their car was struck by a drunk driver on the passenger side. Sam was driving. He was hospitalized for numerous injuries."

Scarlet's stomach suddenly churned. "And the fiancée?"

"DOA."

"Shit. That's harsh." She sank onto a plump sofa cushion.

"Doubly. She was pregnant."

"Oh, Christ."

"Yeah," Bayli concurred with a tinge of dismay. "Sad stuff. According to one of the news articles I found when I started researching him, Sam had just broken ground on a house in Montana that they were going to move into following the wedding. I dug around a little more and discovered he went through with the plan. He has an equestrian estate not far from a little town called Lakeside. Pretty impressive layout. I Google Mapped it and there's some serious acreage there with a gorgeous lodge-style home and modern horse facilities."

THE BILLIONAIRES: THE STEPBROTHERS   55

Scarlet frowned. "Where'd the money come from for all of that? Michael claims he doesn't have access to family funds until he's forty. If Sam was granted some sort of trust when his mother married Mitcham, I can't imagine Sam would be able to get his hands on it anytime sooner than Michael."

"And Sam's mom did not come from money. She was a waitress and also a volunteer docent at a gallery when she met the senior Vandenberg. Struggling, from what I gather."

"Though clearly committed to her passion for fine art."

"Which makes it incredibly difficult to believe she'd be involved in the disappearance of a coveted collection."

Scarlet contemplated this further as the butler entered the suite and set out the coffee and her breakfast, then served her. She dismissed him with a smile and a mouthed, *Thank you*. She took a couple of sips from her cup, then asked Bayli, "Did you come across anything of note with Sam's financials?"

"Haven't gotten to them yet, sorry."

"Don't apologize. Seriously. Everything you're doing is such a huge help. I really need to hire a research assist—"

"*I'm* your research assistant."

Scarlet grinned. Set her coffee aside. "Bay, I know you dig all this cloak-and-dagger stuff, and trying to unearth whatever you can for me, but you do have a job."

"I'm on hiatus, Scarlet. We wrapped the preseason of the travel-and-cooking show and are evaluating all the responses from the test audiences, though the network has already picked us up. I'm just trying to dissect what the viewers really connected with— pertaining to the locales, the food Rory prepared, the chef challenges, and of course my hosting skills. I've been pretty OCD about it all, so a distraction is much appreciated."

"I'd feel better if you let me pay you."

"I don't want you to pay me. And I certainly don't need the money now that I have the show. I don't want Jewel to pay me, either, when I do research for her acquisitions. A girl should have a hobby, Scarlet. And for me, it can't be Christian and Rory. They have their own work to focus on."

Scarlet said, "Yes, I can imagine it'd be difficult to not be all twenty-four-seven about two incredibly sexy men who are more than happy to do your bidding both in and out of the bedroom. I'd still be absurdly jealous if I wasn't deliriously happy following multiple orgasms."

"Understandable. I will say I'm surprised that you pulled an overnighter."

"That would make two of us. I was prepared to put my clothes back on and get the hell out, but Michael was in no particular hurry to see me go." She smiled again. "In fact . . . he has a very sweet side."

"Didn't see that one coming."

"Nor did I." Scarlet's heart did a curious little flip at this more sensitive Michael Vandenberg. It was as appealing as every mysterious aspect of him.

Bayli asked, "So what does that mean, exactly?"

Scarlet shrugged. "I suppose it means I have the hots for the guy. And he might be a little partial to me as well."

"*That* wouldn't surprise me in the least. He just needed to let you pick up his trail and catch up to him. Do you intend to see him again?"

"He said he'd call." Scarlet's teeth sank into her lip for a moment. She said, "Single women all over the world are currently cringing right now, yes?"

"I don't know. On the one hand, Rory told me he'd contact me after that disastrous first meeting with him. And he didn't. On the other hand, Christian was right on it. So . . . there's no telling."

"Well, either way, I have to keep my attention on this case." Though Scarlet felt, deep in her bones, Michael was not the answer to solving it.

THE BILLIONAIRES: THE STEPBROTHERS   57

"What else can I do for you so that I don't go stir-crazy in this huge apartment while Rory is creating a new menu for the next restaurant Christian's plotting in New Orleans?"

"New Orleans? Sweet!"

"Yes, Rory is currently fixated on crawfish—the lobster of the South."

"Um . . . I'm not really sure what to say about that."

"I hear ya," Bayli quipped. "But he's into creating a dozen varieties of hot sauces and making crawfish cool outside of southern boundaries. He might be on to something. You know, once you get past snapping their little heads off."

Rory St. James was a celebrity chef, and his business partner was brilliant restaurateur Christian Davila. Bayli had applied for a position in their newest establishment, Davila's NYC, an upscale steakhouse on Lexington Avenue. She'd wanted the part-time job to help supplement her meager income as a sometime model. What she'd ended up with was a TV show starring her and Rory.

And that was just the tip of the iceberg. What Bayli had ultimately gained was the love of two fiercely protective men who were hopelessly devoted to her.

Bayli wasn't the only one graced with good fortune. Jewel had landed her dream hotel and a vineyard . . . not to mention her own hopelessly devoted men.

Admittedly, Scarlet had been living vicariously through her friends of late. But last night had given her a new burst of enthusiasm and excitement.

Though she was smart enough to play the hand cautiously, not fully knowing Michael's true agenda, even if it didn't involve missing artwork.

Bayli cut into her thoughts, asking, "Want me to comb through the stepbrother's accounts? See what I find?"

"That'd be great—particularly around the period when the

insurance company cut the check. I need to take a shower and then get back to my hotel to check out and get my car."

"I'll call you if anything fishy pops up."

"Perfect. Thanks." They disconnected.

Scarlet went into the bathroom. Once dressed, she called the valet for transportation to the St. Francis.

She'd barely stepped out of the elevator and into the alabaster-marbled lobby when Bayli phoned her.

"You are *not* going to believe this!"

Scarlet's heart launched into her throat.

"Please, God, let this be about Sam," she couldn't help but say, because she needed a different thread to pull that wasn't wrapped around Michael.

"It is," Bayli assured her. "I only had to look specifically around the time frame you mentioned, and lo and behold, his net worth increased by five million not more than three weeks after Michael's did."

"Which could effectively mean . . . there's ten mil from the eighteen the claim paid out."

Except that Michael had insisted his money had come from a real estate transaction. And she believed him.

But damn it. This little revelation—this coincidence—did not bode well for anyone.

Bayli said, "Perhaps the remainder went to whoever actually removed the paintings from the grounds?"

Scarlet's heart sank. "Could be," she reluctantly said, though she was no longer convinced of this theory.

Bayli latched on to it, however. "So the brothers said 'screw you' to the old man and each turned his portion into an infinitely larger fortune? Without Dad's help?"

Scarlet halted at the double doors of the hotel entrance, not passing through them. She said, "That was an initial inclination

I had. It honestly doesn't sit right with me anymore. I need more information. I have to see this Sam Reed guy face-to-face. As with Michael, I need to gauge who Sam is, what he's looking to achieve, what he really and truly wants. He's too much of a mystery to me at this point." And Scarlet wanted desperately to cross Michael off her list of suspects.

There had to be a viable explanation as to how both men had ended up with the same financial disbursements back-to-back.

Bayli said, "I'll track down a Skype number for Reed, if he has one."

"Thanks, but that's not enough. I have to go to Montana."

"Scarlet." Bayli's tone was suddenly filled with concern. "It's the dead of winter."

"And this can't wait. I only have a few weeks, Bay." The sense of urgency hit her hard. "Then all the work I've done will go to waste and I'll fail this assignment. I'll fail my client." Something she simply couldn't abide.

Bayli said, "You've never even been to Montana! Come on, Scarlet. I know you're an overachiever by nature, but this ranch is not going to be easy to find. You could drive for days before you figure out where the hell you are!"

The panic exuding from her friend aside, Scarlet had already made up her mind. She shoved through the lobby doors before a bellman could assist her and stalked toward a valet, saying, "Scarlet Drake. There's a car here somewhere for me."

"Yes, Miss Drake. At the front of the line."

"Excellent. Thank you." The driver appeared and Scarlet slid into the back of the vehicle as she told him, "The St. Francis." Then to Bayli on the phone, she said, "Look, I'm not trying to get crazy here. But this is a cold case for a reason—the good leads have all been exhausted. Yet something in my gut tells me there's more to the story. I want to learn it."

And fully exonerate Michael.

Bayli paused, and Scarlet knew she was stewing over Scarlet's tenacity. She wouldn't be the first; wouldn't be the last.

Finally, Bayli said, "I'll send you all the info you need. But, Jesus, Scarlet. Be careful. Please."

With a soft laugh to ease some of the tension, Scarlet told her, "Relax. It's not the Wild, Wild West. It's just Montana."

"With light flurries later this afternoon, according to my weather app."

"I'll rent a Jeep or an SUV or something. I'm sure they'll put chains on for me or whatever. And again, it's modern civilization. I'll bet they even have snowplows."

"Guess you'll find out."

"Don't worry about me."

"Yeah, right. Like I wasn't stressing when you went on your super-secret date last night."

"I kept you guys in the loop. Thanks for having my back, by the way."

"Oh, we'll be doing that all right," Bayli assured her. "I have new GPS solutions for both you and Jewel, for when she's tracking down her elusive unicorns for negotiations and trading power on acquisitions. The two of you are a bit too Jane Bond for comfort."

"Speak for yourself, danger magnet. I've never been kidnapped before."

"Uh, well, that was just . . . I mean . . . it wasn't so much a kidnapping as—"

"You were trapped, Bay. And it was incredibly hazardous to your health."

"So's the middle-of-nowhere Montana in a snowstorm—especially for a Cali girl."

Scarlet smirked. "I'll be fine. Send the directions I need. And thanks bunches. I love you to pieces."

"Back at ya. And always have your cell close at hand, okay? Promise."

"I swear. Now, I've got to make air and car reservations, collect my bag from my hotel, and do a little winter apparel shopping so I don't freeze my ass off."

"Water, blankets, first-aid kit, power bars, snow scraper, flare gun. Think you can get the rental company to pack all that in your vehicle?"

"Along with ropes for rappelling, a pickaxe, snowshoes, and—"

"Smart-ass."

"Really, Bay?" She laughed. "A flare gun?"

"Yeah, you're right. Fat lot of good it did for the *Titanic*."

"I'll be fine," Scarlet insisted.

"Just keep me posted."

"Of course." They disconnected.

Scarlet set about accomplishing all of her tasks and then drove to San Francisco International Airport.

Excitement rolled through her as she boarded a plane. She felt a trill of curiosity along her spine and her inquisitive mind continued to whirl with myriad possibilities.

What might Sam Reed be hiding . . . ?

SIX

"Good Lord, Sam," Reva Travers said as she pressed a hand to her chest. "That saddle looks better than brand-new."

Sam Reed hoisted the restored saddle from the bed of his truck and carried it past Reva and into her heated tack room as she followed him in. He slung his latest project onto the only vacant stand and then stepped back, propping his hands on his waist.

He said, "Took a little more work than I'd initially thought, but once I got started it became an all-or-nothing sort of deal."

"It sparkles brighter than ever before." She reached for the large red satin bow sitting on a bench and settled it in the seat. "Layton will be so thrilled."

"He deserves this," Sam said of her son, who'd be turning fifteen over the weekend. "He's put tremendous effort into improving his jumping these past few years and now he's got a shot at nationals."

"Not only is he finally tall enough to ride his father's horse, but he'll be sitting high in that beautiful saddle that Hank loved so much." Tears pooled in her eyes. "It was passed down from his great-grandfather. Now Layton can truly carry on the Travers family tradition."

"Hank was a good man," Sam said in a quiet voice as he gently placed a hand on Reva's shoulder. "I'm sorry for your loss."

"I know." She gazed up at him with watery brown eyes. Reva Travers was a pretty brunette who looked like she'd grown up on the Girl Scouts, the 4-H Club, and the advent of the organic veggie movement. And she had. "Been a rough time for Layton lately, especially with Hank's illness incapacitating him for so long. But this will be a highlight after the dark times. Means a lot to him, Sam."

She got a bit choked up. Tried to cover it with a casual laugh as she swiped at her cheek with the sleeve of her sweater.

Sam's gut twisted. Though he told her in an even voice, "We'll get back to training after Layton's birthday. He needs plenty of time on his daddy's horse before the competition season starts."

"It'll help him to have something to focus on following the funeral."

"I agree. Now I have to get back to the ranch."

"Be careful. Couple of hours from now, the snow's going to be fallin' heavy."

Reva's house in Whitefish was about an hour away from Reed Ranch, south through Lakeside. Sam said, "I'll be in good shape before the storm really hits." He gave her a grin. "But I'll be back for Layton's party on Sunday night, I promise."

"He'd be so disappointed if you weren't there. He looks up to you, Sam. More so now than ever."

"I'm damn fond of him, too." Sam gave her a quick, friendly hug, then turned to go.

"Wait," Reva said. "Let me get my checkbook."

Sam glanced over his shoulder. "Don't you dare. This is something I wanted to do. It was a great idea you had, Reva. I'm happy to have been a part of it."

"Sam." She frowned. "I know you have the equestrian facilities and your furniture-making to occupy your time. This project took up even more hours."

"I enjoyed this, Reva. I started fixing up old saddles when I moved here, and I'm getting the hang of it."

"You've done more than that; trust me." She gave him a grateful smile. "At least take the apple pie I made for you."

"Well, you know I'll never pass *that* up." He winked good-naturedly.

She hurried over to the extra refrigerator in the tack room and extracted a pink box with a white satin ribbon up each side and tied into a bow on top. She always did her pies up right.

Handing over the box, along with a small bag from the freezer, Reva said, "There's also a container of vanilla ice cream and some cinnamon."

"You don't miss a thing." He grinned again. Then he headed out.

Reva followed him, saying, "Now don't go forgettin' about Macy Dalton's retirement luncheon in two weeks. We're all expecting you—Macy, in particular."

"I'm not so sure I'm going to make that one," he confessed. "I give back-to-back lessons around that time on Sundays."

"Macy Dalton has twin grandsons who come from a long line of champion jumpers and they'll be ready to climb on the backs of ponies within the year." She gave him a pointed look.

"Then I'll be there."

She nodded. "Had a feeling you'd reconsider."

Sam opened the passenger door of his truck and set the desserts on the floor. The scrawny pup snuggled under the wool blanket on the bench seat stirred and poked his nose out. His dry nose, much to Sam's dismay. The yellow Labrador wasn't doing so hot.

Reva spotted the little hound and leaned in, clapping her gloved hands together. "Oh, my gosh, Sam. He's so adorable. When'd you get a dog?"

Crossing his arms over his chest, he told her, "Wasn't exactly a premeditated decision. I found him alongside the road, not far from the ranch. In the snow, looking damn-near starved to death and brutally kicked around."

Reva gently peeled back the wool and gasped. The pup's pale body was covered in black-and-blue marks, along with several cuts. She pressed a hand to her mouth. More tears sprang to her eyes.

Sam reached around her and covered the Lab up again. "He ought to be okay in a couple of weeks. I'd be happier if I could get him to eat more than a few bites here and there, but it's like he doesn't trust me to feed him proper food or something."

Composing herself, Reva said, "He'll come around. You just have to keep talking softly to him and showing him you're not going to hurt him."

Sam shut the door and he and Reva rounded the front of the truck.

She added, "Take those roads home slow, now. It's starting to get dark."

He chuckled. "You worry a little too much about everyone. I'll be fine."

Resting a hand on his forearm, she stared up at him and said, "I really do appreciate everything you've done for my family since Hank got sick. And to be so concerned about Layton." She seemed to fight more emotion as she told him, "You're very special, Sam. Now if I could just find the right woman for you."

She lightened the mood with her joke. Though she was actually serious.

Sam said, "I'm not lookin' for one, Reva."

"He says that today," she wistfully jested.

Sam tried to keep his expression neutral, forced his shoulders not to bunch. He'd had the woman he'd wanted, once upon a time. A kid on the way, too.

A son.

But one asshole who'd been stupid enough to get behind the

wheel when he'd had too much to drink had altered Sam's future in a flash.

He still hadn't recovered. Could still feel Cassidy in his arms as he'd held her shaking body while sirens had wailed too far in the distance and her blood had covered his chest, his arms, his hands. It'd been impossible to separate where the wounds began and where they ended. She'd been a mangled mess to rival the car.

And there hadn't been a goddamn thing Sam could do to save her.

But he tried really hard not to dwell on the past. To keep the nightmares at bay.

Not dating—not getting emotionally involved—helped with that. He was nowhere near ready to open himself up like that again.

So he politely deflected when it came to Reva's good-intentioned attempts at matchmaking.

She headed toward the tack room, saying, "I've got some more organizin' to do. Sorting out what Layton might be able to use of Hank's and his granddaddies' for the upcoming competitions. I'll see you at the party."

"You take care." Sam slid behind the wheel. The pup shifted under the blanket and all but threw his slight weight against Sam's jean-clad thigh, getting as close as he could, in hopes of body heat or maybe just physical reassurance.

Sam cranked the key in the ignition and warmth flooded the cab. He backed into the turnaround spot and then drove off the property. The light snoring of the puppy filled the silence as Sam headed south on 93 toward Lakeside. It was a raspy, slightly strained sound. But steadier than it'd been when Sam had found the stray a few days ago.

Sam didn't bother putting on music, just ran through his schedule for the week in his mind. As he entered Lakeside, he shifted his thoughts to anything he might need to pick up before returning to his remote home. But he was accustomed to stocking

THE BILLIONAIRES: THE STEPBROTHERS

up for long, hard winters and couldn't think of anything he hadn't replenished or duplicated on a previous trip into town.

So he drove through and continued south. The roads were covered with fresh powder and starting to ice over with the drop in temperature. He was about five miles from the offshoot to the ranch when his cell rang.

Sam yanked off his glove with his teeth and reached for his phone tucked into the inside pocket of his brown distressed-leather jacket with shearling trim to protect against the bitter cold. He hit the connect button. "This is Reed."

"Where you at?" came the deep, staccato tone of his friend Bill Hollis.

"Almost to the house."

"Great. Can you take a call? I just got an SOS for a three-car pileup half a mile south of Lakeside. Sheriff is closing 93, coming and going, in that area."

Sam spared a glance in his rearview mirror. "Happy to know I made it through. Is everyone okay?"

"No medical emergency vehicles requested. For the pileup or the tow call I took. Female driver. Ought to be right up your alley."

"Ha-ha."

"From what she described by way of scenery, she's just shy of the ranch. Red SUV in the ditch. Can't miss her is my guess."

"You tell her to stay put?"

"Not my first rodeo, cowboy."

Sam snickered.

Bill added, "She's an out-of-towner in a rental. Gotta be a bit on the crazy side to be on these roads right now, so I figure she won't mind you in the least."

"Gee, thanks," he deadpanned.

"I don't know what the hell you're going to do with her, since she can't get to Lakeside now. Maybe have her backtrack to Rollins. I don't know where she was headed to in the first place."

"I'll take care of it. You go clean up 93 so folks out this way can actually make it into town come morning."

"Give me a holler when you're done."

"You got it." Sam hung up and pocketed the phone again. Fifteen minutes later, his headlights caught a flash of red and two high beams pointing into a tall, solid bank of snow. "Ouch." He crossed the oncoming lane and came to a stop about six feet from the SUV, facing it, since he had a winch attached to the front of the dually.

Sam tossed off his seat belt and climbed out of the truck. As he approached the driver's side of the other vehicle, the window cracked.

He said, "I hear you need a little help."

"I tried Roadside Assistance and Triple A. They couldn't get a read on my location with their handy-dandy GPS systems. So they gave me a number to a local tow company. Guy should be on his way."

"Yeah . . . he's detained."

"Detained?"

Sam couldn't see inside the SUV because there were no interior lights on, but he didn't actually need to witness the sardonic expression on the woman's face. He could perfectly envision it, thanks to her edgy tone.

He explained, "There's a wreck south of Lakeside. Both lanes are closed."

"Shit." Now disconcertion filled her voice. "I was on my way there for the evening."

"Well, your best bet is to find a motel room in Rollins. Though . . ." He spared a glance up at the sliver of a moon and the clouds thinly shrouding it, glowing with a pinkish tinge. Telling of that heavy snowfall Reva had mentioned earlier. "It's not so wise to be traveling when we're about to get dumped on."

The fat flakes were coming down steadily as it was.

THE BILLIONAIRES: THE STEPBROTHERS

She said, "The forecast called for light flurries only."

"These *are* considered light flurries in Montana. Now . . . do you need water? Are you warm enough? Are you hurt at all?"

"I'm fine. Just a cut on my palm, but I have some napkins covering it."

"Good. Okay, then. Let's—"

"You're a professional?"

"Recreational," he told her between clenched teeth. They were wasting time here. "I do what I can to help folks out."

She let out a long breath. "Of course. I appreciate that. Uh, I tried to check out the damage to the front right tire; that's how I cut myself. On the metal. It's dented in."

"I'll take a look to see if you need stitches." He pulled on the door handle, but it was locked.

She didn't bother releasing it.

Sam resisted the urge to roll his eyes. A woman from out of town—and particularly if she was from a big city—wouldn't trust even an auxiliary tow truck driver without a business card and a sign slapped on the side panel. A half-dozen references on a fancy website.

So he said, "How about I check out the vehicle first?"

"That'd be good."

He left her to inspect the front end with enough illumination from her headlights and the flashlight he retrieved from his truck to discern everything was okay, with the exception of the wheel well on the passenger's side being severely bashed in.

He winced. That could prove difficult. But it was worth a try to attempt pulling her out.

He returned to the cracked window and said, "This could be a bigger problem, but let's at least see about getting you out of the ditch."

"Might as well. It's not as though I'll cause a traffic jam if I end up blocking the lane. I haven't seen another car in over an hour."

"You'd be safer in my truck while I hook up the winch and ease this sucker out."

"Is that really necessary?" she quietly countered.

"I assure you, it's standard operating procedure for professionals and *non*professionals alike."

She sighed. Unlocked the door. "I didn't mean to insult you."

"Lucky for you I'm thick-skinned." He pulled the door open and helped her to the ground.

When she had steady footing in the snow, she stared up at him and asked, "You wouldn't happen to know how far Reed Ranch is from here?"

His gaze narrowed on her, her question distracting him from silky flaming red curls and big green eyes. A beautifully sculpted face. Crimson lips.

Well, not *entirely* distracting him.

He shoved a hand through his hair, dampened by snowflakes. Sam couldn't remember the last time he'd met a woman who stole his breath. This one did it easily. In a heartbeat.

Forcing himself to speak, he countered with, "What business do you have with Sam Reed?"

She smiled slyly, causing his groin to tighten. "That's between myself and Mr. Reed."

"Fine. What business do you have with me?"

Her emerald gaze turned quizzical.

"Sam Reed." He held out his hand. "At your service."

"Oh, shit," she said on a sharp breath. Shook her head. "Doesn't that just figure?"

Now *he* was the one who was puzzled.

She let out a low groan, then thrust her right hand toward him, the one not bleeding. "Scarlet Drake. Insurance fraud investigator."

Didn't that just figure indeed.

He folded his arms over his chest, without the obligatory shake. "You showed up on my doorstep quicker than I expected."

"I'm not actually on your doorstep. But how'd you know I was coming?"

"Michael called me." He dropped his arms, closed the door behind her, and gestured to his truck. "Might as well get in before you freeze to death. I wouldn't want to be blamed for that, too."

She huffed. "I'm not here to accuse. I'm just here to get a few answers."

"How about we start with determining how bad the damage is to your vehicle? Go from there?"

"Right." She marched past him and jerked on the handle of his cab. Then gave a little squeal of joy. "A puppy!"

"Careful," Sam hastily cautioned. "He's skittish."

"Says who?" she asked as the dog all but launched himself into her arms and nuzzled her neck, burying his tiny head in her mass of hair.

"Or a traitor," Sam grumbled.

Scarlet climbed into the truck, and with the cab lights on Sam could see her cuddle with the mutt, who still had his blanket mostly wrapped around him. She appeared to be very gentle with him, though, so Sam didn't say anything about his injuries. Instead, Sam set about connecting the cable from the winch and towing out the SUV. The tire made a god-awful screeching sound as the metal rubbed against it.

Fuck.

That likely meant tire damage. So that even if Sam could pull the dent in the wheel well this evening, he couldn't get her back on the road to Rollins without a new tire. And if the spare wasn't full sized, there was no point in putting it on in this weather. She'd have to wait for a match to be located in stock and delivered or for 93 to be cleared so Sam could pick the tire up.

Son of a bitch.

He just might be stuck with her for the evening.

A woman who likely thought he had something to do with eighteen million dollars' worth of missing artwork.

A woman who'd instantly gotten his blood flowing a bit faster in his veins and had, miraculously, immediately won over the usually cowering pup—who was now nestled so deep in her dark-auburn strands, it looked as though he'd practically crawled around to the nape of her neck and settled in for the rest of winter.

She didn't seem to mind in the least. Appeared quite taken with the little scamp.

Damn it all to hell.

Sam was going to like her.

And didn't that just jack his program to high heaven?

SEVEN

Scarlet was head over heels in love.

The little guy burrowed into the collar of her ski jacket and her hair, one paw at the base of her throat, the other tucked along her shoulder, had squirmed his way into position and now lay perfectly still, breathing a bit uneasily, as though he had a touch of allergies. He was out like a light; she was certain of it.

The other guy wasn't so bad, either.

Sam Reed had a tall, wide build. Athletic. Powerful. He had longish, disheveled brown hair—not quite qualifying as dark, but not quite medium. Bronzed skin, despite it being winter. Apparently, he spent a lot of time outdoors, even during inclement weather. The tan set off his sky-blue eyes.

She stole glances at him as he expertly eased the truck down the empty two-lane highway in reverse, tugging along her rental. When he reached a side road that was barely noticeable with all the snow covering its opening, he plowed right over the soft bank and continued uphill, carefully towing the SUV. His arm was slung over the back of the seat and he gazed behind him, then into the windshield to check on the other vehicle, then behind him again.

No wonder he'd been insulted earlier. He clearly knew what the hell he was doing.

"Sorry about the grilling I gave you," she contritely said.

"Actually, you'd be remiss if you didn't grill me. Stranded out in the middle of nowhere. Not bein' from around here. Granted, it's safe enough, for the most part. We don't get any homicidal tendencies even four months into a biting winter."

She laughed softly. "I'm sure the endless 'flurries' can seem wearing after a while, but so far I'm just astounded. This is really beautiful country. And I don't mind the snow. Except when something with antlers comes galloping across the road and I have to swerve to avoid hitting him."

"Galloping?"

She shot Sam a look. "What do deer do?"

"Sure it was a deer? Could have been an elk."

With a nod, she said, "It was rather large."

"Courteous of you to spare his life. And if it was an elk, you saved yourself fewer injuries than just your hand."

"That was my thinking."

He reached the top of the first slope, with several more rising behind them. They passed under a wide, rounded sign that artistically declared "Reed Ranch" and crested a mammoth clearing at the base of the rolling hills decorated with snow-covered trees.

Sam stopped the truck before an oversized garage and cut the engine. He worked a house key from its ring and handed it over. "To the back door. Careful on the deck. It'll be slippery. Take the dog with you. The fires are going inside to take the chill off. I'll unhook the cable and get your stuff from the SUV. Just . . . be gentle with him." He hitched his chin toward the still-burrowed puppy. "Someone made sport of him."

Her eyes widened.

"Just . . . soft voice. Light touch. That kind of thing."

"Damn it," she whispered, her voice cracking.

"He'll be okay," Sam said with unmistakable emphasis.

Scarlet wasn't sure who Sam Reed was trying to convince more—her . . . or himself.

She said, "I'll be extremely gentle."

"Let me get the door for you."

He slipped out on his side and went around to hers. Helped her out again.

Scarlet crossed to the enormous redwood wraparound deck, the ledge of the railing laden with a good six inches of new snow. She cautiously tromped through the powder and unlocked the wood-trimmed glass door. Inside, the warmth enveloped her and she inhaled the scent of the blazing fires and the hint of apple spice.

This portion of the house boasted an open kitchen with granite counters showcasing an artistically crafted bi-level island. There was an overhead rack that pots and pans dangled from. A double oven built into the wall. A brushed-nickel farmhouse sink, six-burner gas stove with a grill and a griddle, and a gorgeous glass-French-door Sub-Zero refrigerator.

There was also a long wooden table that sat twelve, with a simple runner and a long-and-low fresh-foliage centerpiece with candles. A large dark-brown leather sofa and matching recliners were arranged before the tall, wide hearth, which took up a good deal of wall space. A moderate flame cast flickering light throughout the oversized room.

Smooth river rock trimmed the walls and fireplace. Above, there were open rafters accented with polished wooden beams and a matching ceiling. Old-fashioned fans on lengthy pulleys overhead complemented the décor, along with pendent lighting.

Scarlet wiped her feet on the rug at the entryway and then crossed the gleaming hardwood floor to the island and deposited the key. Sam came in with a gust of wind and she shivered.

The pup stirred.

She glanced at Sam over her shoulder. "He's probably ready for some water. If I take the blanket off, how bad is it going to be?"

Sam left the bags and a pastry box on the counter and reached for a tissue from the dispenser in the far corner. Returning to her, he handed it over.

"Fuck." Scarlet's heart plummeted at the implication she was about to be emotionally devastated. She swallowed hard. Slowly knelt before the water and food bowls already set out on a small mat and carefully extracted the puppy from her hair and placed him on the floor. She gingerly peeled back the blanket. And gasped.

"Oh, come on!" she softly wailed. She leapt to her feet. Moved away and started to pace as her eyes flooded with tears.

"He'll be okay," Sam said once more, in a low tone.

"According to whom?" she quietly demanded.

"I have a vet on call for my horses, and we have a small on-site med facility. Dr. Harmon came out to check on the dog after I found him. Clearly, someone drop-kicked him a couple of times. Tried to starve him. Tossed him out a window on 93, not far from here. We took X-rays. Nothing's broken. There's also no chip implanted, so it's a safe bet to say no one's gonna come lookin' for him. And if they did . . ." His jaw clenched. As did his fists at his sides.

"Yeah. They'd deserve your wrath." She whisked her fingers over her cheeks, though a few more drops fell. She returned to her kneeling position next to the puppy and very lightly stroked one of his floppy ears. "You sure are a cute little bugger."

Since he only gazed at the offering in front of him, rather than partaking, she dipped her fingertip into his water bowl and held it to him. He licked tentatively. She repeated the gesture, lowering her hand, guiding him downward, until he actually stuffed his face in the bowl and lapped enthusiastically.

"Seems you know what you're doing there," Sam commented.

Her head lifted. Slowly. Taking him in from his wet, tan-colored suede boots, up his powerful-looking jean-clad thighs, over the notably impressive bulge between his legs, to the outline of hard muscles beneath his navy-colored T-shirt, since his leather jacket now hung open.

It took a few moments for her gaze to continue upward to his jutting pectoral ledge, then the thick column of his corded neck.

Scarlet tamped down a sigh. The visual assessment was enough to make her burn. Her gaze slid over his squared jawline, his sensual-looking lips, his ruggedly handsome face.

And those blue, blue eyes. Crystal clear and mesmerizing.

She was acutely aware of her chest heaving. Her pulse thumping. Her clit tingling.

"Not a clue," she said of his comment.

Her response held double meaning. She didn't have a clue as to how to treat a battered and bruised puppy. Had less of a clue as to how to handle her second hotter-than-hell man in just two days.

Stepbrothers.

Sam Reed was Michael Vandenberg's stepbrother.

And Michael had called Sam to tell him about her.

What had he told him about her?

The question brought her around. A little bit. She was still swept up in the distressed feelings evoked by a mistreated puppy and the heat flaring within her at the sight of Sam.

She stood and said, "I honestly can't believe someone could do something so vile to a defenseless animal. But of course it happens all the time, right?"

He shrugged. "I wouldn't say *all the time*." Letting out a long breath, he added, "Though even once is too much in my opinion."

He watched the Lab for a few seconds. As did Scarlet. She wasn't sure what was normal for the dog—was he drinking enough? When had he last eaten? Was he freezing his little paws off?

Snatching the blanket from the floor, she asked Sam, "Think he'd be warmer in front of the fire?"

"Actually, I'm more concerned about him eating something."

"What have you been feeding him?"

Sam rubbed his chin with an index finger and said in a contemplative voice, "Well, the vet says he's about nine weeks old, so he's been weaned. He's good for dog food."

"Where do you keep it?"

"Pantry." He hitched his thumb toward a door beyond the fridge.

She headed that way and stepped inside. Her eyes popped. This was no "pantry." It was a huge walk-in storage/laundry room.

On a long counter sat a Science Diet bag. She scooped out some kibble and then went back into the kitchen and dumped it in the bowl. Sam was busy unwrapping the box, which accommodated a pie, and then put a tub of what she presumed to be ice cream in the freezer.

He turned back to Scarlet and said, "Your tire's got a chunk taken out of it. And the idiot with the rental company who serviced the vehicle didn't check to see if the spare was replaced when last used, so you don't have one. I'll need to call around in the morning for a new tire. Pull the dent in the wheel well. Unless the rental company will send someone out for you, there's not much else I can do but offer you dinner and a place to stay for the night. It'll have to be my loft, because the guest bedroom's not finished. But I'll change the sheets for you and sleep on the couch."

"I hate to put you out like that."

"I don't see that either of us has much choice. I'm not inclined to risk my truck as the weather gets worse. Or our lives."

Scarlet knew precisely why, aside from the obvious hazard of being on the road in a snowstorm.

Cassidy Harkins.

She'd been Sam's fiancée.

Scarlet said, "Can't argue with your logic."

"Good. Now how about we see to that cut?"

She tugged off her gloves, one a bit ravaged from when she'd sliced her hand. She carefully removed the bloodied napkins.

Sam took her hand in his, palm up. His touch was surprisingly gentle, though with a hint of roughness from light calluses, indicating he wasn't opposed to manual labor. And like Michael's hand on her bare thigh, Sam's touch sent shock waves through her body. So much so, she jerked her hand back, out of the cradle his larger one had created.

Scarlet's heart bounced off the wall of her chest. To cover her adolescent move and her instant reaction to his skin on hers, she said, "I should rinse this off before I bleed on you."

She skirted him and went to the sink.

He didn't speak for a few moments, the tension stretching between them. Finally, he told her, "I'll get the first-aid kit."

While he disappeared into the storage room, she fought for a steadying breath. All of Sam Reed's six-foot-two-or-three inches of rugged virility were *so* not good for her health.

He came back to where she stood and laid out the canvas-covered kit. Without a word, he took her hand again, dabbed it with a paper towel to dry her palm, and then oozed antibiotic over the wound. It stung, but she didn't flinch this time. Forced herself to remain as still as possible. Hell, she barely even breathed.

Sam placed a cotton pad over the cut and then wound gauze around her hand. After a few passes, he turned her hand over and in a notably gruffer voice than before—was it sexually strained?—he instructed, "Hold this here." He tapped the gauze with his long, blunt-tipped index finger and she did as instructed so that he could cut the end of the strand and then apply two strips of tape to secure the bandage.

"Nice job," she softly said. "Thanks."

"Should be good as new within the week."

He glanced up. Their gazes locked. The air shifted between them.

Everything shifted inside her, too.

Her breathing morphed into a paltry crawl. At the same time, a molten sensation flowed through her from head to toe, seeping into all the cracks and crevices created by years of heartache. Making her feel blissfully warm. A little less alone, a little less hollow.

Because this man had experienced heartbreak and loss as well. And the way he so deeply cared for the well-being of the abused and abandoned puppy told her Sam was a man with vast emotions. Had therefore likely been wrecked to the core over his fiancée's death. And that of their unborn child.

More tears filled her eyes.

He quietly asked, "Did I hurt you with the antibiotic?"

"No."

"Then . . . what?"

"It's just . . . I . . ." She gave a slight shake of her head. Swallowed hard. "I know about the car accident in the Hamptons. I'm so sorry."

"Yeah. That." He carefully released her hand. Made himself busy zipping up the kit and returning it to the other room.

Scarlet felt an odd severing of a sensitive, delicate tie. One that had been woven between them in an instant and cut just as quickly.

While she collected the napkins and paper towel with suddenly trembling fingers because she'd unexpectedly let a wall down that she shouldn't have, Sam stalked back in.

He abruptly said, "I'll tell you whatever I can about the art theft, but the car accident is off-limits, Miss Drake. Absolutely *not* a topic of conversation."

Anger and something much more evocative flashed in his cerulean eyes.

Pain.

It's pain, Scarlet.

And maybe he saw it in her eyes, too.

With a nod, she told him, "I can respect that. And please, call me Scarlet."

"Fine." He shrugged out of his jacket and hung it on a coatrack in the corner by the tall glass panes and the window seating with drawers and cubbies built in underneath.

Scarlet removed her jacket as well, and he hung it with his. Not saying anything further.

A plethora of words welled in her throat, though. An apology. A condolence. And gratitude that he'd helped her out this evening.

If he hadn't come along or taken that tow call, she might still be out there in the snow. Especially with the road outside of Lakeside closed. It wasn't as though there were homesteads lining the countryside. The ranches were few and far between. And there probably wasn't much cause for the locals to be out and about on a night like this, in stormy weather.

She shuddered at the thought of truly being stranded. Though she'd loaded up with provisions to placate Bayli—and because it was the smart thing to do—she had no idea how long the heater would have run. She'd kept the interior lights and the radio off in the event that might aid the battery life, but really, she could have been an icicle by the time someone found her. If not for Sam.

He eventually spoke again, telling her, "You should stand over by the fire. I'll start dinner."

"Let me help."

He eyed her curiously. Or maybe suspiciously. She couldn't quite decipher all of his expressions. There were myriad ones that ran deep.

"All right," he said. "I need the portabellas sliced and we'll do up some baked potatoes." He gestured toward a basket on the island filled with vegetables. All fresh from some sort of greenhouse farmers' market, she was sure. "There's a box of disposable gloves under the sink to protect that bandage from getting wet."

"Good thinking."

Sam reached for a stainless-steel colander overhead and gave it to her for cleaning the 'shrooms and potatoes. He asked, "You're not opposed to venison tenderloin roast, are you?"

"I've never had venison. But I'll try anything once. I'm a bit of an adventure freak."

"I figured as much, since you were driving across Montana in the winter."

She loaded up the colander and took it to the sink. "That was born of necessity."

"Why don't you talk to me about that?" He preheated the oven and set out a broiler pan.

Scarlet said, "The insurance company that paid out the claim on the art collection hired me to basically do a final-attempt investigation to confirm nothing was overlooked in the initial examination of the case. It's a good-faith procedure for their stakeholders, to demonstrate no stone was left unturned and justify the check they cut."

"That's a fancy, nonoffensive way of saying they want to make damn sure my family didn't rip 'em off."

"Why, yes, it is." She smiled and batted her lashes.

"Hmph." He actually cracked a grin. Not much of one, but it was more than she'd gotten out of him thus far.

"So I have Michael's alibi," she said as she rinsed the mushrooms. "I'd like to hear yours."

"I already gave it."

"I'm aware of that, though I haven't yet read the statement. Sometimes it helps for me to hear these things in person."

"Then you came a long way for nothing, Scarlet Drake. Because I don't have a hell of a lot to tell you." He yanked on one of the handles on the refrigerator and retrieved a slab of bacon and the roast, wrapped in butcher paper.

"It's okay if I hear exactly what the FBI did. It's a cross-check. And just plain and simple *Scarlet* is fine."

His glowing blue eyes flitted to her. "Believe me, there's nothing plain and simple about you." His gaze roved her body, from her long hair with the bangs tossed over to one side, down the front of her tight gray wool sweater, to her low-rise jeans and hiking boots. "Scarlet," he added with another quirk of the corner of his mouth.

Their gazes connected again and her pulse jumped.

Bayli had once joked that the way Christian or Rory looked so intensely at her sometimes sparked a physical jolt low in her belly. She called it eye sex.

Scarlet was fairly certain she'd just had it with Sam Reed.

She reached for the potato scrubber on the ledge and went to town on the skins, her blood sizzling, her skin tingling.

And what was going on between her legs mirrored all the zings Michael had incited the night before.

Christ, had that really been less than twenty-four hours ago? Had she only left his bed at the Crestmont this very morning?

And now here she was, hot for his stepbrother. Completely charged by his powerful masculinity and smitten with his contradictory compassionate nature. His obvious love of animals. His broken heart.

Everything about him pulled her in, hooked her. Made her want him the way she'd so desperately wanted Michael within the first few seconds of meeting him.

That was crazy; she knew it.

Not that it wasn't possible to be overwhelmingly attracted to two men at the same time. It'd happened to Jewel over the course of twenty-eight years. Falling in love with Rogen when they were kids and then Vin as they'd entered adulthood. It had happened to Bayli much quicker. About as fast as it was happening to Scarlet.

Perhaps it was because her best friends had experienced

soul-deep emotional and sexual connections with their guys that it
was easily a viable romantic scenario in Scarlet's mind. Plausible,
so that maybe from the onset of meeting Sam she'd subconsciously
been open to the concept of sharing volcanic chemistry with both
him and Michael.

Who knew how synergy and electrifying vibes really worked,
other than to say that they could strike like lightning? And she'd
been zapped twice.

She considered this as she wrapped the potatoes in foil, pierced
them, and added them to the oven along with the bacon Sam was
cooking. Then she found a bamboo cutting board, grabbed a knife
from the block, and began slicing mushrooms at the island.

Sam pulled out the broiler pan when the bacon was only about
half-done and set the roast on the flat strips, seasoned the meat,
then rolled it all up and returned it to the oven.

He washed his hands, moving about stealthily. As he reached
for a sauté pan, his chest grazed her shoulder and it was a wonder
she didn't cut open her other palm from the jarring sensation inside her. Just like Bayli's reaction to eye sex.

Fuck.

She tried to keep her shuddering to a minimum.

Come on, Scarlet. This is serious business.

*Don't get lost in those gorgeous blue irises. That whole sexy, earthy
look the man sported. And the enticing scent of him.*

Scarlet had a small window of opportunity to engage Sam and
find out more about the missing artwork. It was extremely fortu-
itous that he'd been the one who'd rescued her and brought her
here. Even more advantageous that she couldn't make it into Lakeside or back to Rollins, so that she had no choice but to have dinner with him.

To spend the night.

Kismet was shining bright and Scarlet was not fool enough to
turn a blind eye to it. She had the chance to question Sam without

it being the accusatory interrogation he'd originally expected it would be. They could talk. Discuss a few theories. Perhaps Scarlet would learn something invaluable. A key factoid that would explain how the paintings had vanished and where they might be.

Without incriminating Michael and Sam, she hoped. Especially with Sam constantly sneaking peeks at the puppy to check on him. That kindhearted gesture did things to Scarlet. Moved her in a way that would have been significant under normal circumstances, but given Sam's tortured past and obviously still-tormented soul, his concern for the Lab held even more poignancy for her.

She didn't doubt for a second that Sam Reed would have made an incredible father.

And that choked her up again. Literally. She sputtered on a half sob and had to go for another tissue.

"You okay?" Sam asked, the worry much too evident in his rich, intimate timbre, causing her to turn a shoulder on him so he didn't see her dab at tears.

"Yeah, sure," she said, striving for an unwavering tone. Not fully succeeding. "Saliva down the wrong pipe or something," she lied.

"Right. Well, that's probably my fault. I didn't offer you water or anything."

"You did. When you saved me from the ditch." She faced him and smiled softly. "You're a hell of a guy."

He smirked. "I'll try not to let that go to my head. You want some wine? I was planning to open a Malbec to pair with the venison."

"That sounds great. I feel bad that you're going to all this trouble."

"I have to eat, too." He winked.

And oh, God, what that did to her nerve endings! Every single one went haywire. Stealing her breath.

No, he likely hadn't been flirting with her. He'd just made a casual remark and followed it up with a casual facial expression.

Nothing to read into there, Scarlet.

Except that she *felt* the electric current arcing between them. Wanted to bend into it like a reed in the wind.

Wanted to fall into it, to be more precise. Let it capture her, tangle her up. Consume her. Until she lost herself in the moment the way she had with Michael.

That was something she'd never imagined experiencing, had never come even remotely close to experiencing. And while she would concede that it was a trifle terrifying to step away from a reality she'd always clung to, the fantasy of releasing the tether on her tightly contained emotions had led to one seriously amazing night with a man who'd known exactly how to give her everything she'd needed.

Those trusty gut instincts of hers told Scarlet that Sam Reed was as intuitive as his stepbrother when it came to satisfying a woman.

That naughty thought chased away the sentimentality that had crept in on her. She tossed the tissue and picked up where she'd left off with the portabellas.

Out of the corner of her eye, she noted that Sam still studied her closely, trying to read her. Then he gave up and crossed to the rustic six-foot-long, two-foot-wide riddling racks mounted to the wall separating the kitchen from the great room, which featured double-story, asymmetrically cut windows overlooking the property and another gorgeous fireplace centered between them.

He selected a bottle of wine and uncorked it at the island. Poured two glasses and handed one to Scarlet.

They clinked rims and said, "Cheers," at the same time.

She took a sip and nodded her approval. "Very nice."

After a long drink, Sam set his glass aside and collected the green beans from the veggie basket. He prepped the sauté pan, then tossed in the beans. Meanwhile, Scarlet chopped some fresh parsley to go with the mushrooms.

Five minutes passed with a comfortable silence lingering in the air. Scarlet had more questions for him, of course. But for the moment, she absorbed the crackle of the fire and the atmosphere.

Sam removed the beans from the heat and dumped them into a serving bowl. Then he shaved almonds before sliding them into the pan to toast. When they were ready, he also added them to the bowl. Last, he sliced an onion and started to caramelize the strips.

Scarlet asked, "Anything else you need?"

"Chopped thyme, if you wouldn't mind."

"Not at all."

"I'll give the onions a good twenty minutes and then mix them with the beans, almonds, and thyme and finish cooking them all together."

She went back to work. Then sipped some more.

The aroma of the venison roast and the onions filled the vast room. The puppy took interest in the new scents and rounded the island, sniffing curiously.

Scarlet grinned. "Maybe starting him on dog food could take a backseat to a little human food. Can I give him some carrots?"

"Sure."

She made chunks small enough for easy chomping and then knelt before the pup and held her palm out. He did more sniffing, then started to nibble.

"He really likes you," Sam said.

She glanced up. "He likes you, too. Trusts you. Dogs have great instincts, you know?"

"It's too damn bad they can't choose their owners."

The puppy polished off the snack and waddled toward Sam, brushing his nose against Sam's leg.

Scarlet laughed quietly. "I think this one has."

Sam gingerly lifted him into his arms and the Lab settled easily, finding his happy spot.

"Are you going to name him?" she asked.

"Not while he's in such a sorry state. When he's healed and feeling better, I can get a read on his personality. Pick a nice strong name for him."

"That's a good idea."

They stared at each other across the span of the kitchen. It was unnerving to see this big, strapping man cuddling a tiny, defenseless puppy. Heart-wrenching, really, because said pup was covered in bruises and cuts. But he looked perfectly comfortable and cozy nestled against Sam. More important, he seemed to feel safe in Sam's arms, in his care. As though he already knew this man would protect him and love him from here on out.

Scarlet cleared her throat to combat the emotion threatening to overcome her again. She went to the stove and poked at the onions to ensure they cooked evenly. Or just make herself useful and not so teary-eyed.

Over her shoulder, she said, "Tell me when to start the bellas."

Sam grabbed another pan and set it on a burner, not jostling his now-sleeping bundle. "Another ten minutes or so. Enjoy your wine."

She slid onto a high-backed stool and lifted her glass. She asked, "Can we talk about the night of the art theft?"

He gave a slight shrug. "Not a lot to say about it, as I told you."

"Where were you around eleven o'clock?"

"In the guesthouse." He grinned, a bit mischievously. "With two very beautiful socialites. Misty Ferrera and Pembroke Peters . . . Peterson . . . I can't remember which."

"Peterson," Scarlet confirmed. "Adopted by her mother's third husband." She took another drink and asked, "What about Michael? He claims to have been in the guesthouse as well."

"Sure. He was there."

"Interesting. He didn't mention your presence when he gave his statement."

"Obviously, from mine the FBI could put two and two together."

"Or four," she muttered. "You, Michael, Misty, and Pembroke."

"Not exactly." He propped a hip against the ledge of the counter and speared her with a pointed look. "Me, Michael, and Misty. Then me, Michael, and Pembroke. Follow?"

Her jaw slacked. "That's some serious stamina."

The pointed look turned downright wicked. "We were all there for a few hours."

Curiosity—and the sexy expression on his devastatingly handsome face—got the best of Scarlet. Prompting her to ask, "Do you two do that often? Share the same woman?"

"We've been known to on occasion." He shoved away from the counter and sought out his own wineglass.

Scarlet let this new revelation, this sinfully delicious tidbit, seep through her veins.

"Wait a minute," Sam said as he eyed her over the rim of his glass. "You don't look the least bit surprised. Or, I should say, you don't appear the least bit fazed."

Her brow crooked. "About you and your stepbrother engaging in threesomes? No. Doesn't faze me at all."

Excites the hell out of me is more like it.

And she squirmed a little in her seat at the sudden tickle along her clit.

She added, "I have two sets of friends who enjoy a ménage à trois arrangement. Quite successfully, in fact."

"Huh. Guess I didn't think you'd approve of the alternative lifestyle."

"Well, I *am* from California," she told him. "And as *I* told *you*, I like some adventure in my life."

She instantly clamped down on her lower lip. *Oops.* Was that opening a can of worms or what?

Had Scarlet just implied that *she* was more than amenable to a threesome?

Releasing her lip—thankful the lipstick she typically wore in her signature crimson color was of the stay-put variety—she squared her shoulders and brazenly returned his gaze.

"Interesting," he said, his tone low and soul stirring. His blue eyes blazed bright enough to melt her right off her stool. "Why'd you only read Michael's alibi?"

Scarlet's mind faltered. For the first time, she was having trouble keeping up with the quick-fire questioning. Because her brain was stuck on the forbidden.

Sam and Michael enjoyed pleasuring one woman at the same time.

Holy Jesus.

"Scarlet?" Sam prompted her, a tinge of amusement in his tone.

He knew exactly the direction in which her thoughts ran. She was certain of it.

Scarlet cleared her throat again.

How was this all getting so complicated?

Focus!

It was no easy feat, but she got her brain to shift to business again. She said, "Michael caught my attention because five million dollars had been deposited into his account right around the time the insurance check came in."

That was basically an auto-reply, because it was insanely difficult to concentrate on her case when her body was going up in flames. Her nipples pebbled behind her lacy bra and she was damn certain she was wet. Again. As much as she'd been the night before.

What the hell were these men doing to her?

She'd gone a couple of years without so much as a spark. Now in two days she'd met two men who had her revved to the core of her being.

But she wouldn't drop the ball. So she added, "Unfortunately, I discovered that you'd received the same amount." She gave him a hard look. "Just three weeks after Michael."

To his credit, Sam didn't seem even mildly taken aback. He said, "Michael had inherited some property and he flipped a portion of it. That's how he started building his fortune."

"And where'd the five mil come from that you ended up with?"

Sam stepped away and carefully settled the snoozing dog in his bed. Then he washed his hands again. Checked on the onions. Finally, he rested his sinewy forearms on the countertop and leaned toward Scarlet. Close enough that she could inhale the faint scent of some ultra-manly cologne and his natural heat.

She resisted the compulsion to close her eyes and take a deep breath, draw in his very essence. Let it ribbon through her, caress her heart, her soul. Stroke her slowly, blissfully. Until she was drowning in him.

It was damn near impossible not to cave to this new desire. But she fought its allure. Remained dedicated to her inquisition.

"About the money in your account . . . ?" she asked, all breathy and not the tiniest bit professional sounding. Christ, her eyes were probably all soft and seductive.

His gaze still holding hers, Sam said, "My windfall was an inheritance, too. I moved into the Vandenberg estate when I was sixteen, with only a couple of nickels to rub together. My mother wasn't much better off. She'd moved us from Colorado to New York because she was hoping to get in at an art gallery—as more than a volunteer. She hadn't realized she needed a degree, not just book knowledge."

He sipped his wine, then continued. "While living in Mitcham's house and the perks improved our situation astronomically—I was given a car for my birthday, had all the stuff a guy wants when he's growing up—I didn't actually have any cash that was mine. There was an allowance, sure. But it came with plenty of strings."

"Were you willing to let Mitcham Vandenberg pull those strings?"

"To an extent," he admitted. "Existing in the Hamptons requires a working income if you're going to leave the grounds. So I followed some of the rules."

"But not all of them?"

"I wasn't interested in taking the corporate helicopter into the city after school to put in late hours at Vandenberg Enterprises. I suspect that's one of the reasons Mitcham never elected to adopt me or even broached the subject with my mother."

Scarlet's head tilted in contemplation. "Did you want him to adopt you?"

"No." Sam tore his gaze from hers and straightened. He went for the wine bottle. As he refreshed their glasses, he said, "All I wanted was for my mom to be happy. Did I enjoy the sports car and the parties and the royal treatment because I lived on the estate? Naturally. Who the hell wouldn't? But was I willing to jump through massive hoops to make Mitcham love me or treat me like his very own son? No."

"Because you had a close relationship with your real father?"

"I don't know who my real father is. Disappeared without a trace when he found out my mother was pregnant. She tried to find him, but she's convinced he went so far as to change his name to keep from having any sort of connection to us or financial responsibility. That's all I really know, all I really care to know. I've never considered him to be my father, not in the true sense. I don't subscribe to running away from your commitments. . . . Even as a kid I couldn't abide by it."

"Yes, that is pretty shitty."

Sam nodded.

Getting back on track, Scarlet asked, "How'd you get into Princeton? Expensive school."

The angst left Sam's eyes, so he presumably preferred this line of questioning to anything pertaining to his deadbeat dad.

"Princeton is one of the few Ivy Leaguers to offer grants," he explained. "I had the grades and the accolades to apply for one, plus I received a partial football scholarship. I'll confess that I told the Admissions people my stepfather was Mitcham Vandenberg, alumnus, and my stepbrother was Michael, who'd been immediately accepted into the university, as though ordained. The name-dropping greased the wheels." He rapped his knuckles on the granite, pensive. "I still had to work my ass off to survive, though—both academically and with a part-time job."

"I can imagine. You were an architecture major. That had to be all-consuming unto itself."

Sam regarded her a few moments, then asked, "Is there *anything* about me that you don't know?"

"Plenty, I assure you."

"Well, I'm feeling at a slight disadvantage."

"Fair enough." She slid off the stool and grabbed the cutting board with the 'shrooms and went to the stove. As she drizzled olive oil into the pan and turned on the burner, she said, "Ask me whatever you'd like. However, I regret to inform you up front that unless you're fascinated by unsolved mysteries and sketchy locales and shady characters you'll be sorely disappointed."

"I'm interested in *you*," he said, his voice a low, arousing rumble.

Scarlet's stomach fluttered. She glanced at him over her shoulder. He stared intently at her with those glowing blue eyes of his, making her think that the inquisitiveness radiating from him had less to do with wanting to know her backstory and more to do with her silent admission and acceptance that the idea of a ménage scenario with him and his stepbrother titillated her.

Exhilaration trilled through her at the image of their naked bodies entwined flashing in her mind. All other thoughts fled her usually sensible brain as she fixated on the mental trailer playing in her head.

Geez, Scarlet. Get it together.

Speak!

Her mouth worked like a gaping fish trying to expel a hook lodged in its throat as she fought to free the words on her tongue.

But not a single one materialized.

So she turned back to the stove and continued what she was doing while also trying to block the fantasy of Michael and Sam working in tandem to make her come. Over and over.

Her nipples tightened further. Her pussy ached.

These two men were preying on her senses. Did they both know how quickly, how deeply, they were ensnaring her?

"Why don't we start with the basics?" Sam proposed. "Where in California do you live?"

Okay, an easy question.

Breathe, Scarlet.

Just breathe.

She sucked in a long stream of air. Though her body thrummed from a rush of adrenaline, she managed to say, "River Cross. Wine country about an hour and a half outside of San Francisco."

"Lived there your whole life?"

"Mostly. I had an apartment in the city with friends when I went to SFSU."

"What'd you study?"

"Criminal law."

She heard the grin in his voice as he said, "That was a given. Sorry I asked." Then he added, "How long have you been an insurance fraud investigator?"

She scraped the baby bellas into her pan with a spatula and

said, "I interned with a company during college, then moved back to River Cross and hung my own shingle after I graduated."

"Ambitious of you."

"Yes."

Behind her, she heard Sam leave the island. He pulled open the fridge again. A heartbeat later he was at her side. He yanked the cork out of a bottle of white wine and splashed a small amount into her sauté pan, making it sizzle.

"Adds an extra punch," he said with a coy grin. "Better for the garlic-cream sauce I'll whip up to top the roast with."

"How are you such a good cook?" she asked, quite pleased she was finally capable of speech after she'd lost her voice earlier. Kind of surprised it didn't vaporize again with him standing right next to her but pleased nonetheless.

"I'm a bachelor," he simply said. "It's either learn or starve."

"Makes sense. Not exactly convenient takeout or delivery service in these parts, I surmise."

"That is correct."

"Though you don't seem to lack for homemade desserts."

With a sexy chuckle that reverberated deep within her, he said, "No, I do not. It tends to be the payment around here when you do something nice for someone."

Her gaze slid along his corded throat, up to his strong jawline, to his mesmerizing eyes. She said, "I bet you do a lot of nice things for the single ladies of the county."

His Adam's apple bobbed ever so slightly as he swallowed hard. He told her, "I don't exactly provide the kind of services you're thinking of."

"You have no idea what I'm thinking."

"Really?"

"Really."

They stared at each other. At an impasse.

While Scarlet would guess he had more than his fair share of admirers and likely gave his affection to one every now and then, she didn't take him for a womanizer. And given that he wasn't concerned about having a new woman at his place, unexpectedly, and he was accustomed to cooking and picking up after himself, she would venture to say there was no revolving door to his bedroom.

He didn't seem like the type. Even if he was too damn hot for words and made her want to strip him bare and crawl all over him.

She had no idea how much time ticked by as they were both swimming in each other's eyes. But he eventually stepped away and said, "Don't forget the mushrooms."

Scarlet didn't exactly snap to attention. In fact, she felt boneless and much, much too warm for comfort. She tended to the veggies, then had no choice but to haul her sweater over her head and drop it onto her stool. She wore a white tank top for extra layering, and even that felt too clingy, too oppressive.

If she had any sort of excuse for opening the refrigerator door, she'd just stand there and let the coolness wash over her.

Sam took note, naturally. But didn't say a word. Instead, he checked on his roast. Then tossed the green beans and almonds into the pan with the caramelized onions. Scarlet put herself to good use—and welcomed the distraction—by trolling the kitchen for plates and flatware. Napkins.

She set the table as Sam finished up dinner. He served while she poured more wine. The puppy expressed mild interest in the festivities and ambled over. It touched her heart that he wasn't just a lonesome ball of fur on his thick pillow.

Sam set out bread and she tore off a hunk for the mutt, who gobbled it down. His appetite was growing by leaps and bounds.

Not that Scarlet could blame him. Her stomach grumbled at the sinful scents permeating the house. She hadn't eaten since

Spokane many, many hours earlier. But it wasn't just the delicious aroma that had her so ravenous. It was also Sam.

She had to tamp down that particular craving, though. Focus instead on dinner.

"This looks incredible," she said of the feast spread before her. "And smells even better."

Sam surveyed the bounty, then told her, "I didn't think to put out a salad."

"Screw the salad." She speared a baked potato with her fork and hoisted it onto her plate. "That's just a waste of space in my mind."

He grinned. "Careful there, darlin'. I'm starting to like you."

She couldn't resist the flirty look she threw his way as she said, "Feeling's mutual, cowboy."

And Scarlet was suddenly dying to know if he'd do anything about it. . . .

EIGHT

Sam had been 100 percent certain he knew what the hell he was doing from the moment he'd taken the tow call.

Now?

Not so much.

Scarlet was alluring. Riveting. Tempting.

So very, *very* tempting.

Which he tried not to think of as he passed the butter, sour cream, and chives for her baked potato. Then carved the roast.

He wasn't a man to get spun up over a beautiful woman. Granted, it'd been a long time since he'd seen one *this* beautiful. Even longer since his testosterone had shot into the stratosphere upon first glimpse. Then there was the matter of his gut twisting when he'd gotten all caught up in feminine tears and empathy.

Trying to put it all on the injured Lab would be reasonable. Sam himself was all messed up inside over the beating the dog had taken. What kind of sick motherfucker would do such a thing?

But aside from being wrapped around the axle by the woman with loads of verve sitting across from him, Sam was also feeling the bonfire low in his groin that hadn't burned in years. He'd nearly forgotten how all-consuming it could be. Hadn't felt it even when he'd been prowling his way through Manhattan after Cassidy had been killed in the car crash.

Mostly he'd used sex that first year without her as an attempt to counteract the insidious hell he'd been thrust into. Even though he and Cassidy had only been together six months before he'd proposed and she'd gotten pregnant just a month after their engagement had been announced, he'd loved her to the point of distraction.

And when she'd been taken from him—his child as well—he'd gone numb inside. Had stayed that way on some levels. Not even fully realizing it until Scarlet Drake had slipped out of the SUV and he'd gotten a good look at all that silky red hair, those vibrant green eyes, her curvy body.

Christ, the curves this woman possessed . . . They made his pulse race and his cock strain against the button fly of his Levi's.

She'd snagged his full attention from the get-go. But then she'd gone and taken her sweater off while cooking and now she was driving him wild with plumped-up breasts that crested the low neckline of her tight tank top, the thin straps resting on her bare shoulders. Her nipples were tightened into enticing little buds and it was pretty much all he could do to keep from forgoing dinner, taking her in his arms, and whisking his thumbs over the taut peaks, making them harder.

That wasn't all that lit him up. The honey-colored skin exposed was soft and satiny looking. She had a narrow waist and shapely hips. A great ass.

Sam couldn't help but wonder if Michael had already enjoyed it. His stepbrother hadn't gotten into the particulars when he'd phoned, since he'd been about to board an airplane. He'd only told Sam that Scarlet would likely be hot on his trail, because she hadn't dug up anything substantial on Michael to help her case along.

And that was what Sam really ought to concentrate on. That she was prying into his personal affairs.

Though he was interested in prying into hers as well.

He asked, "What do you like so much about being a fraud investigator?"

She set aside her wineglass and said, "I'm obsessed with recovering jewelry, art, antiquities . . . anything, really, that's reported stolen or lost and doesn't turn up somewhere for resale."

"And how do you track down these items?"

"With help from my friends." She smiled craftily. "One of my best friends, Bayli Styles, is a research nut. Plus, I've built a global network of black market and auction house contacts. Library and museum curators. Special agents in the insurance industry who can confirm whether private sales have been made or if new policies have been taken out on missing pieces."

"Now that actually does sound fascinating. Not to mention dangerous."

"Yes, there is that." She sampled the venison, her eyes growing wide. "Wow, this is spectacular."

"Glad you like it."

He didn't press her further as she enjoyed more of the roast, though myriad questions still rambled through his brain.

Apparently through hers as well, because she washed down a bite with some wine and then asked, "So about this inheritance of yours. Where it'd come from?"

Sam chuckled. She was like a dog with a hambone. He told her, "Mitcham had a brother. Phil Bert. Funny little man. Hated being called Phil. Hated Bert. But together, *Phil Bert* was just fine. Suited him, too. He was quite a character. You would have liked him."

"So . . . not as intense and intimidating as Mitcham?"

One of Sam's brows lifted. "You've met my stepfather?"

"Not in person. I phoned his office early on in my investigation. We spoke for all of five seconds, I'm sure. And it wasn't a pleasant five seconds."

"I wouldn't expect it to be. He doesn't like being under fire. Doesn't appreciate anyone second-guessing him."

"Like father, like son." The corners of her mouth quivered, as though she held back a smile at the mention of Michael.

Sam opted to latch on to that nugget. "So you and my stepbrother . . . the two of you are involved?"

"I wouldn't say that. Not so much." She polished off her green beans and sipped more wine.

Sam said, "He told me you had a couple of drinks together last night."

She eyed Sam steadily. "What else did he say?"

"Nothing more. Just that you were looking into the stolen goods."

Scarlet took a deep breath, her chest expanding. Sidetracking Sam's thoughts for several seconds and sending a shitload of blood to his cock.

Her gaze unwavering, she said, "We did more than have a couple of drinks. I woke up in his bed this morning."

"Can't say I'm surprised." *Envious? Yeah. That was a huge possibility. But surprised? Nope.*

Sam told her, "Michael has exceptional taste. He's selective, make no mistake. Can go extensive periods without sex until he finds just the right woman. I'm sure he wanted you from the moment he laid eyes on you."

She bypassed her seemingly customary minimal wine sip and downed a bigger gulp. Then asked, "And what about you? Do you go extensive periods without sex?"

Sam's jaw tightened at the invasive question. He had a very cut-and-dried answer, yet wasn't certain it was one she'd want to hear. But did that really matter?

Pushing his empty plate aside, he confessed, "I was much less selective after my fiancée died. More interested in quantity versus quality. All based on desperation, really."

"Oh?"

He didn't like the grilling. Oddly, he didn't put a stop to it. He told her, "At first, I was desperate to forget how much I loved Cassidy. Later, I was just desperate to *feel*. Something. Anything."

Scarlet's gaze dropped to her food and she picked at the remnants with her fork. Not eating it, though. Like she'd lost her appetite.

He'd heard the pain in his voice and could see it disturbed her. But there was something more. And he experienced a peculiar surge of dark pleasure when she told him, "I understand that sort of desperation. I felt it myself when my parents passed away. I was twelve."

"And what became *your* vice?" he asked, instantly pulled into her trauma.

Her gaze snapped up and met his. Burned through him as she said, "Danger."

"Scarlet . . ." His brow furrowed. His gut clenched.

"I instantly lost the fear of death." Her eyes misted. "Because if I died, then I could join them. We could all be together again. A family."

He let out a long breath. Rubbed the sudden knot at his nape. "What did you do?"

She tilted her chin, almost defiantly, and told him, "I started sticking up for the kids in my school who were being bullied. If someone got pushed around, I pushed back, instead of just walking away and letting it be another person's problem. When I saw someone doing something suspicious or underhanded, I confronted them. But I also got a rush by taking more physical risks. You know, like standing in front of a speeding train to see if I could hold my ground or if I'd chicken out. Obviously, I always chickened out. But . . . trains became an addiction."

His stomach twisted further. "Why trains?"

She broke the eye contact and stared off into the other room, as though debating how much she wanted to share. Or rather, how much she was *capable* of sharing. He suspected that was more accurate.

Sam knew from his own emotional tug-of-wars to just sit and let her take her time. Not force anything.

And eventually, she did come around. Her gaze returned to his. "My parents were killed in a train wreck," she said. "A horrific one. They were in Europe investigating a case for the law firm my father worked for; my mother was consulting. They'd booked rail tickets from Switzerland into the Czech Republic in early spring. Living in Montana, you know how massive accumulations of snow can shift when the sun melts it and then the temperatures dip and freeze the banks, then more flurries build on top."

"Oh, Jesus." He had a good idea where this was headed.

She said, "They were on a mountain pass when either the give of all that accumulation or the vibration of the tracks triggered an avalanche. Took out the midsection of the train within seconds. Completely obliterated it."

Sam's heart wrenched. "They were in one of those cars."

"No. Unfortunately."

His gaze narrowed on her. *"Unfortunately?"*

"Yes. Had they been, they would have died instantly. Instead, they were in the back. So they likely saw the avalanche as it hit. And then when it did, the inertia plowed the train off the tracks and over a cliff. Dragging both ends with the middle. My parents were alive when they plummeted several thousand feet. With no way to escape. They were trapped. And they must have been terrified, because they couldn't save themselves or anyone else."

Tears trickled down her flushed cheeks.

Sam shoved back his chair and went for the box of tissues, depositing it on the table at her elbow.

He returned to his seat. "I'm really sorry to hear that, Scarlet. I know you were devastated by their deaths. But to torture yourself over details like—"

"You didn't do the same?" she challenged. "Still don't?"

"Cassidy died in my arms." That was all he said.

"Then you understand how deep hopelessness can cut. How it makes you do reckless things."

He stared hard. "Tell me you're not reckless anymore."

"I'm not," she said with conviction in her velvety tone. "What happened on that road this evening wasn't recklessness. It was self-preservation. I knew slamming into that elk would have hurt much worse than putting my vehicle in a ditch."

"That's very true." He probed further, "What about with Michael?"

Scarlet gave a small smile through her tears. "That wasn't recklessness, either, Sam. It was passion. Somehow, I sensed he needed to experience it as much as I did. You said yourself he's selective. And he said he hadn't been with anyone in a while. I believed him."

Sam nodded. "He wouldn't have any reason to lie about it."

"Nor would I when I told him I hadn't been with a man in two years."

"That's a long time."

"A hell of a long time," she corrected.

"Yeah." He got to his feet again, the subject matter hitting a bit too close to home in too many ways. He took his plate to the sink and rinsed it.

Scarlet joined him with her dish and then they cleared the rest of the table in silence, each lost in their own thoughts.

For Sam, it was troubling to be so candid. To zero in on such touchy topics. He didn't know this woman. Not really. Yet oddly, it seemed as though he did. He connected with her. Wasn't quite so guarded with her. Maybe that was what truly unsettled him.

Or maybe it was because she comprehended his pain. Lived with her own agony.

If he wanted to take the analysis a step beyond all that, he would concede that it wasn't just envy that had flared within him when Scarlet had confirmed she'd slept with Michael. Guilt had also edged in on him. Because even though he'd fucked numerous nameless, faceless women during his grieving stages, none of those empty encounters had meant anything to him.

So now the guilt encroached because with Scarlet, not only did he want to make love to her—not fuck her just for physical gratification—but also because he knew that with her it *would* mean something.

She'd already infiltrated his senses, ignited his desire, touched places inside him that had been off-limits and sealed from the moment Cassidy's eyelids had dipped and she'd drawn her last sliver of breath.

He'd been shattered.

Time had helped to fix some of the broken pieces, yes. People either caved when faced with tragedy or powered through. They might not be the same person they were before. They might even turn on themselves—as Sam had with his sexual exploits and Scarlet with her daredevil ways.

He'd never condoned his actions. But when the dust settled, what was most critical was what rose from the ashes.

And in all honesty, all Sam had wanted from the day he'd finally shaken off some of the turmoil and emerged from his abyss was to be a better man. To be the man Cassidy had fallen in love with, had trusted with her heart. Had trusted with her baby.

The accident had not been Sam's fault. A drunk driver had run a red light and T-boned their car. Like Scarlet's parents, there'd been nothing Sam could do but watch in horror.

Yet because he'd been behind the wheel, he'd heaped a shitload of blame onto himself. Still felt a great deal of it. Knew it would never fully go away.

At the end of the day, however, he knew all Cassidy would want for him was to go on. To tuck the memories away and start living again.

He had no doubt Scarlet's parents would want the same for her. Sam understood. Though it was never that easy.

Which was why this complexity of being instantly and vehemently attracted to Scarlet was such a catch-22 for him.

He wanted her.

But he didn't want to want her.

Because that felt like a betrayal. Even when he logically knew it wasn't.

He also knew there was no point in stewing over it. She was here to investigate a crime. He had nothing case-cracking to contribute. She could ask him all the questions she wanted; he didn't have any pearls of wisdom to impart. That put them at a stalemate—times two because he wasn't willing or ready to do anything about the erotic sensations crawling through his veins.

So he stuck to safer territory, asking Scarlet, "Do you want pie? It's apple with vanilla ice cream and cinnamon."

"I saved room."

"Smart girl."

When they sat down again—this time in front of the roaring fire—she reminded him, "We were talking about Phil Bert, but I don't think I got the whole story."

"Right," Sam said. "So Uncle Phil Bert was a horseman and that's probably why we hit it off so well. Instantly. I spent a lot of time with him, learned a lot about horses, did some jumping, discovered I had a knack for training, and essentially just enjoyed being on his property."

"In the Hamptons?"

"Yes. Though he wasn't a fan of the high-society scene. He was very low-key. Salt of the earth. And those are the kind of people he tried to surround himself with. Needless to say, he and Mitcham weren't the best of pals, despite being brothers. *They tolerated each other* is the best way to describe their relationship."

Scarlet bit into the slice of pie he'd heated up for her and swallowed it down before asking, "Did Phil Bert like Michael, or just tolerate him as well?"

"He liked Michael. Didn't see too much of him because Michael's never been one to hang around the stables. But they had a good rapport and found other things in common."

"Yet Michael didn't get five million dollars in cash from his uncle—his biological uncle—when he passed. And you did. That's a little strange, don't you think?"

"Not really," Sam said. "The majority of the estate was liquidated and went to numerous horse farms—mainly a couple of facilities that take in retired or lame race champions so they're not mistreated or euthanized. Or ground up for the meat."

"Ugh." She crinkled her pert nose.

"It happens. Anyway, Uncle Phil Bert knew his father had bequeathed an entire sugar plantation to Michael. Took some time for all the legalities to be worked out, but eventually that land was Michael's. He was able to subdivide and sell a plot. The end result was that he had acreage in Hawaii, a business, and available funds."

"And you had . . . ?"

"Still just a couple of nickels to rub together," he told her.

With a small nod, she said, "So Phil Bert evened the playing field."

"In a manner of speaking, yes. He left me the exact same amount as he knew Michael had made on the flip. Along with two horses. And a lifetime of knowledge that allowed me to start up this equestrian ranch and pursue a passion I'd never have known existed within me if I hadn't met Phil Bert. If he hadn't taken an interest in me. Hadn't trusted me to take good care of his horses."

"That's very heartwarming. But . . . How'd Michael respond? Did it cause any sort of rift between the two of you that Phil Bert had bequeathed you something and Michael nothing?"

"Michael's not that way. Yes, I know he can be very intense and completely wrapped up in acquisitions and the market and building a bigger and bigger empire. Yet one thing that both vexed and shaped him as a person was Mitcham's decree that Michael and I were supposed to make it on our own. If we wanted what Mitcham had, we had to figure out how to achieve it without simply being handed a golden ticket."

She seemed to give this thought, then said, "Michael did mention this, though he phrased the dynamic a bit differently. Basically, he summed it up by saying he was privy to luxuries, but they weren't really his by right until he'd earned them."

"Precisely."

Scarlet stared off into the tall flames for a few seconds. Likely piecing together some of the puzzle before posing her next round of questions.

Sam admired her profile. Found her just as mesmerizing when she was lost in thought as he found her when she was gazing intently at him. Or flirtatiously. He wondered if she knew the latter came so naturally to her. That he responded to it innately.

He finished his pie with the exception of some of the crust and fed that to the pup. He really did need to name the little guy. Especially since the Lab was finally starting to come around, eating more, and he'd drained his bowl of water. Was doing his business regularly.

In addition to the multitude of toys, the bed, the food and treats, and the other accessories and supplies Sam had splurged on at the pet store in Kalispell, he'd also picked up a stretch of fake turf that emitted a feral scent that enticed the dog to relieve himself there, rather than on Sam's expensive hardwood floor. Since the pup was only a few inches from the ground at this point, he couldn't get through the mass of snow that had piled up. And Sam hadn't had the chance to use the blower on the deck and walkways during this latest storm.

As the mutt wandered off, Scarlet turned back to Sam. She asked, "How's the relationship between your mom and Mitcham?"

"Good. Strong. She's crazy about him. Was from the time she met him. She didn't even know who he was at first. That was probably by design on his part. But he fell hard for her, too. I honestly believe he'd do anything for her. He's a different man when he's with her."

"Not quite the forbidding hard-ass?"

"Not quite." He grinned.

"Hmm. So you approve of their marriage?"

"Initially? No, not really. I had no desire to move to the Hamptons. But the fringe benefits made up for that hesitation. And then seeing how happy she was . . ." He shrugged. "What more could I have wanted for her?"

"What indeed."

They put their plates in the dishwasher and Sam said, "I'll show you to the loft. Take your bags up for you."

"Thanks. It's been a long day. And I appreciate the hospitality."

"Anyone in these parts would have done the same."

She gazed up at him and smiled beguilingly. "Maybe."

It took a few seconds for him to come around. He collected her belongings and headed into the great room, which she took interest in. On either end of the split-level room was a curving stairwell made of wood and brushed-nickel railing. The railings also extended across the open rooms upstairs. Sam's office on the right side, his bedroom on the left.

At the top of the stairs, Scarlet stepped into his private space and marveled over it with soft "oohs" and "ahhs" as she noted the oversized sofas and chairs, the enormous fireplace, the big bed. Farther beyond was a large bathroom and walk-in closet, both of which separated the suite from his office.

She glanced up at the wood-trimmed ceiling and said, "You have skylights. I've only ever seen them in home magazines."

"Mine are heated with a drainage system so that the snow

doesn't accumulate. Just melts and runs off. If the sky were clear tonight, you'd be sleeping under the stars."

"That must be incredible."

"I do enjoy it."

"You really have the perfect place here. Impressive. How come you never joined a firm?"

He popped into the bathroom to get the clean set of sheets. As they stripped the bed, he told her, "I'd planned to work in Manhattan after I'd graduated. But I had some freelance design jobs that kept me busy. Then I realized I wasn't into the rat race, wasn't too keen on the Wall Street way of life, and decided to try something different. I came out here for a visit when I was twenty-four. Fell in love with it. Decided what I really wanted was a wide-open space for a house and horses."

"A man who follows his dreams," she mused as she tucked in corners of the fitted sheet. "Even more impressive."

"Well, I couldn't have done it on this grandiose a scale were it not for Phil Bert or Michael."

Her brow knitted. "What do you mean—Michael?"

Sam snapped open the top sheet and they settled it on the mattress as he said, "Michael advised me on how to take my five million and turn it into twenty-five million. Took some time, mind you. I had to start out with a small slice of this property, plop a single-wide trailer on it, and live there while I built the house myself. Eventually from investments, I had enough capital to buy more land, finish the house, and add the outbuildings."

"Commodities?" she ventured.

"That and some real estate investments we partnered up for."

"Quite the whirlwind existence you've led thus far."

As they draped the bronze-colored down comforter over the bed, he told her, "No more so than establishing a global network of black markets, auction houses, and curators."

"Let's not forget all the ins I have with domestic and international police departments and federal agencies. Mostly because of my gran."

"Who does what . . . ? Work for the CIA or MI6?"

"Hardly." Scarlet laughed softly as she reached for a pillow, discarded the former case, and slipped on a new one. "She's L.C. Seymour."

"Ah." Sam whistled under his breath. "So the inquisitive nature runs in the family."

"Exactly."

They finished up and then Sam brushed his teeth and grabbed his drawstring pants and a fresh batch of clothes for the morning. He stoked the fire and told Scarlet, "There are plenty of blankets under the bench seat at the end of the bed if you get cold in the middle of the night. Help yourself to anything."

"Actually, it's perfectly toasty up here. And absolutely stunning. I like your style, Sam Reed."

He stared down at her, knowing it was foolish to get lost in her eyes, but it was so damn easy. He said, "You are insanely beautiful, Scarlet Drake."

She stretched on tiptoe and kissed his cheek. "Thanks for everything, cowboy. You're a real hero."

"I don't know about that." He had too many hellish nightmares of the car accident to buy into her compliment. "But I appreciate the sentiment."

He continued to gaze at her. And couldn't help but lower his head and brush his lips over hers.

He'd only been wanting to do that all damn night. . . .

NINE

Scarlet felt the heat. The lust. The high-voltage current.

It was a simple kiss, really.

Sam's supple lips sweeping over hers.

Feathery light. A whisper of a kiss, in truth.

One that was amazingly perfect.

One that kindled every fiber of her being.

Her lids had fluttered closed for the briefest of seconds. Now she looked up at him and wondered how on earth she'd step away and go about her business. Let him go about his.

Because that wasn't at all what she wanted to do.

Her heart stammered in her chest. Adrenaline flowed through her veins.

She waited with bated breath for him to make another move. For him to recognize that she was still standing there, open to whatever came next.

But the "next" seemed to trouble him, for Sam was the one to take the step back. Physically as well as mentally, she noted with dismay.

He said, "I'll let you get some sleep. Don't worry about your tire. I'll call over to a guy I know in Lakeside and we'll get it worked out."

"That's very kind of you." What else was she going to say? He was retreating.

From the torment in his eyes, clouding the blue irises, she surmised he was torn by the idea of staying and what that might entail . . . and leaving when he apparently believed that was the right thing to do.

Because of his fiancée?

Because he still felt loyalty to Cassidy? And Scarlet wasn't just a bar or a nightclub pickup?

She didn't know of course. Could only speculate. But the uncertainty in his eyes made her heart ache for him.

To ease both their consternation, she said, "Dinner was wonderful, and I know I'm going to get a good night's sleep. Thanks again."

"Yeah. I'll see you in the morning." He dragged his gaze from her. Then took the stairs to the first floor.

Scarlet watched him go, catching his reflection in the oversized windows.

Sam was definitely the soul-stirring type.

But he was clearly caught up in emotions and memories that plagued him. Didn't loosen their hold on him.

Scarlet could relate. At the same time, a burning desire to help him assuage that pain he clung to—that continued to claim him—gnawed at her insides.

She slowly circled his room, her fingertips gliding over his books, his knickknacks, his furniture. It was a damn shame the bed wouldn't smell like him, because she found warmth and security in his virile scent. Had the overwhelming urge to snuggle against him. To be close enough to him to be enveloped in his presence and surrounded by his muscles.

A wholly unfamiliar sensation.

Then again, when Michael had climbed into bed behind her last night and spooned her she'd been thrilled and aroused to be engulfed by him. That, too, had been a wholly unfamiliar sensation.

One she craved to feel again.

She craved a lot of forbidden pleasures when it came to these two men.

As Scarlet removed her tank top and bra and unzipped her jeans, she imagined Sam doing it. While Michael watched.

Although her internal temperature soared, she went into Sam's closet and found sweaters folded in dresser drawers. She selected a navy-colored one that almost matched the hue of the T-shirt he'd worn this evening, which complemented his lighter eyes, and pulled it on. Then she settled in the large bed, thinking it was way too much space for one person. And finding that reality a somewhat disturbing one, particularly on Sam's behalf.

He should have gotten his full dream. A wife. A child. Maybe several kids. Hell, he had the acreage to add on. Fill this house with tons of laughter and lots of puppies.

A tear formed on the rim of her eye. Whereas Michael appealed wholeheartedly to the adventurer in Scarlet, Sam's damaged soul called to hers.

Not exactly something she was comfortable owning up to. It would be in her best interest to keep all of her past pains locked up tight. Not speak of her parents and their tragic, harrowing deaths.

It was saner that way.

Yet she couldn't deny that hers and Sam's heartbreak made them kindred spirits. And Scarlet found solace in that.

So much so, she was able to stare up at the glowing pink clouds and the soothing snowfall captured in the hint of moonlight and breathe a bit easier. Although it was apparent there was a need for release from the overwrought emotions that permeated this gorgeous house, a surprisingly peaceful synergy flowed through her.

At first, Scarlet had no idea how that could be possible—when two wrecked people and one abused puppy were currently residing under the same roof and the entire space was rife with distress, she shouldn't have found even a small measure of tranquility.

But she did.

Because the fires snapped and crackled, warming the air.

The snow fell in fat, pristine-white flakes.

The scent of venison roast and caramelized onions still lingered. Mixed with the tinge of apple-cinnamon.

So beyond the suffering, there was an inviting degree of serenity.

No hustle and bustle. No shoving thoughts and dismal feelings under the rug, because they'd pretty much been laid at both Scarlet's and Sam's feet. Like Michael, Sam had many layers to him that she wanted to strip away. In due time.

Admittedly, her interactions with both men helped Scarlet to expand her tunnel vision on work and humanize the case she was focused on.

Not something she normally did. But in this instance, it felt right.

Michael wasn't her thief.

She was convinced of that.

Nor was Sam.

So . . . Who was?

Mitcham had nothing to gain, aside from recouping the initial expenditure on the collection. But seriously. The man was worth more money than she—and pretty much most of the global populace—could comprehend. So that didn't make sense. Not to mention, he'd purchased the artwork for his new bride. What sort of monster would gift the woman he loved with such a rare treasure and then turn around and rip it from her hands?

It wouldn't exactly be a clever way to welcome her into his home.

And Karina wasn't a fathomable suspect herself. By marrying Mitcham, the woman had just scored everything she could possibly want—a rich, handsome husband, a mansion, and a prestigious art collection.

So who the hell would benefit from stealing the works?

An aficionado outside the mansion walls, sure. As Michael had implied. But something crucial Scarlet had learned from Jewel when it came to high-end collectors was that they wanted to show off their prizes. Put their acquisitions—no matter how those acquisitions had ended up in their possession—on display. Like trophies.

If one couldn't brag about such an impressive array of paintings without drawing suspicion—and the authorities to their doorstep—then what would be the purpose of procuring them? Especially under such high stakes?

Scarlet's brain churned as her thoughts ran rampant.

She'd be exhausted tomorrow if she kept this up, but she'd yet in her twenty-eight years of existence figured out where the off switch was.

So she mulled over more scenarios and possibilities. But like the FBI, she was coming up empty-handed.

Fatigue would eventually catch up to her. Until it did, she allowed everything from the probable to the absurd to traipse through her mind. Knowing if she hit upon one tiny feasible concept, something bigger might gel. . . .

Morning came with the soft rays of sunlight penetrating the thin clouds and the glorious aroma of strong coffee wafting through the air. Scarlet grinned while still in that groggy state between a sinful dream of two magnificently built men in the form of Michael Vandenberg and Sam Reed and the reality of a hearty cup of joe awaiting her.

She wouldn't have left the two magnificently built men in lieu of coffee, of course, were they not a mere dream. One beyond her reach.

Shoving away the covers, she didn't think of dragging on her jeans and top while she brushed her teeth, swept a hand through her hair, and then headed downstairs. Wearing nothing but Sam's sweater and a thick pair of socks.

She followed the delicious scent of caffeine and breakfast. Jonesing for both. And for Sam.

Strolling into the kitchen, she was greeted by a lumbering puppy. His paws were a bit too large for his short stature, and then there was the matter of him being in obvious pain that made it difficult for him to actually scamper across the hardwood floor.

Prompting Scarlet to ask Sam, "Did the vet prescribe anything for the bruises and cuts?"

"Low-dosage aspirin and an antibiotic. I've been giving him both."

"Right." Scarlet really had nothing ingenious to contribute on the subject of healing a dog. "I've never actually owned a pet, so I have no clue what taking care of an injured one entails." Still, she gently scooped the pup up into her arms. And was rewarded with a soft lick on her cheek. She laughed.

Sam said, "My experience with animals is that TLC can sometimes be the best medicine."

"Yeah. You have a point there. Rudy seems to respond to it."

From his place at the stove as he scrambled eggs, Sam jerked a brow at her. *"Rudy?"*

She eyed the pup and gave a slight shake of her head. "I don't know. *Fido* is so not right. *Spot? Jack?* Ideas?"

"I'm thinking more along the lines of *Cletus.*"

Scarlet stared at Sam. "Seriously?"

"Why not?"

"Cletus," she slowly repeated. Gave an even slower shake of her head. "Gotta tell you, I'm not seeing it."

"Hmm. Then it just might be Rudy."

She snickered. Told the Lab, "He's totally humoring us. But I like Rudy. How do you feel about it?" Another lick, this one just under her left eye. "I'll take that as a yes."

Sam chuckled. "One little good-night kiss and you're namin' my dog?"

"Someone has to do it. And that kiss might have been little, but it packed a hell of a punch."

"Sort of like you running around half-naked in my house, wearin' my sweater. Pretty sure those are my socks, too."

"They are. You did tell me to help myself to anything."

His gaze slid up her bare legs and he grinned. "Trust me, I am not complaining."

Heat rushed through her. Scarlet put the dog in his bed and then set the island for two, now that she knew where everything was located. She poured a cup of coffee for herself, then topped off Sam's mug. Next, she retrieved the tiny pitcher of creamer from the fridge, along with the orange juice.

Sam flipped pancakes on the griddle and added two small stacks to side plates. He put out a serving bowl filled with the eggs and another plate with bacon and sausage links. Added toast. Scarlet went back to the fridge for the butter and two kinds of jam.

They worked well together. Perfectly in sync. Not bumping into each other. And again, the comfortable silence that stretched between them was enthralling. Enjoyable.

Scarlet was a chatterbox by nature, because her mind was always whirling. But that peaceful feeling she'd experienced last night as she'd lain awake in Sam's bed and stared up at the snowy pink heavens remained with her this morning. Even after he'd mentioned their brief kiss and following the way he'd so hungrily taken her in from head to toe a few moments ago.

It was too damn bad he'd felt compelled to shower and fully dress before starting breakfast. She would have liked to see him fresh from slumber, in pajama bottoms and nothing else. His brown hair tousled, sleep still in his sky-blue eyes. His voice low and rumbling.

She bit back a moan as desire flared against her clit. She couldn't imagine anything sexier than waking up between this man and his stepbrother. The three of them naked and huddled together. Their bodies entwined. Sam's and Michael's hands on her. Sam kissing her lips, Michael nipping at her neck.

Scarlet pulled in a raspy breath.

Sam eyed her curiously. "What are you thinking over there?" he asked as he settled next to her, on the end of the raised counter.

"Honestly? That you're wearing too many clothes."

His laugh was light and stirring. But then as he reached for his coffee, his expression darkened. His eyes glowed seductively, though she didn't miss the glimmer of something troubling around the fringes.

Scarlet debated whether she should make an inquiry as to the latter or let it lie.

But since beating around the bush wasn't really her style, she bucked up and said, "You're sending a lot of mixed signals, Sam."

"Yeah." He gave a slight nod. "I know." He sipped his coffee, then set his mug aside. "On the one hand, I was sort of hoping you'd get lonely in that big bed all by yourself and come downstairs. Crawl under the covers with me, in front of the fire."

She swallowed down some OJ and a lump of uncertainty before saying, "It's not like the idea didn't cross my mind. It was a very appealing notion. But you backed off after that kiss, so I figured me joining you wasn't what you wanted."

"It was exactly what I wanted," he said with conviction, pinning her with a solid look. But as was usually the case, there was contradiction rimming his irises. "It was also *not* what I wanted."

Needing to get to the heart of the matter, because Scarlet wasn't one for riddles or games, she ventured, "This is about Cassidy, isn't it? This was going to be her home. The two of you were going to live here."

"She never set foot in this house," he vehemently said, his sudden intensity taking Scarlet by surprise. "So there are no ghosts haunting me here."

"But in your mind . . . ?"

"I have reservations," he confessed.

"You mean demons."

He stared at her.

Scarlet told him, "I never, ever talk about my parents' deaths. In fact, I rarely speak of them in general. I didn't have much difficulty doing it with you last night. I can understand how you feel. I empathize with you. And I will admit that my inability to really process what happened to them and release all of my horror and pain makes it extremely hard for me to get close to people. It's why I don't date. Anything could happen, and I don't feel I'm fully equipped to deal with another personal tragedy. But then again . . ."

She chewed over this new direction of conversation and a piece of sausage. Sam waited patiently for her to gather her thoughts. They were still a bit murky; her insides a bit tangled.

Eventually, Scarlet said, "I feel as though I know precisely what you're going through. Maybe it's not fully true, but I do have a good idea. And so I understand that you wanted to kiss me, but that you didn't want to. That you wanted me to come to you last night. But that you didn't want me to. The desire is there. But so, too, are the demons."

"I've always been aggressive when it comes to my desires. No–holds–barred. But with you?" His eyes bored into her. "There's something about you. Something that tells me it wouldn't just be sex."

"And that bothers you."

"Bothers you, too," he pointedly said. "Otherwise, you really would have crawled under the covers with me."

Scarlet considered this as she finished her breakfast. She couldn't deny he'd hit the nail on the head. The problem was, she couldn't exactly say it was *just sex* with Michael, either. Because she continued to think of him. And wanted to explore more with him.

This was all getting very convoluted. Scarlet suspected a little advice and perspective from Jewel and Bayli might be in order.

But now wasn't the time for that.

Sam pushed back his stool and stood. He gathered dishes and took them to the sink to rinse them off and load them into the dishwasher. Scarlet helped him, not saying anything. Not entirely sure what it was she was supposed to say.

She relished the nearness of him. Inhaled his scent, purposely brushed her arm against his as they worked. Felt all the sparks and exhilaration he'd so easily incited from the second she'd gotten out of her rental and absorbed the full effect of Sam Reed.

Lover of horses. Rescuer of abused and abandoned puppies. Savior of damsels in distress. Builder of breathtaking homes.

He was like the Horse Whisperer, John Wayne, and Frank Lloyd Wright all rolled into one.

With the exterior of a Hugh Jackman–Chris Hemsworth mash-up.

It was no wonder she was having premature hot flashes.

Sam rounded up the silverware, put it in the basket, and turned on the cycle. Standing behind Scarlet, he reached around her on both sides to wash his hands at the sink she blocked.

He sniffed her hair and said, "I see why Rudy burrows against your neck."

A sensuous shudder chased down her spine. Leaving her a little breathless as she said, "You're not really going to call him that."

"It's starting to grow on me."

"Clearly *Old Yeller*'s out of the question."

"Clearly." He wiped his hands, then added, "I have work to do in the stables. Your tire will be delivered this afternoon, so make yourself at home."

"I have emails and such to catch up on. I brought my laptop, so I'll be fine. I assume you have WiFi?"

"Indeed I do."

"Well then. I'm all set."

He gazed at her a few seconds more. Eventually he said, "I didn't have any involvement in the disappearance of my mother's art collection, Scarlet. In fact, I was angry that it happened, because it really broke her heart. That gift from Mitcham meant a lot to her. I don't give a damn that Michael and I have trouble relating to him. Somehow, Mitcham clicks with my mother. If you saw them together, you'd be shocked, I'm sure. But you'd also get what I'm talking about."

She sighed in resignation. "I can see how the FBI ran out of suspects."

He swept his warm fingertips over her cheek. "You believe me?"

"Hard not to. You have a solid alibi. Misty and Pembroke corroborated Michael's story and I'm sure there were plenty of witnesses to see the four of you enter and leave the guesthouse at the times you and Michael both stated."

"I don't have any reason to lie about it."

"No, I suppose not." She was contemplative a moment, then added, "I also rely on character. I'm a great judge of it, and I have no reason to doubt either of you. Michael's a bit pissy with me when it comes to my questioning, but I can recognize now what that's all about. He was born with a phenomenal foundation, but he had to build the walls on his own. He doesn't appreciate someone taking a hammer to what he's constructed. I'm an intruder and that sets him on edge."

"Very astute." Sam's head bent to hers and he gave her another of the feathery kisses that teased her senseless. As much as she wanted him to just haul her up against his hard chest and kiss the hell out of her, the way Michael would do, she found Sam's emotional and physical tug-of-war titillating. Perhaps because she knew that when the dam broke they'd both be overpowered by lust and longing.

And that was a sexy thought, rife with anticipation and danger.

He grinned at her, as though reading her mind and liking the fantasies she wove. Then he spun on his boot heels and headed out.

Scarlet released another long breath. Fanned her flaming face with her hand.

She had the distinct feeling that she and Sam were on a crash course to spontaneous combustion.

And it was going to be explosive.

TEN

Sam took an all-terrain vehicle to the stables, adjacent to the indoor and outdoor arenas. There were several trucks in the drive. Some belonging to his employees, who maintained the grounds and facilities. A couple belonging to his students or their parents.

Sam had learned from Phil Bert how to train horses and riders. Sam had been into roping at first, upon his initial exposure to horses. Then he'd taken an interest in jumping. Had studied the mechanics of it, spent time at competitions to catalog everything associated with the approach, takeoff, and execution. Had competed himself. Sam had a natural talent for riding, and his horses had always been sturdy and steady beneath him.

He'd also spent ample time observing as Phil Bert had instructed champion riders of various ages and stages of expertise.

Bonding with a horse was probably one of the greatest joys in life, Sam surmised. They were intelligent, fascinating creatures. They emitted and absorbed emotion. And, quite frankly, when you were mostly an inner-city kid who'd never visited so much as a petting zoo suddenly being surrounded by these magnificent animals—and watching them soar through the air, clearing fence after fence—was not only thrilling but also therapeutic.

Maybe that was why Sam preferred viewing and studying "free jumping." The absence of a rider gave the horse freedom from that additional weight burden, and Sam could evaluate the animal's skills and trajectory. Its temperament and fluidity. Just admire it for its grace and beauty.

Sam headed into the enclosed arena and spent a couple of hours with two junior female jumpers. Then he stopped in the stables, where more of his employees tended to the horses. The stalls were large and each one had an attached outdoor corral. Sam tried to create as much room as he could for the horses to safely roam. And he was fortunate to have a number of skilled trainers and caretakers on hand. Even the vet stopped by once a day. Inclement weather be damned.

Sam made the rounds with the horses, because he enjoyed their company and always wanted to ensure they were in tip-top shape. Then he went to the utility sink to wash up, cranking on the faucet.

"Son of a bitch!" He swore a blue streak as water shot out, drenching his T-shirt and face.

Sixty-something gray-haired Winston "Win" Daughtry ambled from the main office and asked, "Everything okay, boss?"

Sam tossed him a smirk. Flicked a hand at his wet chest. "Does it look like everything's okay?"

Win chuckled. "Sorry about that, boss. I forgot to tell you the faucet's broke. I called Harvey. He's coming out tomorrow. So, uh . . . Don't use the sink until then."

Sam yanked a few paper towels from the dispenser, pressed them to his chest, and sardonically said, "Thanks for the heads-up."

His employee and friend told him, "I would have mentioned it sooner, but I've been on the phone with Jeanette Hadley, who's willing to come up from Phoenix and work with Layton Travers and his horse to help groom them for nationals. Like you wanted."

"Layton's ready for the big time. Jeanette will be an additional asset to his training."

"So good news there. Might wanna change your shirt, though." Win returned to the office.

It was noon, so Sam made his way to the house. He found Scarlet at the dining table tapping rapidly on the keyboard of her laptop while also speaking into her Bluetooth earpiece. She'd taken a shower and changed into a sweater and jeans with hiking boots. Too bad. He'd liked her in his clothes. Liked her bare legs even more.

When he entered she dropped off her call and said, "I made venison stew with the leftover roast. I hope you don't mind. I got the recipe off the Internet and it was really about the only thing I could whip up. Not so handy in the kitchen, you know?"

"I think you've been doing just fine." He went down on his haunches to get a good look at Rudy, huddled under the table at Scarlet's feet. "And *you* are definitely loving every minute of it."

"He yipped," she said.

Sam's head popped up. "Pardon me?"

She snapped the lid of her computer closed and said, "He heard a noise coming from the driveway, took a few seconds to decide whether he actually wanted to get to his feet, finally did, then yipped. Just once. A little one. It was cute. Not exactly authoritative, but let's keep that between the two of us. No need to give him any sort of inferiority complex."

Sam grinned. "He must've heard Brent with the snow mover. Comes by after a good dumping and clears it all out so folks can get up that long drive."

"Lots of activity around here."

"Yeah, it's kind of nice."

"And what's with the wet look?"

Sam glanced down at his soaked chest. "Small accident in the stables." He shrugged out of his jacket and hung it up. Then he stalked into the laundry room. Went to the back where the machines were, stripped off his shirt, and tossed it into the dryer. He grabbed a clean T-shirt from a recently folded load on the shelf and turned to head into the kitchen.

Scarlet was standing along the pantry counter, where she'd apparently been gathering a few treats for Rudy from the box. But her gaze was fixated on Sam, her hand mid-air. She gaped.

A surge of testosterone had him taking a few steps toward her, another grin on his face.

The long cords of her neck pulled tight as she drew in a deep breath.

Sam said, "Like what you see, darlin'?"

She was drinking him in. Looking a bit spellbound.

He closed the gap between them, until they were mere inches from each other. He tossed the shirt on the counter. Placed a hand on her hip. She released the treats in her fist and instead gripped the granite ledge behind her.

Sam's thumb slid under the hem of her sweater and swept over her silky skin. Brushing back and forth.

His head lowered to hers and he said, "No mixed signals here. I'm telling you exactly what I want. Touch me, Scarlet."

She continued to stare at him. The anticipation mounted. His cock throbbed in wild beats.

Finally, she pried her good hand from the ledge and her nails skated over his abs, the light touch causing his muscles to flex. Her fingertips moved slowly upward to his pecs. She clearly marveled over him and that excited him even more.

As her palm skimmed over his shoulder and down his biceps, she offered him her other hand. "Take the bandage off."

He carefully removed it. Then she used both hands to roam his chest and stomach. His back. Setting every inch of him ablaze. Until he couldn't stand the torment another second and his mouth pressed to hers for but a brief moment before their lips parted and their tongues tangled.

He kissed her deeply, passionately. Red-hot desire flashed through him. An erotic awakening only she could spark. Her fingers threaded through his hair as she succumbed to him, let him pull her in, kiss her more fervently. His hand under her sweater grazed her rib cage before he cupped her breast and squeezed. Roughly, no doubt conveying his need for her.

His other arm encircled her waist, keeping her close to him. Christ, she made him hard. So quickly, so painfully. All he could think of was sliding into her warm, wet depths.

Well, he had something else in mind first.

Breaking the kiss, he shoved the sweater up and over her head, heaping it on top of his discarded shirt. He palmed her breasts and kneaded them through the lacy material of her bra as his lips glided over her throat. A soft moan escaped her, spurring him on. Jesus . . . making him even harder.

"You feel incredible in my hands," he murmured against her skin. And felt the shiver run through her.

"I have extremely sensitive nipples."

Sam groaned. His pulse jumped. He peeled back the lace from one breast, tucking it under the plump mound. The pad of his thumb whisked over the taut center. She pulled in a sharp breath. He pinched and rolled the little bud, tightening it further. Her chest rose and fell heavily. Her fingers in his hair tugged on the strands and her body writhed against his.

Sam cupped her breast again, bent his head, and curled his tongue around her nipple, then fluttered the tip over the pebbled peak.

"Oh, God," she said on a throaty sigh. "That makes me crazy."

"I'm going to do more than that," he assured her. "I'm going to make you come."

He drew her nipple into his mouth. Sucked hard.

"Sam!" she cried out.

As he tongued the puckered bead, one hand pressed to the

small of her back and the other went between her legs, his fingers massaging, teasing her through her jeans.

She clasped his biceps, her nails digging into rigid sinew. He could feel her tremors and he suckled again, inciting a fierce tremor within her that reverberated to *his* core.

"You're making me so wet," she whispered.

That drove him out of his mind.

He deftly unbuttoned her pants and slid the zipper down the track.

"I want you dripping for me," he said. His hand slipped into her thong panties. He rubbed her clit as his mouth returned to hers.

He kissed her heatedly. Greedily. All the reservations—the demons—that had been tormenting him since he'd met this woman didn't stand a chance of holding him back now that he'd tasted her lips, caused her body to respond ardently to him, felt the pearl at her apex swell under his touch.

She released her vise grip on him and twined her arms around his neck, clinging to him. Her breasts were pressed to his chest, one still covered in lace that rasped over his skin, taunting him as much as the nipple he'd exposed.

God, she felt like a slice of heaven as she squirmed in his loose embrace, her arms tightening as though she couldn't get close enough to him.

His hand at the small of her back shifted lower into her jeans, his fingers easing beyond the thin strand of her thong nestled in her cleft. He penetrated her pussy from behind, working two fingers into her slick, narrow canal while he continued a slow, circular motion on her clit.

And damn, she really was dripping for him.

He tore his mouth from hers and lightly bit his way down her neck as she moaned and writhed. Her inner walls contracted around his fingers, released, contracted stronger, insistently.

"You're close, aren't you?" he murmured.

"Yes. God, yes."

He picked up the pace at her apex, stroked her pussy quicker. Her breathing escalated. Her fingers twisted in his hair again.

"Sam," she said, her wisps of air teasing his temple. "I want you between my legs, crushing me beneath you, with all of these muscles against my body, surrounding me."

"You want me inside you."

"Yes. Desperately."

The urgency in her voice called to him, struck all the right chords.

"Come for me first," he quietly demanded. Then drew her nipple into his mouth with a forceful suction that jolted her.

Her breath caught and her body tensed.

A heartbeat later, she called out, "Sam!" as she shattered, every inch of her quaking. "Oh, fuck," she said. "Oh, God."

She held fast to him and her orgasm. Whimpering softly.

Sam waited until she was a little steadier on her feet and her body relaxed a bit. Then he withdrew from her and palmed her ass cheeks. He lifted her up and her legs instantly wrapped around his hips. He carried her through the kitchen to the couch he'd slept on the night before, the sheet still draped over the distressed-leather cushions, a fur blanket tossed over the back of the sofa. There was a mound of pillows in the corner, and he settled Scarlet there.

He hastily whipped off her hiking boots, which looked to be brand-new, followed by her socks and jeans. He paused, simply taking in the arousing sight of her in skimpy white lace.

A strangled sound lodged in his throat. "Damn, you're gorgeous."

Her gaze followed his, along her body. Her lingerie was slightly disheveled. "I'm a mess."

"One hell of a sexy mess," he said, lust tinging his tone.

"So why are you still standing there?" She crooked a finger at him. "We should be naked by now."

"I'm all for naked." He toed off his boots, then ripped open the fly of his Levi's and shoved the denim down his thighs.

A sharp, "Oh," fell from Scarlet's parted lips. Her emerald eyes feasted on the bulge in his shorts.

Sam rid himself of the rest of his clothing, then had her out of her bra and panties two seconds later.

As he joined her, he asked, "Did Michael use a condom?"

"No. And, yes, that part was reckless. But I did believe him when he told me gets tested."

"He does. So do I. Though I was very careful during my short-lived promiscuity."

"I'm not holding that against you, Sam." She swept hair from his forehead. "Everyone copes differently."

"I don't mean to press my luck here, but—"

"I want you to come inside me." She stared into his eyes. "I want to feel you—*all* of you."

His lips skimmed over hers, so warm and soft, like the rest of her. He loved having her beneath him, their bodies melded together, his cock gliding over her slick folds with each deep breath they took.

"You make me so damn hard," he said. "I didn't think I could get this hot for someone."

"I like that you took your time reaching this place in your mind. I understand, you know?" She kissed him.

Sam could easily lose himself in this woman. And he wasn't even inside her yet. Was merely savoring every single second of flesh on flesh. Her wicked tongue twisting with his. Her hands skating down his back and to his ass. She gripped his cheeks and squeezed.

A silent plea.

One he answered by shifting his pelvis ever so slightly until his tip nudged her opening. Her nails dug into his butt. His pulse spiked. His cock thrust into her.

She broke their kiss and cried out.

Sam's hips rocked with hers as he pumped slowly.

"You're so fucking tight," he said against her lips. "So wet."

His shaft slid smoothly along her inner walls. He slung one of her legs over his hips, forcing her to relinquish her hold on him. Her palms flattened against his shoulder blades instead, keeping him plastered to her. Sam's hand on her ass angled her hips just so and he plunged deeper into her. They easily fell into a sensual rhythm that had them grinding together and Scarlet opening further to him.

"Yes," she whispered. "You feel amazing."

His thrusts were long and full, unhurried despite the adrenaline rushing through his veins. He kissed her possessively, amping up the passion and the need that arced between them.

This wasn't at all what he'd experienced with those other women, following Cassidy's death. Those encounters had been brief. Minimal to no kissing. Mostly anonymous with her bent over a desk in a hotel room or pressed up against the door. Quick and physically gratifying, but no more than that.

With Scarlet, he could stay buried in her warm depths forever. She moved in sync with him. Tasted as sensational as she felt. Even the hint of her floral perfume seduced and enticed him. Sam was completely consumed by desire, but she also stirred something inside him. Tugged at heartstrings he'd long since thought had been severed.

Also knowing that she'd been with Michael sparked dark yearnings. Sam couldn't help but think of how mind-blowing it would be for him and his stepbrother to pleasure her at the same time. Turn her soft whimpers into throaty moans. Make her come twice as hard.

Spurred by that fantasy, his hand glided along the cleft of her ass, down to where their bodies were joined, and he collected some of her cream on his middle finger, then circled the rim of her anus.

He asked, "Did Michael—"

"No," she hastily said in a breathy tone. "Not there."

"Has anyone been here?"

"Just toys."

Fire roared through him. "That's good to know." Both in terms of him being her first—and the fact that she was already primed for what he wanted to do to her.

As he pumped into her pussy, his finger penetrated the small hole and she let out an excited cry.

Sam's hips rocked faster and she maintained the tempo with him. He drove deep, working her from both angles. Her broken breaths filled the quiet room and resonated within him, pushing him close to the edge.

Her body felt so fucking good against his, and she milked his shaft with her inner muscles, clenching and releasing until his own breathing was ragged and his pulse echoed in his ears. His heart hammered and the blood in his cock surged and throbbed.

He kissed her once more, turned on by her supple lips and velvety tongue. His hips bucked harder, faster. She didn't miss a beat. Her nails clawed at his back and her leg that was wrapped around his waist tightened so that he was pinioned to her.

Shudders ran through her. She practically vibrated beneath him.

Tearing his mouth from hers, Sam murmured, "Come for me."

"I couldn't stop it if I tried." Her eyes glimmered and danced. Her cheeks were rosy and her lips were swollen from his kisses.

She was even more stunning in the throes of passion, and Sam committed every little thing about her to memory.

"You're so deep inside me," she said. "Perfect spot. It's so fantastic—everything you do to me is so incredible."

He would have kissed her again, but she clamped down on her

lower lip. Her eyelids dipped. Her pussy clutched him firmly and Sam thrust harder into her.

"Yes," she moaned. Her head fell back. "Oh, God, yes. Just like that."

He kept pumping, pushing her higher.

"Yes," she said. "Oh, Christ—*yes!*"

She clenched him tighter and called out his name. Sam lost it, too.

"Ah, fuck!" His body convulsed, his cock pulsated, and he filled her pussy with his hot cum as she continued to move with him, drawing out every ounce of their orgasms.

Sam hadn't thought he could ever come so explosively after Cassidy.

He'd been wrong. *Way* wrong.

ELEVEN

Scarlet couldn't catch her breath. Nor did she relinquish her hold on Sam. She wanted him to stay right where he was, buried inside her, his hulking body covering hers.

God, that felt so wonderful!

She still quaked beneath him. Still rode the residual high of a powerful release. Still savored the scintillating sensation of him filling her.

Whether her heart rate would ever return to normal was debatable. Certainly not while she was around this man, she suspected. Or his stepbrother.

She could only imagine what it would have been like to be Misty Ferrera and Pembroke Peterson the night of the art theft. Those were two seriously lucky women.

So, too, had been Cassidy Harkins, she had no doubt. Even if Sam and Michael hadn't both been involved with her, knowing what she knew of Sam, Scarlet was sure his fiancée had landed herself one hell of a man.

Said man was currently leaving feathery kisses along Scarlet's throat when the back door swung open and Rudy yipped again.

Scarlet's eyes flew open. Sam slowly lifted his head and gazed beyond the end table and the lamp sitting on it.

"Well, hello there, Jesse," he said.

Jesse? Scarlet mouthed.

Sam grinned at her as he casually reached for the fur blanket on the back of the sofa and draped it over them.

He said to the intruder, who was obviously a friend, "You're a bit earlier than I expected."

"Your tire came in an hour ago. Thought I'd bring it out to you. Help you pull the dent while I'm here."

"I appreciate that," Sam said. "Meet the woman who needs that tire. Scarlet Drake. Scarlet, this is Jesse Wilks. From Lakeside."

"Nice to meet you, Miss Drake." She heard his footsteps on the hardwood floor and—wholly mortified because she was naked and lying beneath Sam—she thrust an arm over her head for Jesse to swoop in and give her hand a gentle shake. "Sorry for the interruption."

"Nice to meet you as well, Jesse. And *Scarlet*'s fine."

She didn't dare look at him since he'd only see the horror on her face. Instead, she glared at Sam. Who chuckled.

He told her, "Darlin', I'm gonna have to leave you for a few minutes so Jesse and I can fix up your SUV."

"I'll try to survive without you," she caustically said.

Sam's laugh was heartier this time. "Trust me, I have a preference of where I'd rather be. But Jesse did come all this way."

"And I'll be outside gettin' the tire from my truck," Jesse chimed in.

When the back door closed behind him, Scarlet narrowed her gaze on Sam. "Stop looking like the cat that ate the canary."

He kissed her, then said, "Any man on the planet with air in his lungs would get a kick out of being walked in on when he had a woman as beautiful as you underneath him."

"Save your flattery," she told him in a dry tone. "I'm likely turning three shades of red."

"And it's damn pretty." He kissed her forehead. Then hauled himself off of her, though he covered her back up with the blanket. "I won't be long."

Scarlet watched him scoop up his jeans and boots and strut bare-ass naked to the kitchen sink, where he washed his hands and then dressed. He ducked into the storage room for his T-shirt, put his jacket on, and shot her a brow-wagging look before walking out.

A long breath blew through her parted lips.

Sam Reed was sexy as hell.

And she was thoroughly captivated by him. So much so, it took several minutes for her to compose herself and toss off the blanket and retrieve her clothes.

It was only noon, so she figured she could have a quick lunch with Sam before she hit the road while there was a break in the storm. In this weather, it could take her five hours or so to get through Montana and Coeur D'Alene, Idaho, and then into Spokane.

She decided to check on flights out of Kalispell, a faster route. But she didn't have any more luck finding availability into San Francisco than she'd had when she booked the round-trip airfare. So Spokane it was.

Sam returned not more than thirty minutes later, declaring success. He joined her for stew and then Scarlet packed up. Sam escorted her to the SUV.

Admittedly, she was reluctant to leave. But time was still of the essence with her case.

Sam put her bags in the front on the passenger's side and then rounded the vehicle to the driver's door where she stood. He'd turned the rental around so it was ready for her to easily depart. The engine was running to warm it.

He asked, "You really have to go now?"

Her heart fluttered at his hint of disappointment. "You're officially a cold lead. I have to find a hot one."

"Hey, I think I take offense to that."

She kissed him, then said, "You know what I'm saying. I still have work to do. And as much as I'd love for you to distract me for another evening, or a half dozen more of them, I have a prior commitment."

"A woman with a work ethic," he quipped in a mock-grave voice, and rolled his eyes for dramatic effect. "Onward, then. Though I hardly took you for the love 'em and leave 'em type."

She smiled. Her nails trailed along his pecs as she said, "You know I'm not. So I expect you to call me."

"Already slipped my number into your laptop bag."

"Excellent." She kissed him again. "Then I'll call you. Now . . . I really do have to be on my way. It's going to snow again tonight and I'd rather be at the airport when it starts."

"Agreed."

He opened the door for her and she slipped into the seat and latched the belt.

"Be safe and call me if you need anything more from me," he said.

Sadly, Scarlet already did need something from him. Another go-round on his sofa. But that was an issue she couldn't rectify at the moment.

And for God's sake, when had she become a nymphomaniac?

With an inward snicker, she had to contend it was right about the time she'd met Michael Vandenberg. Then his stepbrother, Sam Reed.

Yeah. Too hot to handle—times two—but so worth the try!

She left the ranch and rambled through Montana, picking up I-90 into Idaho. All the while, her brain was divided. She contemplated her next moves with this investigation. Yet thoughts of Michael and Sam invaded her mental strategic-planning efforts.

So Scarlet decided a couple of things had to happen. First, she'd address the never-ending sizzle consuming her by consulting with Jewel on how to juggle two men. Then she'd talk to Bayli about picking up another scent to follow with the case.

Perhaps then she could find a modicum of harmony between her personal and her professional lives.

The next morning, Scarlet breezed into Jewel's office in River Cross, where she was busy with preparations to break ground on hers, Rogen's, and Vin's new inn and winery.

Jewel's beautiful face lit up at the sight of Scarlet. "Thank God you survived Montana!"

She laughed. "Really, you and Bay worry too much."

"Well, driving across three states in a blizzard isn't exactly in your normal travel repertoire."

"It wasn't a blizzard, but you're right. And it *was* touch and go there for a while on the inbound side. I hadn't factored elk dashing across the highway into my master plan."

"I'm just glad you're okay."

Scarlet sank into a chair in front of Jewel's glass-topped desk. She was a striking blonde with sapphire eyes and an infectious smile. That likely had something to do with her living arrangement with both Rogen and Vin.

"I'm fantastically okay," Scarlet assured her. "As you know, stellar orgasms will do that to a girl."

Jewel's eyes widened. "*Oooh,* do tell."

"The stepbrother is just as irresistible as the real estate tycoon." Scarlet beamed. "And by *irresistible* I mean Holy Mary Mother of God. They are both so amazingly gorgeous, but it's more than that. . . . I can't even explain the attraction—it's not just physical. There are so many facets to Michael and I'm dying to find out who that man really is. And with Sam . . . Good Lord. He's the complete package, but so very, very damaged."

Jewel's brow knitted. "That could prove dangerous, emotionally. For a girl like you . . ."

"Yes, I know," she admitted. "Believe me, I had time to give this its due consideration as I passed state border after state border. But the chemistry was much too overwhelming not to cave in to it. Oh, and from what I've learned of Sam's alibi, these men are quite familiar with pleasing one woman at the same time." She mockingly gawked. "How enticing is *that*?"

Jewel's jaw dropped. "You've been here for five minutes and didn't lead with that juicy tidbit? You really are rusty at titillating your friends with sexy tales."

"As if I've had any sexy tales for titillation. Please. Even the last guy I hooked up was so unmemorable, I can't pinpoint when we'd gotten together, where, or even what the hell his name was. I mean, that's just sad. Ridiculously so."

"Amen, sister."

"So as much as I've been lamenting the lack of action on my part when you and Bay have been having all your fun, it's been a blessing in disguise. Who wants to settle for mediocre when there's earth-shattering sex out there? Honest-to-God, rock-you-to-the-core-of-your-being sex?"

"That's what I'm talking about," Jewel said with a smirk. "So yours has been fully worth the wait?"

"And then some. But . . . It's more than that." She sighed. "I've totally hit a dead end with the investigation, and I'm suffering some serious guilt from sleeping with both of my persons of interest. Very unprofessional. Yet . . . To have missed out on either one of these men. What a travesty that would have been."

"Agreed. I can tell that just from the sparkle in your eyes." Jewel drummed the end of her fountain pen on the leather blotter in front of her. "If you're not able to make ends meet with Michael and Sam as suspects, well, then, hell . . . there's no longer a conflict of interest in my mind."

Scarlet gave her a dubious look.

"Okay, total gray area, sure. But if there's nothing conclusive and you're just barking up an empty tree when it comes to these two, then you've done your due diligence, right? Move on to the next possibility on your list."

She cringed. "That would be Michael's father and Sam's mother. Like that won't rub all parties concerned raw."

Jewel made a face. "I guess this is why they always say don't shit where you eat."

"I am so fucked?"

"Well, there's an obvious retort for that comment, but I'll spare you." Her friend grinned mischievously.

"Ha-ha."

"Sorry." Jewel looked contrite. "So now what are you going to do?"

Scarlet pushed out of the plush white chair and started to pace. "Good question. I really have no clue. I want to see Michael *and* Sam again. But I'm still poking around in their private business."

"And what if you actually do unearth something that reflects poorly on either one of them, even if it's indirectly?"

Scarlet tapped the tip of her nose. "Bingo. I'm digging a huge hole for myself here. I know this. The sensible side of me really and truly comprehends that getting involved with Michael Vandenberg and Sam Reed is such a bad idea in the grand scheme of things. But on the flip side—imagine having sex with Rogen once, or Vin once, and then never having it again."

"I'd wither away and die."

"Yeah." Scarlet slumped into her chair and heaved a breath. "I feel the same way. Worse, I'm so intrigued by them and so desperate to know them better that I can't just let this go. On the flip side—what am I really going to discover?"

"Well," Jewel said in a tentative tone. "There's the possibility that you won't discover anything incriminating."

"Sure, not toward Michael and Sam, but once again, indirectly there's the chance that something could crop up related to someone else in the family. I mean, we're talking about eighteen million dollars' worth of artwork that just vanished!"

"Yes. And anything you might unearth that's attached to the Vandenberg name would look bad for *everyone* involved."

"Precisely. So here's my big dilemma," Scarlet said. "I can't give up on this investigation regardless of how prickly it could get. I need to continue my questioning. *Someone* has to have seen *something*. Someone has to know something. Where the hell are all those goddamn paintings?"

She threw her hands in the air in exasperation.

With a nod, Jewel said, "I'm following you."

"I just have to work this all out in my mind. I've been fairly boggled. I had no idea how I'd respond to Michael. I had less of a clue with Sam. But that all has to take a backseat to this assignment. I'm fully dedicated to it."

"There's only a couple weeks left to the statute of limitations," Jewel reminded her. "So finish with your investigation and then see what's what. Right?"

Scarlet wanted to believe it was all that easy to compartmentalize. But it wasn't. Yet what other choice did she have than to push her romantic encounters to the dark shadows of her mind? At least until she was done with her job.

Because she really did need to uphold her professional commitment and reputation. As far as the big picture went, that was currently most important.

So she left Jewel's office and returned home, a three-bedroom Tudor-style house with two dens. She shared the space with her gran, who typically would be pounding the keys of her laptop at this time of day, working on her latest novel. Except that she'd apparently run out to get the mail.

As Scarlet entered from the garage, L.C. came through the front door. They met in the middle.

Scarlet's grandmother was a petite woman with pale-green eyes and silvery hair styled in a chic bob. She wore four-inch heels and wispy scarves and was quite fashionable and sophisticated.

Thrusting a few envelopes at Scarlet, L.C. said, "The usual nonsense. Credit card solicitations and AARP still wants to sign you up."

Scarlet gave a half snort. "I'm only twenty-eight years old."

"So they start campaigning when you're at an early age?"

"They're killing a lot of trees with this crap."

"Indeed. So how did your interview in Montana go?"

Thank God Scarlet wasn't sipping anything at the moment or she would have spewed all over her gran.

Interview . . . Wasn't that an interesting word?

She said, "Another suspect whose name I'm pretty sure I can draw a line through. Airtight alibi and nothing to gain from the larceny. In fact, less of something to gain than suspect number one. Though he's a lost cause as well. I'm not finding any solid ground here."

"What's next?" L.C. asked as they walked toward the back of the house, where their respective offices were located, utilizing the dual den space.

"I'm not sure," Scarlet told her. "I'd really like to question the father. But he's a beast of a man. Bared teeth, menacing growl, and all. And getting close to the wife? Oh, for the love of God . . . I'm going to need a crossbow and a spear to get within a ten-foot radius of that woman while Mitcham Vandenberg is still breathing."

"Why is he so defensive if he has nothing to hide?"

"First, he has yet to proclaim he has nothing to hide—just

abruptly told me to go to hell. Second . . . it might not exactly qualify as defensiveness but rather his inherent desire to keep nosy people like me at bay. I've been warned that the Vandenbergs don't want anyone looking too closely into their affairs."

"Those are the best people to interrogate." There was a wicked glint in L.C.'s eyes. "Push enough buttons and Lord only knows what will pop out of their mouths. Mostly that's when you get the real answers to your questions."

"Very true. But gaining access to these people is point A. And there are plenty of barriers."

L.C. gave her a quick squeeze around the shoulders and said, "You'll come up with something. Let me know if there's anything I can do to help." She veered off in the direction of her workspace and Scarlet continued on to hers.

Her first order of business was to record her interactions with Michael and Sam as they pertained to her case. After that, she took the opportunity to read through the FBI report, since this was the first time she was seeing it. A kernel that had lodged itself in the back of her brain kept trying to make its way to the forefront, so she called Bayli.

"Interested in more research?" Scarlet asked.

"Always!"

Scarlet smiled at her friend's enthusiasm even as she said, "This one falls into the Mission Impossible category. I want to know who Sam Reed's father is."

"Hmm . . . Did you ask him?"

"Funny," Scarlet deadpanned. "He doesn't know. Mom and Dad were never married, and Dad split before Sam was born."

"Sounds familiar," Bayli lamented.

"Sadly, yes. And like you, Sam hasn't been inclined to learn the man's identity or track him down."

"Then why would you do it?"

Scarlet switched on the speaker feature so that she could pace behind her chair. She said, "I'm not entirely sure. I just like to know all the players in the game."

"But this guy clearly isn't in the game."

"Correct. Yet he was previously. A real winner, too, from what Sam says. He thinks the asshole even went so far as to change his name to make it more difficult to associate him with Sam and his mother and keep him from having any sort of legal or financial responsibility to a newborn."

"Which means chances are good he's not included on Sam's birth certificate."

"That would be my guess."

"Wow." Bayli whistled under her breath. "This one's a doozie. I've researched many a missing item for you, but never a person whose name I don't even know."

"Well, I wouldn't want you to get bored with me or anything."

Bayli laughed. "Not a chance. So I'll start with Sam's birthplace and I'll also see if I can pick up any leads under his mother's name. I read in the FBI report that they were originally from Colorado, then the Bronx before movin' on up. Or rather *out*—to the Hamptons."

"Total needle in the haystack, but let me know what you find. In the meantime, I've got to figure out how to engage the senior Vandenberg without him biting my head off."

"Gads, good luck with that."

"Yeah, thanks," she said in a dry tone. Not so thrilled with the prospect.

"Before I go," Bayli added, "tell me how it went in Montana."

Scarlet sank into her chair and told her friend, "Professionally? A complete bust. Personally? Holy. Moses."

Bayli let out a playful squeal. "Oh, my God! Spill!"

"Michael Vandenberg is devilishly handsome. Sam Reed is *devastatingly* handsome. And I couldn't keep my hands off either one of them."

"You naughty girl."

"You're one to talk. But yes. Yes, I am."

"*So* delicious—stepbrothers!"

Scarlet squirmed in her seat. "And they are as different as night and day. Though both equally addictive."

"Are you planning to see one of them again? Or maybe . . . *both* . . . of them?" There was a teasing lilt in Bayli's voice. Scarlet could practically see the other woman's dark brows wagging suggestively.

"I'm not sure exactly how this will all pan out," Scarlet admitted. "I haven't spoken with Michael since 'the morning after.' He alerted Sam that I was investigating, so I figure Michael assumed I'd make the trek to Reed Ranch. I'm hoping that's the reason he hasn't called me yet—giving me time to question Sam. As for *that* man . . ."

She crossed her legs as the thrumming started up between them.

Scarlet said, "Definitely the sort you want to stay snuggled in bed with on a snowy day."

"Sooo," Bayli ventured, "if he doesn't want to know anything about dear old Dad, should you really be trying to locate the sperm donor?"

Scarlet contemplated this a moment. She hadn't thought of it being such a murky subject but could now see that discerning this information when Sam had never gone looking for the guy himself might muddy the waters.

Still . . . she liked to connect as many dots as possible during an investigation. Wasn't above interviewing Misty Ferrera and Pembroke Peterson to clear them of any involvement—for all Scarlet knew, they could have been decoys to keep Michael and Sam out of the mansion. The fewer people roaming the hallways, the less chance of someone observing the theft.

The only problem with this approach was that Scarlet would

have to curb her raging desire to ask the women an entirely different set of questions. All centered on what it was like to be the
cream filling between two hot and hunky bodies.

Her eyes squeezed shut and she drew in a staccato breath.

Oh, the sexy images and sensations that notion conjured!

"You still on the line?" Bayli asked.

Scarlet's lids fluttered open. She sighed. "Just having a moment," she mumbled. Then added, "I can see where me hunting
down Sam's father could be an issue, but I'd like to go through
with it, anyway. I'm lacking *everything* here. Witnesses. Suspects.
Motive."

"Maybe it's exactly as you said from the beginning. Mitcham
Vandenberg reported the collection as missing, but it's actually
safe and secure somewhere in his possession until the statute of
limitations runs out on filing a criminal indictment or a civil suit."

Scarlet got to her feet and walked her office again. "I wouldn't
discount my own theory so hastily, except that Sam was adamant
about how broken up his mother was over the theft. Those pieces
were a gift and they meant a lot to her. I can't fathom Mitcham
giving them to her only to take them away. And that's one of the
reasons I don't believe Sam was involved."

"Not to add to your troubles or anything, but did the orgasms
cloud your judgement? You're letting this one off the hook pretty
easily."

"Trust me, if you met this man yourself you'd also be convinced that he'd never do anything to purposely hurt someone he
cared so deeply about. There's enough he believes he should atone
for; stabbing his mother in the back simply doesn't jibe with his
personality."

"Well, you did minor in psychology, so I'll take your word
for it."

"Unfortunately, that leaves me empty-handed."

"Scarlet," Bayli said in a sterner tone. "The FBI didn't crack the case. The insurance company paid the claim. It isn't your fault if this mystery is never solved."

"Gran would say the same. But not before she jumped on the bandwagon and tried to tie it all together. I can tell she's already chomping at the bit to get involved."

"Might be best if she sits this one out. At least until you decide what you're going to do with your two men."

"That's actually left up to Michael and Sam," Scarlet said. "Because I know where I stand. No sane woman would walk away from these guys."

"I hear what you're saying. Believe me when I reiterate that *double the pleasure* is the way to go."

"I have no doubt. But what am I supposed to do? Just come right out and tell them I want my very own threesome?"

"That's probably not even necessary. These types of men just *know*. It's in their blood or something. It's second nature. And if they're each aware that you've been with the other . . ." Bayli let out a lusty sigh. "They'll be on the same wavelength regarding a mash-up."

"So it's not something that just accidentally happens."

"Well, it could, of course. Too many cocktails, both of them get frisky without anyone discussing how the scenario might play out, whatever. But seriously, Scarlet. If Sam knows you've been with Michael and Michael knows you've been with Sam . . . ? Then they're likely already plotting a three-way collision in their heads."

Scarlet gnawed her lower lip a moment, holding in check a Cheshire cat grin. She really shouldn't be traveling the path of wishful thinking. Not until she wrapped up her investigation, at any rate. But neither Michael nor Sam was under her microscope anymore. So Jewel's "gray area" wasn't so shady, right?

Oh, hell. I could be getting all worked up over absolutely nothing.

Michael still hadn't contacted her.

She had yet to call Sam.

The two men were just recent hookups and who was to say they'd become anything more?

And it was hardly something for her to dwell on; the sand in her hourglass was rapidly running out.

So Scarlet booted up her laptop to look at her case notes while she told Bayli, "I should get back to work. Thanks for your help. And for lending an ear."

"Keep me posted on your progress—with the investigation and with your new lovers."

"Here's hoping they weren't just one-night stands."

"Something tells me you're going to have plenty more hot and heavy encounters with these two."

Scarlet mentally crossed her fingers. "From your lips to God's ears, girlfriend."

"Talk to you later."

They disconnected the call and Scarlet went back to her business, with forbidden thoughts simmering in the back of her brain, keeping her sexually charged. And brimming with anticipation of what might come next where Michael Vandenberg and Sam Reed were concerned.

TWELVE

"This redesign of the department stores is fantastic," said Anna Christie, Senior Vice President of PR and Marketing, as the group sitting around Michael's executive conference room table viewed the final mock-ups on a projection screen. "Revolutionary, even."

"It'll put us a bit off our budget," added Michael's CFO, Thomas Vance. "A couple million over, but when I do a reforecast we might be able to balance the scales better."

"We'll make those two million back immediately following the reopening of each store," the COO chimed in.

"And then some," Thomas concurred. "Especially since we're retooling the restaurants in each one."

"I want Rory St. James to work up the menu," Michael announced from the head of the table. "Internationally acclaimed and his and Christian Davila's restaurants hold three Michelin stars. We'll have a formal dining room at the top of each of our buildings and I want every one of them to be starred."

"He won't be easy to hire," Anna said. "Not with the success of his newest steakhouse and culinary show."

"Or cheap," Thomas lamented.

Folding his arms over his chest, Michael told the group of

senior execs, "Our department stores will rival Harrods from the onset. But I want them to surpass that benchmark. Exceed expectations. The restaurants are critical when it comes to elevating the prestige of our collection, just like the locations I selected: Dubai, Paris, Milan, and New York."

"Chef St. James has a restaurant in Paris," Anna noted. "Do you think he'll open another restaurant in that city?"

"We'll make it worth his and Davila's while," Michael assured everyone. "I'm already laying the groundwork."

Thomas raised a finger. "Now, Michael. I already said we're going to be over budget on this project. This isn't like our usual mergers and acquisitions. We're keeping this collection of stores in our portfolio. The operational costs alone—"

"Will not impede our profit margin," Michael interjected. "We'll make a fortune on this acquisition once we've remodeled and re-launched. The crowning jewel will be St. James/Davila-designed dining rooms. The epitome of elegance, the height of sophistication. Panoramic views, an impeccably trained staff, and a menu that will put us up there with the 'best of the best' restaurants globally."

For over half a decade, Michael had been dreaming of this transformation of a well-known chain that hadn't been keeping up with the changing times and was hemorrhaging cash at a horrific rate. He had watched the decline over the past six years as location after location was closed. The flagship store was in New York, and even though Michael would be gutting the place and almost starting from scratch—not to mention he was adding his name to the original branding—he wanted to maintain the exclusive Fifth Avenue address and the centuries-old history of the chain.

It'd taken a long time and some very bold and daring investments to reach the point where he could purchase the flagship and the square footage in his other desired cities. But it'd finally all come together. He'd signed on the dotted line following that

dinner meeting at the Crestmont. Intuition told him this most en-
terprising endeavor would also be his most lucrative one. Particularly if he could get celebrity chef St. James onboard.

Michael wrapped up the meeting and headed down the corridor to his office. He had a number of calls to return and emails to
read, as well as additional meetings scheduled for the afternoon.
But he managed to find a few minutes to phone Scarlet.

"I was starting to feel the sting of a brush-off," she teased.
Though Michael did not miss the hint of vulnerability in her voice.

"My apologies," he sincerely said. "I've been busy. And . . .
I figured you were immersed in your investigation."

"Yes. Montana turned out to be an adventure. Scenic, hazardous, and a dead end."

"So you went to see Sam." Michael hadn't had time to follow
up with his stepbrother. Nor had Michael been able to project how
long Scarlet might be with Sam. A couple hours? A couple days?
So he hadn't pestered her. Let her do her work. Though he was
curious as to the outcome of the visit, so he asked, "How'd the two
of you hit it off?"

She said, "I definitely enjoyed his company." Now there was a
suggestive tinge to her soft tone.

Michael grinned. "I'm sure. Most women do."

"Speaking of . . . Why didn't you mention that he was in the
guesthouse with you and your 'wildly passionate brunette and luscious Scandinavian blonde'? I do believe those were your exact
words."

"Beautiful and a mind like a steel trap." Michael chuckled.
"How is it that you're still single, Scarlet Drake?"

"Answer my question first, please."

Michael knew better than to be evasive. She'd pin him down
one way or another. So he told her, "I was just trying to get a rise
out of you the night we discussed my alibi."

"Assert your sexual prowess?"

"Something like that."

"Okay. But you also didn't specifically mention Sam's presence when you gave your statement to the FBI."

"He'd already been questioned. I didn't feel the need to be redundant. Or go into detail as to what the evening entailed."

"Yes, Sam did that for you. . . ." She paused. Then added, "I got the big picture from him."

Michael's groin tightened. "And what was your reaction to the *big picture*?"

He heard her draw in a long breath. Let it out slowly. "Misty Ferrera and Pembroke Peterson are extremely fortunate women."

His grin returned. "Did you tell Sam that?"

"Not in so many words. But he likely got the sense that I found the idea of your threesomes . . . intriguing."

"You can't just admit it makes you hot?" he challenged.

"Wet," she brazenly said. "It makes me wet."

A low growl escaped his parted lips. His cock sprang to life. Christ, how she revved him in a heartbeat.

"You realize I could make this happen," he said. An unabashed warning.

Did she really know what she'd be getting herself into?

"I would have put a stop to this conversation the second it started if I didn't want you to make it happen."

Adrenaline shot through him.

It'd been years since he and Sam had shared a woman. Michael had missed the intensity of the lovemaking and the way he and Sam were so damn good at working in unison to get off the object of their desire—and the explosive orgasms it had led to for him and Sam as well.

He told Scarlet, "I want to clear up all of your inquiries regarding the case before we go any further."

"I told you that I believe you weren't involved. I believe Sam, too."

"But you still have your eye on my family?"

"Yes. I'd like to speak with your father and Karina, though that's proven even more difficult than reaching you."

Michael stood and crossed his office to the windows overlooking Madison Avenue. A light snow fell and black umbrellas dotted the sidewalk twenty stories below.

Thinking quickly, he said, "I imagine you want to see the estate as well. Snoop around? So why don't you come out for the weekend?"

"To the Hamptons?" she tentatively asked.

"That is the scene of the crime."

"Yes. And you're just going to invite me out for the weekend, knowing the exact reason I'm there?"

Michael snickered. "That won't be the *only* reason you're there. I'll sweeten the deal and call Sam. All you have to do is tell me when to expect you at the airport and I'll have the helicopter waiting for you to take you to the estate."

Silence filled the line.

He'd pressed her back to the wall. How would she respond?

She could finish her investigation into his family and put that to rest. Have her cake and eat it, too, because he and Sam would take advantage of the convenient situation of holing up in the guesthouse for the weekend.

A win-win all the way around.

One corner of his mouth lifted. A bit devilishly. Michael didn't have a doubt in the world that his stepbrother would be all in with this particular threesome. Scarlet was irresistible. And both men had similar tastes. He was certain the temptation had been as difficult for Sam to fight as it had been for Michael.

Now he just had to get Scarlet to consent.

"You still there, sweetheart?" he prompted.

"Yes. Um . . . just checking my calendar . . ."

His brow lifted. Was she really? Or was she stalling?

Had he called her bluff?

Was all of her bravado a load of crap?

"Scarlet—"

"I'll be there Saturday afternoon."

He heard the clicking of her keyboard in the background and assumed she was already looking at flights. That ratcheted his excitement to all-new levels. He'd never wanted a woman as fiercely as he'd wanted Scarlet from the time they'd met. To share her with Sam . . . Christ, that would be the ultimate in sizzling affairs.

Michael told her, "Send me your itinerary when it's booked. I'll let Sam know his presence is requested in the guesthouse."

"Do you really think he's going to want this?" she tentatively asked.

"Hell, yes," Michael assured her. "I was more concerned about whether you'd agree."

"I'm a bit mind boggled we're even talking about it."

"We're doing a lot more than that, sweetheart."

"Right." Another long pause. Then she said, "For the record, I've never been in this sort of situation before. But I do know what I'm doing. At least, in a sense. My two best friends have enlightened me with their ménage relationships."

"And you're sure you want one of your own?"

"I'm sure that I want both of you." Her tone dropped an octave, sounding sultry and evocative.

"Then pack light."

She sucked in a breath.

Michael smirked. "What did you expect me to say?" he taunted. "I've seen you naked. Now I want to see you naked while Sam's fucking you."

"Jesus," she said on a moan. "How am I supposed to get any work done with you talking like that?"

"I have to make it through the next two days myself. And chances are good this erection isn't going away anytime soon."

"You had to give me that visual."

"Fair play and all that," he taunted. "You did tell me you were wet. You don't expect me to have a physical reaction to that?"

"Which begs the question . . . Whatever it is that's going on between us—is it purely physical?"

She'd caught him off-guard. Though that shouldn't have been the case. Scarlet obviously wasn't one to leave loose ends. He liked that about her. Respected it.

So he very earnestly told her, "I've had significant trouble concentrating on business this week while wondering when I'll see you again."

"Yet you're not bothered that I was with Sam?"

"No," Michael insisted. "Had it been any other man? Yes. But it's different with Sam. We have an understanding. We're typically on the same page when it comes to a woman we're both attracted to. I don't really know how to explain it, except to say that from the first time we partnered up to satisfy one we learned how to share her beyond the physicality of the situation."

"Were either of you in love with Misty or Pembroke?"

"No."

Scarlet took a moment before posing her next question: "Have you ever been in love, Michael?"

"No."

She sighed. "But Sam has."

"Yes. Unfortunately, it ended tragically."

"I do feel bad about that."

Michael nodded in agreement, even though she couldn't see the gesture. He asked, "What about you? Ever been in love?"

"Deep like a time or two. That's about it. I guess since I was a kid coping with the sudden death of her parents, I sort of phased that out of my life plan. My philosophy has always been that I could do without the additional heartache if something goes awry."

"And you automatically assume something *will* go awry?"

"Yes."

He was interested in her position on this because Michael had always had a similar concern. His mother had passed away when he was sixteen. And his father had remarried less than six months later.

Less than six months.

That'd seemed outrageous to Michael back then and still did today. Made him wonder if his father had ever truly loved Michael's mother. Whether Mitcham had been as broken up about her death as Michael had been. It was difficult to tell, because Mitcham hadn't shown his emotions during that time. Or his face, in all honesty. He'd mostly spent his days and nights in the city, at the office, while Michael was at the estate.

Then, suddenly, Karina had arrived. The wedding ceremony and reception had been held at the mansion with a small gathering. At least that had provided a show of respect for Michael's mother—that the newlyweds weren't flaunting their relationship in an ostentatious way. Still, Michael couldn't fathom how his father had moved on so damn quick, and it'd been a source of contention between the two men ever since.

Because Mitcham Vandenberg was not a man who had to explain himself. Plain and simple.

Oddly enough, though, the new union was one of the things that had bonded Michael and Sam. Sam got what Michael was going through. And Sam had been just as disturbed at how Mitcham could bury one wife and marry another one in such a short span of time; however, Michael's stepbrother had expressed that what mattered most to him was that his own mother was happy. She was. Mitcham made sure of it.

Another conundrum: Michael's usually tightfisted and uncompromising father would give Karina the moon and the stars if she asked for them. That Michael was aware of, she never did. Karina had not done anything in the fourteen years he'd known her to give him cause to label her a gold digger. From the start, she'd seemed genuinely, madly in love with Mitcham. Always did whatever she could to please him, without expecting anything in return. In fact, when he gifted her with jewelry or a car she appeared taken aback. And wholly appreciative.

Admittedly, Michael liked her. Would have cut her more slack when he was still living in the mansion had she not replaced his mother so hastily. So out of the blue.

Scarlet interrupted his errant ruminations by saying, "Thank you for being more amenable to my questioning."

"About the theft?"

"About *you.*"

He said, "How else will we get to know each other better? And, Scarlet, I do want to know you better."

"That means a lot to me, Michael."

"I'll let you go now. Don't forget to send me your flight information."

"I'll see you on Saturday."

She hung up. Michael grinned. He hadn't missed the elation in her tone. And couldn't wait for the weekend.

But he had one more call to make. He gathered his iPad and a thick file folder for his next meeting and hit the speed dial number for Sam on his cell as he left his office.

"I'd wondered when I'd hear from you," was the first thing his stepbrother said.

"Apparently, it's my day to be harangued for my lack of communication skills."

"I just figured curiosity would be burning a hole in your brain."

"Indeed it is. I was speaking with Scarlet a few minutes ago. She seems a bit taken by you."

"I assumed the same regarding you."

"And doesn't that bode well for the two of us?"

Sam was quiet for a few moments. Then said, "She's the first woman since Cass who really struck a chord with me. I wouldn't say I jumped right into something with Scarlet, but it didn't take long to accept that there's a mystique about her that crawls under the skin and stays there."

"Yeah, I know exactly what you're talking about."

"Certainly I enjoyed her on my own," Sam said. "But I'll confess that I've been thinking what it'd be like if the three of us got together."

"That was one of our topics of conversation."

"You don't say?"

As Michael made his way down the corridor to his conference room, he told Sam, "She's flying out here on Saturday. Staying the weekend at the estate. Why don't you join us?"

"Ah, damn," he groaned. "That's almost impossible to pass up."

"So don't pass it up."

"When it involves Scarlet Drake, I wouldn't. Except . . . I've got a lot scheduled for the weekend." He shuffled papers that Michael heard over the line. Then said, "I do have a trainer coming up from Phoenix. She could take over my lessons."

"Had a feeling you wouldn't want to miss this opportunity."

"Not sure it's a golden one. I hate to rain on your parade, but if Scarlet's investigating the family that's going to put a damper on things if Mitcham and my mother are around."

Michael explained, "I have a perfect solution for that. They'll be in the city Saturday night for the opera and I'll arrange for us all to have brunch on Sunday at the mansion. That gives Scarlet the chance to look around and appease her inquisitive side; then we have the evening to ourselves. She can interview Dad and Karina before she leaves and that'll put an end to her suspicions."

"Provided Mitcham allows an interrogation."

"She doesn't interrogate."

Sam chuckled. "No, she doesn't. She's quite good at turning her questions into general discussion."

"That's not all she's good at."

This time, Sam let out a strangled sound. "Yeah. That woman possesses one hell of a body. And she knows how to use it."

"She fits the ideal for us both."

"Yes, she does."

Michael said, "Then make arrangements for the weekend."

"And let's hope she doesn't set off Mitcham."

"Never any guarantees there."

Michael dropped off and entered the conference room to start another series of meetings. While he also considered what lay ahead for him, Sam, and Scarlet.

THIRTEEN

Saturday couldn't come fast enough for Scarlet.

Unfortunately, it brought with it a bout of nerves.

She had a hell of a time mentally mapping out her strategy to engage the senior Vandenberg and his wife, even though she had the entire flight from coast to coast to mull it all over. She was much too obsessed with her impending sleepover with Michael *and* Sam.

She sipped a glass of chardonnay in first class as she fought the jitters. She'd told Michael she had a good sense of what a ménage was all about. But that was all based on theory and conjecture. Scintillating tidbits relayed from Jewel and Bayli.

Scarlet had no idea what it was truly like to be pleasured by two men at the same time. Given her emerging prurient nature, she was relieved the subject had been broached not only with her best friends but also with Michael. For something like this to have happened impulsively would have thrown Scarlet for a major loop. She needed time to absorb the implication, process it, dissect a few scenarios, and just plain fantasize about Michael and Sam seducing her, kissing her, touching her, making her come.

Oh, Lord.

Already knowing how magnificent each man was in his own right, how it felt to have their hands and mouths on her body, how downright sinful it was to have each of them inside her, doubled her arousal.

Thank God they'd be spending the night in the guesthouse. Because it was *not* going to be a quiet evening.

She'd brought along some sexy lingerie. Didn't really anticipate wearing it, though. At least, not for long.

Despite her fear of the unknown, Scarlet was probably more excited and eager than Michael or Sam. This was old hat for them, after all. Not their first go-round with the same woman. But she hoped their most memorable one.

A second glass of wine helped bring her anxiety down a few notches. So that maybe she wouldn't be a rambling, bumbling fool when she reached the estate. Though the buzz would likely wear off by then and she just might end up tripping all over her tongue.

As the plane touched down on the runway, Scarlet primped with her small compact and then ran a brush through her long, beachy curls.

Her pulse was a bit erratic as she walked the jetway, but she could breathe, thanks to the alcohol. Her skin tingled, though. And a little shiver of delight shimmied down her spine.

She was about to be very, *very* naughty.

Since she hadn't checked her Rollaboard, she bypassed Baggage Claim and moved toward the exit Michael had texted as her pickup location. She searched the crowd for a driver holding a sign with her name on it but only saw one man.

Sam.

She smiled brightly at the sight of him and gravitated toward him like a magnet to steel.

"This is a surprise," she said as he swept her into a fierce hug. "Michael indicated he was sending a car to get me to the helicopter."

"He did. I got here a half hour ahead of you, so we can ride together."

Sam loosened his embrace slightly and dipped his head. He kissed her the way only Sam Reed could. Softly and deeply. Scarlet nearly melted at his feet. Luckily, he still had a good hold on her.

When Sam finally broke the kiss, she was breathless.

He murmured, "Damn, you feel even better against my body than I remember."

"Flattery will get you *everywhere* with me." She winked.

With a low chuckle, he said, "Careful there, darlin'. Michael will be disappointed if we start the party without him."

"Then let's get going."

Sam grabbed the handle of her suitcase and put his other hand at the small of her back to lead her out the sliding double doors. They walked toward the front of a long procession of executive cars and limos. A chauffeur alighted from a sleek black Mercedes limousine and opened the back door for them, then took Scarlet's Rollaboard and Sam's weekend tote and put them in the trunk.

Settled in the back of the vehicle, Scarlet was once again a bundle of nerves. Thrilled beyond all belief, too. Sam's kiss had lit her insides. Tightened her nipples. Made her clit throb.

To distract herself from all the erotic sensations consuming her, she asked, "How long will it take to get to the Hamptons?"

"We'll be at the estate shortly."

"Great. I'm dying to see it."

Liar.

In truth, Scarlet's previous obsession with getting a good look around the place had vanished the second Michael had told her he'd invite Sam along for their rendezvous.

Sam said, "The mansion can be a little overwhelming, I'll forewarn you. I got lost the first couple of weeks I lived there. Had to memorize some landmarks to know which direction I was going, like the Italian vases are arranged on display stands in the back portion of the east wing and the French ones are scattered on tables in the front part of the west wing. Things like that."

"Hopefully I'll be able to find a bathroom."

"Not too difficult," he said with his easy grin. "There are twenty-two of them."

"That's helpful," she deadpanned.

"Also eight bedrooms. Six suites. Numerous living and dining rooms. A library and fitness center."

Scarlet blanched. "Oh, Jesus."

"Don't worry. There's always someone in the hallways cleaning something who can send you to the right place."

"So when you said it was a little overwhelming at first . . . That was a total understatement."

He kissed her forehead and told her, "Don't stress. We'll mostly be in the guesthouse."

"And how many bathrooms does that have?"

"Just four."

"*Just* four, he says."

Sam took her hand and gave it a gentle squeeze. "You hardly strike me as the type to be intimidated by real estate."

"Usually not. One of my best friends, Jewel Catalano, grew up in a mansion in wine country."

"Then no worries."

"The difference is, today I'm invading the turf of someone I have to consider a suspect in a crime. Two someones, to be exact."

"You did just fine when you suspected both Michael and me," he reminded her.

"Well, Michael was a bit gritchy with me in the beginning. Not quite pissed off enough to keep from asking me out on a date, though. And as for you . . . You had me off the scent the second I saw the puppy."

He laughed but said, "That's not true. It took more convincing than that to get you to realize I honestly don't have a clue as to what happened to the art collection."

"Well, someone has to know. By the way, how's Rudy?"

"Doing much better. Eating more and he looks less terrified of snowflakes and a stiff breeze. The vet took him for the weekend. I figure that's a good thing, so he can get looked over again and we can make sure he's on the solid road to recovery."

Her heart swelled. "You've been really worried about him."

Sam's sky-blue eyes glowed warmly. "I'm really happy about him. He's a survivor. A tough pup. And I'm glad I found him."

"That's very endearing. And I bet he's damn glad you found him, too." She brushed her lips over Sam's and felt that now-familiar jolt low in her belly, along with the stirring of emotions deep within her.

He let out a sexy groan and told her, "It's a good thing we're here. Or we'd be getting into a lot of trouble in the back of this limo."

"I've become a big fan of trouble lately."

"Hmm. A different kind of living dangerously."

"The fun kind."

He kissed her again, slowly and tenderly. Scarlet easily gave herself over to the firestorm he ignited. Let it burn through her.

She was still incinerating when the car door opened. It took a few seconds for the sound to register in her mind. Sam's as well, apparently. Because neither of them instantly pulled away. It took some effort for her to finally drag her mouth from his.

On a heavy breath, she said, "You could make me forget my own name."

"Yeah, I know the feeling." He slipped out of the limo, turning to offer his hand to her.

Sam guided her through the executive terminal with the driver following behind them, their luggage in tow. Sam checked in at the desk and they were told the copter was all prepped and waiting for them, so they headed out to the tarmac and the helipads.

"I've never been in a helicopter before," Scarlet said. "It's not going to make me queasy, is it?" Something she should have considered previously, but she'd been much too caught up in the *after* they arrived at the estate scenario to give much thought as to *how* they'd arrive.

"You'll be okay," Sam told her. "Smooth-as-silk ride, I promise."

They climbed aboard and Scarlet's jaw dropped. There was rich burl wood trim, gold-plated light fixtures, a large tan leather sofa against one wall of the cabin, and two matching oversized chairs opposite it. A chiller of champagne was set out and Sam popped the cork on the bottle and poured. He handed over a crystal flute to Scarlet and they clinked rims.

He said, "Despite the reason behind the visit, I'm glad you came to Montana."

"Me, too."

They sipped. Scarlet couldn't take her eyes off him. He wore his distressed-leather jacket and jeans, along with the boots she was used to seeing him in. The light wind had ruffled his thick brown hair. His shimmering irises mesmerized her so that she barely even noticed when the copter lifted off the ground.

She was drowning in lust and they hadn't even reached the Hamptons yet, where Michael awaited them.

Of all her adventures, Scarlet had to admit this was the most scintillating one. The most exciting one.

She knew what she was barreling toward. Yet . . . not fully. So that the prospect enticed her and the uncertain reality teased her senseless. Along with Sam's heated gaze.

In the back of her mind, Scarlet tried to recall that she wasn't just on a pleasure trip. There was business to conduct as well.

And then there was the matter of what she and Michael had briefly discussed when he'd called her. That whole love issue.

Scarlet wasn't looking to fall head over heels for anyone or have her heart slaughtered.

She was fairly certain Michael and Sam felt the same. Especially Sam.

So what they were doing was dicey. Although their affair was all under the guise of sexual attraction, it was evident more existed amongst them.

The cautionary tale didn't deter her. She drank her champagne and let the exhilaration run rampant.

They'd polished off the bottle by the time they arrived on the estate grounds. They were shuttled to the mansion and someone took their bags to the guesthouse. She followed Sam through the cavernous entryway with two curving staircases on either side that led up to an open mezzanine. The décor was modern, with ecru and black marble in intricately designed patterns and complemented by medium-colored glossy wood trim. Tons of glowing chandeliers and mirrors and sconces hung from the ceilings and walls. All very elegant and inviting.

Breathtaking and intimidating, yes. But inviting nonetheless.

They entered one of the many living rooms and found Michael at the wet bar, pouring a scotch for himself.

He glanced over his shoulder when he heard them approach. Gave his signature devilish grin.

"Excellent timing," he said. "Dad and Karina have already left for the Met."

"Do they know I'm going to be here?" Scarlet asked.

"Of course. Dad's prickly about it, which puts Karina on edge," Michael told her, "but she'll get over it because *Tosca* is her favorite opera and that's what's opening this evening."

He handed his glass to Sam, who accepted it and took a gulp while Michael cupped the side of Scarlet's face, leaned in, and kissed her.

She was still reeling from Sam's sexy kiss and now Michael's hot, passionate one was sending her soaring.

When he finally pulled away, he asked, "What can I get you to drink?"

"Nothing, thanks. We had champagne on the way over." Given the electricity humming through her veins, it really was a miracle she could speak. And coherently, even.

It was a bit surreal to have Michael kiss her in front of Sam. She hadn't thought that one through. But it didn't seem to faze Sam. He looked as turned on as she felt.

Michael suggested, "Why don't we give you the tour before dinner?"

"To placate me?" she jested.

"Something to cross off your list so you can enjoy the evening."

He took her hand and the three of them traveled the maze of long, wide corridors adorned with intricately designed tables, elegant side chairs, elaborate mirrors, sculptures, and paintings. Michael pointed out all the rooms and she could fully understand how Sam had gotten lost in the beginning. The place was huge. And clearly, no expense had been spared.

It was a good hour later when Sam opened double doors at the end of one wing and announced, "The art gallery. Such that it is these days."

Scarlet stepped into the massive room. She surveyed her surroundings, mentally noting the framed pieces and more sculptures. Then she did a closer visual inspection of the walls. There were some empty spaces, but the gaps didn't necessarily indicate there'd recently been a painting hanging there—and would be again as soon as she left the premises. There were no holes from nails, no variance in the shade of paint that might suggest those holes had just been plugged and touch-ups performed that looked fresher or newer than the older paint.

Of course, that didn't mean the entire room couldn't have

been repainted in the two days since Michael had summoned her and she'd arrived. Yet Scarlet did not get the sense that the missing artwork had been returned to this gallery and was thus stashed away during her visit.

It was all very peculiar. Where the hell were those paintings?

Certainly not here.

She said, "Everything looks to be in order. Do you mind if I interview random staff members?"

"Suit yourself," Michael confidently said.

Scarlet stopped to speak with a few housekeepers and an electrician, two of whom had been on-property the evening of the theft, though they'd been outside mostly, working the party. Scarlet had a feeling that would be a common response, since hosting five hundred people at an outdoor event likely required all hands on deck—and because that had been the answer given when employees had been quizzed by the FBI.

The trio made their way to a dining room. A smaller, less formal one, much to her relief. The table was already set for three and a sommelier was on hand to discuss wine selections and pour. The meal was exquisite, though Scarlet's appetite was a bit scarce. Partially because her mind was wrapped around the disappearance of the art collection. But mostly, she was thinking beyond dinner. Specifically, what would transpire when she, Michael, and Sam retired to the guesthouse.

Butterflies took flight in her stomach and she felt a little giddy, which she could maybe blame on the wine but knew better what the real reason was. She was antsy over the rest of the evening. Anxious to see Michael and Sam naked and hard.

Wanting her.

Heat burst on her cheeks. This was quickly becoming the longest dinner ever.

Both men kept the conversation light and she was grateful for that. She wouldn't have been able to concentrate on anything too mentally taxing.

They had crème brûlée and coffee in a separate room, in front of a tall fireplace. The drapes on the windows and patio doors were pulled back to showcase the grounds and the falling snow. It was all very lovely and even cozy, despite the enormity of every room.

When dessert was over, Michael said, "We'll take a car to the guesthouse. It sits on the back portion of the estate."

Anticipation could be a real bitch. It clawed at her. Hitched her enthusiasm. Made it difficult to breathe.

Michael and Sam escorted her to the foyer, where they were handed their coats by the butler. Sam helped her into hers. They left the main house and Michael drove them down a winding paved path carved into the trees that lined each side of the estate as well as the acreage beyond the mansion. The three-bedroom guesthouse had a gorgeous wood-accented entryway and sweeping staircase, numerous windows, and a heated swimming pool and spa.

Sam built a fire in the living room hearth as Scarlet admired the views through the glass panes along one wall.

Michael stole behind her and whisked her hair over her shoulder. He kissed her temple, then asked, "Do you want wine or water? Anything?"

She gazed at his reflection and smiled. "I want to know that the two of you are still going through with this."

"We're here, aren't we?"

She faced Michael. His mouth sealed to hers. His hands clasped her hips just as her fingers fisted the front of his shirt. The searing lip-lock went on and on. Until Scarlet was completely breathless.

She pulled away . . . but still wanted more.

Her gaze landed on Sam, standing alongside the fireplace, watching them. The vibrant glow in his beautiful blue eyes spurred her on. She crossed to him, slid her palms up his chest to his shoulders. Then downward where she clutched his bulging biceps. He kissed her slowly, evocatively, their lips and tongues twisting and tangling. He palmed her ass and squeezed before pressing her firmly against him. She felt his erection and it thrilled her even more to know how quickly he responded to her. To the sight of Michael kissing her and the wicked promise of what was to come.

Behind her she smelled Michael's distinct scent, and her excitement ratcheted as he moved in close and his lips skimmed along her neck. He nipped the skin as Sam continued his sensuous kisses. Already she was careening toward sensory overload. And they'd just started. . . .

Between kisses, Sam murmured, "Let's take this to the bedroom."

Desire flared deep within her. She was really and truly going to get her wish. Her fantasy.

Michael stepped away. Sam scooped her into his strong arms and carried her upstairs with Michael hot on their heels.

Scarlet's fingers raked through Sam's lush hair and she nibbled on his earlobe. Then whispered, "Nothing's off-limits as far as I'm concerned."

"Careful about granting carte blanche, darlin'. Michael and I will take advantage of it."

"I know what I'm doing. What I want."

She'd spent the past two days preparing herself with her toys. She'd boldly asked her friends about double penetration, and both Jewel and Bayli swore by it. Just hearing them describe how amazing it was to have both of their men inside them at the same time had gotten Scarlet's juices flowing.

They entered a room and Sam set her on her feet. Then he flipped the switch for the gas fireplace and sank into a chair next to it. Michael propped his shoulder against the doorframe and folded his arms over his chest.

Scarlet eyed one man, then the other. What were they up to?

The suspense drew out as they both stared at her. Taking her in from head to toe and back up. She wore a tight black tank dress with a caramel-colored leather jacket over it. Black thigh-high stockings and four-inch heels. Michael appeared transfixed by her legs. Sam's gaze remained on her breasts.

Eventually, Michael spoke.

"Strip for us," he quietly commanded.

Scarlet's entire body went up in flames.

It was one thing to have Michael or Sam peel away her clothing. It was something altogether different to do it herself while they both watched. While they each knew the other was getting hotter and hotter with every layer removed.

Christ, *she* was getting hotter and hotter just thinking of it.

She gripped the lapels of her jacket and slid the leather slowly down her arms. Let the garment fall to the floor. Then she strolled to the end of the bed and kicked off one shoe. She planted her foot on the bench at the end of the mattress and rolled the top of her stocking along her thigh. She bent at the waist to continue rolling the nylon down her calf, knowing the short hem of her skirt had hitched up far enough to give her captive audience a glimpse of her G-string and bare ass cheeks.

Holding the position a few seconds longer sexually charged the air. Then she kicked off the other shoe and repeated the process. Lingering once more. Until Sam shifted in his seat, his crotch apparently too tight for comfort. Served him right.

She kept her gloating smile in check. Instead, she turned to face them and eased a thin strap along her shoulder, letting it slip to the crook of her arm. The other strap followed. She worked the material over her breasts, stomach, and hips. It pooled on the hardwood floor and she flicked it away with her foot.

She stood before the men wearing nothing but her strapless bra in black satin, matching panties, and a diamond tennis bracelet.

"The bra first," Sam instructed.

Scarlet reached behind her and unhooked the clasp. Tossed the lingerie aside.

"Now the panties," Sam said. "Slowly. And bring them to me."

Her pussy clenched. She should have known the men would turn this into a sexy game that stimulated her as much as it did them.

Crooking her thumbs in the strands at her sides, she dragged the satin downward. When she reached her knees, she bent at the waist again. Stepped out of the G-string. Took her time straightening, her gaze first landing on Michael, then sliding to Sam.

She walked over to him, crisscrossing one leg in front of the other with her gradual progression. Sam's eyes were glued to her. When she reached him, she dropped the panties in his lap.

"Per your request." She smiled slyly.

He rubbed the scant material between his finger and thumb and his irises darkened with lust. "You're wet." He lifted the lingerie to his nose and inhaled deeply. "Fuck, you smell good."

"She tastes even better," Michael informed him in his deep, intimate voice.

"I'm about to find out." Sam gazed up at her and said, "Put your foot on the top of my thigh."

She did, balancing on one leg.

"Stick your finger in your pussy," Sam told her.

Scarlet slid her hand along her hip and to her apex. Her fingertip glided over her clit and then dipped into the tight canal.

Sam said, "Now brush that finger over your lips."

Her pulse jumped. She wasn't even sure anymore who was more aroused—them or her.

She followed Sam's lead.

"Kiss me," he demanded in a low, smoldering tone.

Scarlet's foot slipped from his thigh and she pressed her knee to the cushion at his hip so that she could lean over him. Her mouth swept against his. Sam's tongue darted out and swiped at her lips.

"Nice," he murmured lustily.

She engaged him in soft, playful kisses.

But it was a huge mistake to think *she* was in control.

Michael joined them, alongside her, and his fingers grazed her cleft. Then one slid inside her and he pumped assertively. His other hand was between her legs in front and he rubbed her slick folds.

"Oh, God," she said against Sam's lips.

He discarded the panties and insisted, "Keep kissing me." Sam cupped her breasts and massaged roughly. His thumbs whisked over her hard nipples.

Scarlet moaned as heat blazed through her. Her forearms rested on Sam's shoulders. She bowed her spine to thrust her breasts firmly into his large hands and also lifted her ass for Michael. He worked a second finger into her pussy and stroked faster. He targeted her clit with the pads of two fingers at the same time Sam pinched and rolled her highly sensitive nipples.

She let out a small cry.

Scarlet felt moisture trickle along her inner thigh.

Sam kissed her hungrily as he continued to knead her breasts. Michael wedged in a third finger and picked up the pace.

Scarlet had not doubted that it would be sensational to have two men pleasuring her, but she really couldn't have known just *how* sensational it would be.

Her pussy squeezed tight and released, her clit pulsated, and her nipples tingled.

Sam broke their kiss and told Michael in a dark tone, "Make her come." Sam shifted slightly and flicked his tongue over one aching bead, then drew it into his mouth. He sucked hard.

"Yes!" she called out. "Oh, God, yes. I'm so close. So . . . so . . . Oh, God!" Everything within her collided and erupted and she screamed.

Her heart hammered in her chest. Tremors shot down the one leg supporting most of her weight.

Michael withdrew his fingers from her and Sam guided her to straddle his lap as she quaked. He kissed her neck while she gasped for air. When the vibrations within her lessened, he stood and carried her to the bed and set her in the middle of the mattress.

Her chest still rose and fell quickly as she watched Michael undo his cuff links and tie and then unbutton his shirt. Every inch of smooth, tanned skin exposed made her mouth water. He shucked the shirt, toed off his shoes, and divested himself of the rest of his clothing. He was rock-hard. And Scarlet was certain she wouldn't be pulling in a full breath anytime soon.

Her gaze flitted to Sam, who was hauling his sweater over his head. He jerked open the fly of his Levi's and was out of his clothing just as fast as Michael. Her eyes feasted on Sam's thick cock and she honestly felt as though she could come again. From the vision before her and the mere thought of both men slipping into bed with her.

But neither actually happened—the orgasm or them joining her. Instead, Sam returned to where the chair was positioned and snatched her panties from the floor. He strutted back over to the bed and said, "Give me your wrists."

Michael grinned. Scarlet's insides sizzled. There was a tickle of hesitation in her brain. But then Sam wagged a brow at her, silently reminding her of the carte blanche she'd given. All reluctance flew out the window. She offered him her wrists and he bound them with the strands of her G-string.

"Lay back," Michael told her. "Arms over your head."

"This isn't exactly fair," she claimed. "I want to be able to touch you. Both of you."

"You will," Sam vowed. "When we're ready for that."

She gazed at his cock, then Michael's, and said, "You look plenty ready to me."

"Maybe a little *too* ready," Michael confessed. "You are damn good at getting us both worked up."

"And we want you to come again before we fuck you," Sam said. He leaned toward her, kissed her, then added, "We want to make sure *you're* ready for us."

"Michael told you how wet I am. Feel free to check for yourself." Her tone was flirty but held the tinge of the desperate need she had for them.

Sam said, "I intend to get you wetter. Now lay back."

As she did their bidding, Sam climbed onto the bed on one side of her. Michael did the same on the other.

Scarlet momentarily feared cardiac arrest.

She'd told them she could handle this, but could she really? They were both so gorgeous. So skilled at getting her off—and so perfect when they did it together.

Michael kissed her. His hand glided over her skin and he caressed her breast. Sam palmed the other one and his tongue flicked against the taut peak. The internal fire they ignited burned brighter than the flames in the hearth.

Sam drew her nipple into his mouth while his fingers skated along her belly and to her sex. He stroked her dewy folds, making her writhe on the bed. Then he rubbed her clit in a slow, circular motion.

Michael's mouth left hers and instead lowered to her chest. He tended to her other nipple and Scarlet thought she'd go half out of her mind at the dual suctioning that alternated with the flittering of their tongues. She'd never experienced anything quite so intense on that particular erogenous zone.

While they lavished her breasts with affection and Sam hastened the tempo between her legs, Michael thrust two fingers into her pussy and pumped with force, pushing the air from her lungs.

Her legs were spread wide and she planted her feet on the bed, providing leverage so she could raise her hips. They undulated in rhythm to the men's ministrations.

With her arms still above her head Scarlet was able to grip the edge of the mattress, and she held on as her body moved and wriggled of its own accord, seeking the pleasure Michael and Sam so willingly gave her.

She wanted more. So much more.

And they knew it.

They didn't let up on her breasts, and her nipples were insanely hard and throbbing. Michael withdrew his fingers from her and eased a long one into her anus at the same time two of Sam's fingers filled her pussy and the heel of his hand rubbed her clit.

"Oh, God!" she cried. "Oh, fuck!"

The climax loomed, the sensations mounting.

Her men stroked faster, plunged deeper, sucked harder.

Scarlet's eyelids closed. Her hips rolled. Her breaths came on choppy moans.

"So fucking wet," Michael said again, his warm breath blowing against her nipple. Her cream oozed from her pussy to her cleft and coated his finger as he thrust into her. "Come again. Come for us." His mouth was on her breast once more. Pushing her to that beautiful precipice.

Scarlet's nails dug into the bedding and mattress she fisted. From her fingers above her head straight down to her toes, everything pulled tight inside and out, her muscles straining, her core clenching.

A breath later the sensations burst wide open.

"Michael! Sam!" she said on a sob. "Oh, Christ!"

She came harder than ever before.

Twice as hard.

FOURTEEN

Scarlet was stretched out on the bed as Michael and Sam cared for her, unbinding her wrists, taking turns kissing her, stroking her skin.

She had yet to open her eyes. There was something enthralling about distinguishing between the way Michael smelled versus Sam. The way they tasted. The way they touched her. Even the difference in the sexy growls they made was exciting.

Michael was clearly more aggressive in nature. Sam was a bit more sensitive. Both were phenomenal at selflessly giving pleasure.

How they'd learned to do it together, how many women besides Misty Ferrera and Pembroke Peterson they'd practiced on, didn't matter to Scarlet. First, that was a part of their past. Second, Scarlet was reaping the benefits.

The more interesting thing about this particular expertise Michael and Sam possessed was that there was no competition between the two men to be better than each other when they were satisfying a woman—because what they did in tandem elevated their personal game. Scarlet hadn't just experienced that; she'd also *felt* it. They'd wanted to make her lose it for them. For *both* of them. That was where their focus had been. On her. Not proving who was more masterful at what. They worked together and the end result deserved equal praise.

Which brought up another tidbit. Scarlet had always been a little perplexed over Jewel's and Bayli's declarations that their feelings for their men were equally strong. When it came to Rogen and Vin, Jewel didn't love one more than the other. The same applied with Christian and Rory for Bayli.

Now, however, Scarlet had a clearer understanding of that undivided affection. Because Michael had qualities that appealed to Scarlet. So, too, did Sam. And their inherent ability to fall into sync with each other when it came to her intensified the emotions and admiration. Scarlet cherished them both. Not one over the other.

She smiled when Sam kissed her, and she muttered, "Even after endless fantasizing and quizzing my girlfriends, words cannot describe how incredible it is to be with you both."

Michael's lips brushed over her stomach. Her flesh quivered. He nipped at the rim of her belly button and she gasped.

Sam said, "I thought Michael and I were past this, because we weren't meeting a woman we both wanted . . . let alone one we'd both want for more than a night."

Her lids fluttered open and she gazed at Sam. "You think you're going to want me again? After tonight? After you've explored every inch of my body?"

He grinned. "There's a laundry list of things I want to do to you. It'll take quite some time to get through it."

She tore her gaze from him and stared at Michael. "And you? Bored with me already?"

He bit her again, jolting her in that enticing way she was now addicted to. "Not even close."

"Thank God."

Sam asked, "How are you feeling?"

With a coy smile, she said, "Wondering if you wore me out?"

"Just checking to see if you need a break. A cocktail. Anything."

"Just the two of you." She rolled onto her side to face Sam and kissed him.

Michael stretched out behind her.

Scarlet's hand skated over Sam's chiseled pecs, down his abs to his cock. Her fingers coiled around the shaft and stroked him slowly.

Michael's lips and tongue glided up her spine, making her tremble from the sensual touch.

When he reached her nape he brushed away her curls and kissed her flushed skin. Bit lightly.

She broke her kiss with Sam and a throaty moan tumbled from her lips.

Michael whispered in her ear, "I'm going to fuck your ass. Can you take Sam in your pussy at the same time?"

"We'll be careful," Sam was quick to assure her.

"I trust you. Both of you. And you know what you're doing."

"I just need you to not tense up too much," Michael instructed her. "I don't want to hurt you. This isn't about pain. It's about the pleasure that we can all give each other. The pleasure we want to give you."

She craned her neck so she could kiss Michael. Then she murmured, "This means a lot to me. That you're so concerned about me. That you both want me."

Michael let out a low groan. "So fucking much."

She turned back to Sam. Kissed him as well. Against his lips, she said, "I am *so* ready for you. Don't make me wait any longer."

Michael lifted her thigh and draped it over Sam's hip. Then Michael shifted away and she heard him rummage in the nightstand drawer. Heard the tearing of foil and a few seconds later there was a drizzle of lubricant along her cleft.

He said, "I'm going to enter you first. So you can get used to how I feel. If it's too much, sweetheart, just say it."

She glanced over her shoulder and smiled softly. "Thank you. But I've done my homework."

He kissed her, then said in a teasing tone, "Of course you have."

To Sam, she asked, "You'll be able to feel him, too, when you're inside me?"

"Yeah."

"And that turns you on?"

"Not in the way you think," Sam explained. "It'll turn me on to know he's buried as deep as I am and that you're getting the ultimate in fulfillment."

"That's a lot for a woman to process."

Sam chuckled and the low rumbling reverberated within her.

Scarlet added, "I've had the most amazing fantasies about the two of you." And they had her teeming with excitement as much as the reality of lying between these two highly arousing men.

Sam kissed her again as his hand massaged her breast. From behind her, the tip of Michael's cock nudged that small, forbidden hole. As much as she'd become a fan of these men's brand of *trouble*, she was also fascinated with the *forbidden*.

Michael pressed slightly into her. She broke her kiss with Sam as a tiny cry leapt from her mouth. There was a mild searing, but it was mixed with exhilaration. Her inner muscles naturally tightened.

"No," Michael said on a strained breath. "Try to stay relaxed. It's a damn snug fit as it is and I'm barely in. I want you to feel all of me."

Scarlet wanted to scream for him to thrust into her. *She* wanted to feel all of him, too. But she also knew that the position required delicacy.

It was just that both men were stoking the internal flames

and it was all so scorching hot. Sam's hand left her breast and he rubbed her clit, keeping her dripping. He tongued her nipple, then suckled, and that distracted her enough that she didn't clench Michael's cock as he eased farther into her.

She craned her neck just enough so that she could see Michael. He captured her mouth in a sizzling kiss. A moan lodged in her throat. He was bigger than her toys—and felt a million times better. Supple skin covering rigid muscle. His cock throbbed and it stimulated the sensitive tissue.

The more he gave her, the more her pleasure intensified, darkened.

When he pressed as far as he could and his balls were nestled in her cleft, Scarlet ripped her mouth from his.

"Oh, God!" Heat raged through her veins.

Michael quietly said one word: "Sam."

She kept her gaze on Michael as Sam slid two fingers inside her, apparently to help her assimilate to the double penetration.

"That feels good," she told them. "*So* good."

Michael remained still behind her, but Sam stroked her pussy while suckling her nipples, giving them equal attention. The pressure mounted within her again. She could come just like this. But she wanted everything they had to offer.

Her gaze fell on Sam. Her hand slipped from his biceps to encircle his shaft. She pumped, eliciting a primal groan from him.

"I need you, too. Inside me," she said. "I'm ready. God, I am so very ready."

His fingers withdrew from her. Scarlet released him.

Sam stared deep into her eyes as the head of his cock glided along her moist folds, then her clit, sending shock waves through her.

"Stop torturing me," she begged. "I *need* you. As much as I need Michael." Whose muscular chest was melded to her back. He kissed her neck, driving her wild.

Sam gripped her thigh and hoisted her leg higher so that it

was slung over his waist and she was fully open to him. His tip pushed in, ever so gently, ever so slightly, with the same caution Michael had employed.

While her pulse raced at the great care they took with her, Scarlet's body yearned to be filled by them.

Her sensible mind told her to keep her mouth shut and let them do precisely what they knew how to do. Her newly developed lascivious side longed to plead, or demand, or do whatever the hell she had to in order to convince Michael and Sam that she could handle this—and that she was dying to experience them at the same time.

Sam entered her. Slowly. Seductively slow. Scarlet's eyes nearly rolled to the back of her head.

"Oh. My. God." She caught her lower lip with her teeth. Tried to catalog every single sensation, but there were just too many of them all at once.

Both men were huge inside her, stretching her, making her feel . . . complete. But it was more than that. The sensation swelled far beyond that. She was engulfed in every physical, emotional, and visceral nuance. Surrounded by Michael and Sam, everything about them infiltrating her senses and entrancing her. So that she wasn't just filled with their cocks but by their very essence.

At first, she couldn't move. She simply soaked it all in. Let the beauty of the moment overtake her.

And they let her.

Then her hips began to undulate and the men fell into pace with her. Sam's mouth returned to her breasts, keeping her nipples puckered. Michael's hand slipped around to her front and he rubbed her clit.

Scarlet knew she wouldn't last long. How could she? It made her head spin and her heart hammer to be the recipient of such ardent affection.

She wasn't the only one enjoying the ride. Both men's breath labored. They pushed a little harder, a little deeper, inside her. Scarlet was floating on some mystical cloud, wholly losing herself to the feeling of them both stroking her inner walls, both nipping at her skin, both touching her in ways that were incredible individually but exceptional in tandem.

"Oh, God," she whispered. "I . . . Oh, fuck." There was too much happening to her body to think or speak cogently. Except that some sort of carnal responsiveness overcame her and Scarlet heard murmurs from her lips that she couldn't control, didn't even know what she was about to say before the words rolled so easily off her tongue.

"Fuck me," she said as Sam stared into her eyes again. "I want more."

His jaw clenched. His sky-blue eyes darkened. His cock pumped faster.

"Yes," she told him, her pulse soaring. "Make me come." She dragged her gaze from Sam and it locked with Michael's over her shoulder. "Please," she insisted. "I'm so close. I need this. Make me come. Make us all come."

The three of them moved together, the cadence hastening, their breathing escalating. Until Scarlet reached the breaking point. It was all too much—in the most phenomenal way.

Sam thrust deep. Michael massaged the pearl between her legs as his cock slid along her narrow canal.

"Yes," she mumbled as the sensations bloomed. "Oh, God, yes!" Everything erupted within her and Scarlet screamed in pure ecstasy.

"Goddamn!" Sam ground out. "You're squeezing me so fucking tight. Jesus, Scarlet. Yes!"

She felt the violent tremors through his body. Felt his hot seed fill her as his cock pulsated.

Michael continued stroking inside and out. His warm breath was on her neck. His body was tense and she knew he was damn close, too.

Sam was still buried in her pussy, keeping the excitement thrumming in her veins.

"You feel so fucking good," Michael ground out. "Too damn good." The quaking overtook him, too, as he exploded inside her, calling her name.

Scarlet's inner muscles clenched and released, milking their cocks, drawing out their pleasure, and sparking more of hers until another orgasm rippled through her, stealing her breath.

They remained entangled, the air around them crackling. Scarlet's eyes were closed and she basked in the afterglow. Her skin tingled and flames licked at all her most sensitive areas.

There was absolutely nowhere on the planet she'd rather be than lying between these two incredible men, their limbs twisted, their breaths coming in heavy pulls. It was a high Scarlet didn't think she'd ever come down from. Made all the more scintillating because neither Michael nor Sam seemed inclined to unravel from the threesome.

When she finally opened her eyes, she found Sam watching her, his irises shimmering warmly. He swept his fingertips across her cheek. Kissed her softly as Michael's lips whisked over her shoulder and along her neck. Scarlet's entire spirit ascended to some higher plane she'd never experienced before. She was beyond elated. Had never felt so satisfied. So fulfilled.

Michael asked, "Are you okay?"

"Better than okay," she told them. "Stellar, in fact."

He chuckled. "Glad to hear it."

"I had every right to be jealous of Jewel and Bayli," she said. "What a gold mine I tapped into."

Sam lightly bit her bottom lip. "Michael and I are also fortunate. You're amazing. Sexy and seductive."

"Smart," Michael added.

"Wow. I must have done something right by the universe to warrant all this praise," she quietly joked.

Sam kissed her again.

Eventually, Michael withdrew from her and ducked into the bathroom. She and Sam followed suit. Then they all crawled between the sheets with Scarlet happily nestled in the middle. She spooned Sam. Michael spooned her. It was bliss.

And a fantastic night's sleep.

In the morning, Sam and Michael were flipping through the newspaper at the kitchen table while Scarlet got ready in the bathroom.

Michael sipped his coffee, then said, "That was a hell of an evening."

Sam nodded. "I didn't think we'd have another one like that after Misty and Pembroke. I met Cass and the two of you didn't spark. And the past several years, neither one of us has met a woman we wanted to introduce to the other."

"Then Scarlet stalked me." Michael grinned. "I took one look at her and had to have her. I was pretty damn sure you'd feel the same."

Sam set aside the sports section and said, "I didn't want to, admittedly."

"Yeah, I figured as much. There's no replacing Cassidy. You know I feel like hell over what happened to her—to *you*."

"I appreciate that."

"And it's understandable that you haven't connected with anyone else on that level. Or remotely close to that level. But now . . ." Michael sat back in his chair and folded his arms over his chest. "It's different with Scarlet, isn't it? You're really feeling something for her."

"You're not?" Sam coyly countered.

"That's complicated."

One corner of Sam's mouth jerked up. "Indeed. Very unexpected and yet totally undeniable."

They stared at each other across the table. Several moments ticked by. Michael wanted to say that he could control his involvement with Scarlet. That he could keep it all contained, compartmentalized, whatever, so that he didn't get attached. So that she didn't get attached to him.

He had a shitload of work on his plate. This new department store project—especially with the restaurant concept he had in mind—was pretty much an all-consuming venture. He'd wanted this for a long, long time and couldn't afford to get sidetracked. Not from a momentum standpoint or a distraction one. Literally and figuratively. He wouldn't blow his budget further out of the water or drop the ball.

But it would be an outright lie to say he wasn't interested in pursuing more with Scarlet, even if he only admitted it to himself.

And something told him Sam shared his interest.

No, it was more than that. From the moment Sam had arrived at the estate, Michael had seen on his stepbrother's face and in his eyes that he was already hooked on Scarlet.

Michael also comprehended the natural conflict with that attraction. Sam didn't want to want anyone as much as he had Cassidy. That was easy for Michael to discern. He'd spent significant time with Sam after the accident. Michael was the only one he'd fully confided in. The only one he'd broken down in front of. The only one he'd told that he could never forgive himself for not keeping his fiancée and his unborn child safe. Had not protected them.

It had torn Michael up to see his usually strong, grounded stepbrother fall apart, even if only in private. Michael could accept the situation for what it was—not Sam's fault, yet still a difficult scenario to reconcile in one's mind. Sam had considered himself weak when he'd grieved. Michael had tried to convince him that wasn't the case. Michael related to his pain to some degree, having lost someone he'd loved as well. At the heart of it all, Michael wished that Sam didn't have to suffer. But of course Michael had as much control over that as Sam had had when the drunken asshole ran the red light. Absolutely none.

Yet there was a little something Michael could offer to ease some of his stepbrother's turmoil.

Michael uncrossed his arms and said, "There's no doubt that you and I are not in the best position to get so caught up in Scarlet. Worse timing for us to feel some emotional ties to her. I'd like to think that last night was the one-shot deal we were both missing, both in need of, and then we could just walk away."

Sam's jaw set. A mixture of dread—or guilt?—and acceptance flickered in his eyes.

Michael leaned forward and speared the other man with an intent look. "I'd prefer to believe that I could simply call last night a great fuck and wash my hands of it. I'd bet my entire real estate portfolio that you'd like to do the same. I'd further wager every penny in my bank accounts that that won't be the case for either of us. Regardless of how badly it could screw us over."

Sam got to his feet and started to pace. Customary for him when he was agitated. Michael recognized, however, that this was a different type of agitation. Not a thorn in Sam's side because something wasn't going his way. No, this was all about what Sam had declared a couple of days ago regarding Scarlet Drake getting under the skin. Moving through their veins. Leaving them both jonesing for her despite whatever personal convictions they possessed.

What happened with the three of them in that bedroom upstairs was more than hot sex. They'd created a bond. A powerful one that had not occurred with any other woman the men had shared.

This was what they'd always been looking for. *This* was what they'd both wanted from the time they'd discovered their talent for pleasuring the same woman.

And if ever an object of their desire was going to help Sam past his heartache and loss and also make Michael fall in love, it was this one.

Scarlet Drake.

Sam seemed to know this, too. He drew up short, gripped the back of his chair, and said, "I'm not going to kid myself here. I want to explore what's going on with the three of us. Problem is, you live in the city. Hate the country and horses. And I'm not too fond of Manhattan. Scarlet's home base is California. Exactly how do you envision this all working out?"

"Ah, the logistics." Michael sighed. "You just had to go there."

"Might as well. We're both struggling with the emotional aspect. Let's just heap all the obstacles on top of each other so we're not deluding ourselves. Or Scarlet."

"An additional obstacle unto herself," Michael contended. "She's not into the long term or anything serious."

"She had a tough go of it trying to deal with her parents' deaths. She doesn't want to leave herself vulnerable to another loss."

"You can commiserate."

Sam nodded. "Absolutely."

"But you can't escape this, can you?"

Their gazes locked again. Michael could see the writing on the wall. It was evident Sam could, too.

The question was whether they were all capable of surviving their individual undertows and successfully surfacing so that they didn't let what could be a prime opportunity slip through their fingers.

Sam said, "Let's see what happens today. You and I are discussing this, but it involves Scarlet as well. And at the moment, she's got her hands full with an investigation and the fact that she's going to ruffle feathers in about twenty minutes."

"There is that," Michael lamented. Yet another obstacle. They were setting some sort of record, he was sure.

Draining his coffee cup, he went to the sink and rinsed it, then put it in the dishwasher. He clasped his stepbrother's shoulder and said, "I am glad we met her. I'm happy that she's making you feel something other than anger and agony. I grasp that you won't ever fully recover from Cassidy. That's completely understandable. But to find some measure of comfort, or peace, or just plain excitement has to ease some of the pain."

"It does," Sam told him. "Scarlet's special and I don't want to hurt her any more than you do. Any more than she would want to hurt us. That's why we're all going to have to be up-front about our feelings and intentions. Once we've personally sorted them all out."

"Yes. Now . . . I've got to check my email and then we can get on with the meet-and-greet at the mansion."

"This ought to be interesting." Sam rubbed his nape, the tension already building.

Michael felt it, too. But when it came to this investigation, he wanted his family out from underneath the microscope. He and Sam had enough to deal with where Scarlet was concerned. They didn't need her suspicions looming like a dark cloud.

Clear the air and move on was his current train of thought.

The sooner, the better.

FIFTEEN

Brunch took on a different meaning when Scarlet, Michael, and Sam entered the solarium where the table was set for five. And Mitcham and Karina Vandenberg were already seated. He sipped coffee. She enjoyed a mimosa.

Scarlet felt a twinge of guilt. She'd taken advantage of their hospitality. Their kitchen staff had provided dinner and housekeeping had picked up after the trio. Not to mention Scarlet had spent the night under one of the Vandenbergs' roofs on the estate. Then of course there was the matter of what actually had gone on under said roof.

Did Michael's father and Sam's mother know about the two men's fetish? Were there rumors about the estate or even the revelation following the FBI statements given? Did they suspect what Scarlet's relationship was with their sons?

Heat crept up her neck and spread over her cheeks. This was definitely an awkward situation. But she still had a job to do. Still had all those thoughts and questions spinning in her head. She hoped to quell her internal speculation and wipe the slate clean where this family was concerned.

Michael graciously made the introductions.

Karina Vandenberg, a delicate-looking blonde dressed in classic Chanel, said, "It's so very nice to meet you, Miss Drake. How have you enjoyed your trip to the Hamptons so far?"

"This is a beautiful property, Mrs. Vandenberg. And your staff is above reproach."

"We're quite fortunate."

Scarlet couldn't help but wonder if that comment ran deeper—beyond staff competency to eternal loyalty?

It was possible.

Anyone within these walls could be protecting the family. She needed to be on her toes. Not get stuck in first gear over what had gone on the previous evening in the guesthouse.

Though that was extremely difficult. Because the memories of what Michael and Sam had done to her were next to impossible to relegate to the back of her mind.

Actually, she was good at relegating. The memories just refused to stay there.

So she took the chair that Michael held out for her, across from Mitcham. Who coolly said, "Miss Drake."

"I appreciate this opportunity to speak with you," she told him. "I've been looking forward to meeting you in person."

"I'm sure you'll be disappointed to know I haven't anything more to share with you than when you phoned my office," Mitcham said.

"I'm just crossing my t's and dotting my i's," Scarlet replied. "I assure you it pleases me that everything appears to be on the up-and-up here."

"*Appears* to be?" Mitcham snorted. "Did you find anything amiss?"

Scarlet smiled. She'd been down this road a million times before with people she'd needed to run theories by and she'd met with similar obstinacy and defensiveness. Nothing new here.

She said, "I'm satisfied with the physical inspection. My only qualm, really, is in how the paintings were actually removed from the premises."

"Perhaps we should have brunch before we get down to business," Karina suggested. She gestured to the buffet stations set about the room.

Michael got to his feet and pulled back Scarlet's chair. Beside her, Sam stood. Mitcham assisted his wife.

When they all returned to the table with full plates, Mitcham surprised Scarlet by asking, "What do you think happened to the collection, Miss Drake?"

"Well . . ." She took a drink of cappuccino and then said, "I thought the FBI's theory of the event workers being involved was feasible. But every single employee who'd come onto the property and worked the party was interviewed and there wasn't anything presented as a viable lead. A few arrests were made based on illegal immigration and also two counts of possession of marijuana; however, no solid clues to the crime committed were discerned."

"Then why are you involved?" Mitcham challenged her. His gaze was darker than Michael's. Not a grayish-blue but a much-too-close-to-black for comfort. Mitcham was a tall, muscular man with wide shoulders and salt-and-pepper hair. He was foreboding and it was a bit intense questioning the man on *his* territory. But Scarlet had dealt with his kind before.

She told him, "I'm just performing due diligence for the insurance company that paid the claim."

The senior Vandenberg said, "And your personal theory is?"

"It falls along the lines of the FBI's," she said. "I think the culprits came in through the service entrance with the other trucks that supplied the tents and equipment for the party. Possibly in an unmarked vehicle so that no one could identify or provide a name of the company after the fact. The truck and the supposed 'employees' would be extremely nondescript from the corporate aspect as well as their own appearance. White coveralls, generic Dockers, and polos with ball caps pulled low on the brow. That sort of thing. Point being, anyone who happened to see them coming or going would not consider them of interest nor could they pinpoint anything about them later on."

"So they just breezed in as though they were working the party and then breezed out with over a half-dozen paintings?" Mitcham rumbled. "We've heard that concept before."

Scarlet calmly said, "Yes, as it pertains to the identified event companies. I'm talking about one that had absolutely nothing to do with the setup and teardown of the party. These guys weren't hired, contracted, expected on-property, or able to be tracked down. They were wraiths. Didn't exist. Someone could have seen a blank white service truck parked amongst all the other legitimate trucks and vans, but they wouldn't have been able to provide any further information."

"Even my perimeter security didn't find anything conclusive," Mitcham seemed to reluctantly admit. "I have since extended my surveillance inside the mansion. I'd never believed I'd have to do that. I thought I could trust those within these walls who tend to the estate."

"Your wife just said something similar," Scarlet pointed out. "She agreed they're above reproach."

"That doesn't equate to trust," Mitcham argued. "They can excel at their jobs. It doesn't mean someone who works for me won't steal from me."

"Then you believe it was an inside job?" Scarlet asked.

"What I believe," Mitcham said as he pushed aside his half-eaten plate of food, "is that someone stole something that meant a lot to my wife. And if I ever get my hands on the lousy SOB who orchestrated the robbery, I will happily wring his fucking neck."

He shoved back his chair and stood. Tossed his napkin on the table, bent at the waist to kiss his wife on the cheek, and then stormed off.

Scarlet watched him go. That wasn't just anger that radiated from the man. It was torment.

Because he'd assembled something significant for his wife and someone had been Machiavellian enough to swipe it from under his nose—and devastate the woman he loved.

Scarlet slid her glance to Michael. His prominent features were hard as stone. His fist was wrapped around his Bloody Mary glass.

She shifted her gaze to Sam. He was also visibly disturbed. Scarlet was certain that was because his mother was essentially reliving the nightmare.

Because of Scarlet.

Somehow this had become an even more complex scenario than any other case she'd ever tried to solve. There were too many personal connections this time. Michael and Sam, sure. But Scarlet couldn't deny the admiration she had for Mitcham Vandenberg, a man who'd come across initially as too condescending, too arrogant, too powerful, to give her more than a few seconds of his time. Not to mention a man who found it all too easy to tell her to go to hell when she pried into his business. But he clearly still loathed the fact that something Karina had adored was now long gone.

As Scarlet considered Karina in her peripheral vision, she recognized that the very lovely blond-haired, blue-eyed woman was just as distraught.

But with Karina mostly dropping her gaze to her plate following Mitcham's departure, Scarlet couldn't help but wonder if there was more going on here.

The complication came from having Michael and Sam at the table. It hindered Scarlet because she honestly didn't want to probe deeply when they were here. She wasn't trying to upset either of them. Just wanted to get to the truth.

Unfortunately, in order to do that, she had to push a little harder.

She asked Sam's mother, "Who was the one to discover the paintings were gone?"

"A housekeeper. She was in charge of maintaining the gallery and she performed that duty in the evening so she didn't disturb anyone in the room during the day. I used to take my afternoon tea in there."

"I see. And may I speak with this housekeeper?"

"She's no longer with us."

Scarlet's interest piqued. Skyrocketed, actually, when both Michael and Sam turned rigid in their seats. Her pulse hitched a notch.

"When did she leave your employ?"

"Shortly after the theft."

Scarlet eyed Michael once more. Why hadn't he mentioned this? Talk about suspicious behavior on the housekeeper's part!

To Karina, she said, "Do you have forwarding contact information so that I can get in touch with her?"

"I most certainly do not," Karina huffed, suddenly indignant.

Scarlet's gaze narrowed. They were definitely on to something here.

"If you could please provide her name, that would be helpful," Scarlet encouraged. "I'd like to ask her—"

"Scarlet," Sam interjected.

Beside her, Michael quietly said, "She's dead."

"Oh." Her spirits sank. Her pulse returned to normal. Well, relatively speaking. It was as normal as possible while she was in Michael and Sam's presence.

Karina neatly folded her linen napkin and placed it gently next to her plate. She'd only eaten half a grapefruit with a wedge of dry toast. She crossed her long, slender legs and clasped her hands in her lap.

"Anything else, Miss Drake?"

Scarlet peered at Michael and Sam again. A sense of dread

slithered through her. Because Scarlet was about to go for the jugular. She tried to do it as politely as possible.

Squaring her shoulders, Scarlet asked Mrs. Vandenberg,
"What happened to the insurance money?"

"Scarlet!" Sam shot her a sharp look.

She knew she was creating more strife. But she had the fidu-
ciary responsibility to tie up all the loose ends. Even if it strained
her relationship with Michael and Sam.

She had to persevere. She said, "There were deposits made
into Michael's and Sam's accounts around the time the check was
cut. But they've explained about their inheritances. You, however,
didn't prosper. That eighteen million dollars went into your personal account and then promptly vanished. As mysteriously as the
artwork."

Karina wrung her hands in her lap. Ever so slightly. She took
a few deep breaths and said, "The FBI cleared this family of all
suspicion. Why are you still digging? What do you hope to gain?"

"I'm just looking for the truth, Mrs. Vandenberg. On my client's behalf."

Karina raised her hands in exasperation. "It's no one's business
what I did with the insurance money. The claim was settled. I
cashed the check. End of story."

"My experience has been that there's usually an epilogue when
dealing with this sort of claim."

"Well, in this case, you're wrong."

Scarlet was undeterred. She calmly said, "I understand you
consider this a closed book. I'd like to as well. When I've exhausted
all avenues that are open for pursuit. That's why I'm asking where
the funds went."

"The money was allocated to another project," Karina said between clenched teeth.

"Fascinating." Scarlet smiled, trying to appear nonassuming.
Like they were just two friends having an amiable chat.

Michael glanced at Scarlet and then Karina. He looked pensive and perplexed. It was, after all, $18 million they were talking about.

Sam paced behind his chair, hands on his waist. Clearly agitated, but it was difficult to tell if it was because Scarlet had grilled his mother or because Karina was becoming just defensive and irritable enough to make her innocence doubtful. Still, Sam looked as though he'd jump in at any moment, if necessary.

Scarlet didn't want to give him a reason to. Deep in her heart, she didn't want to shatter his belief in his mother. Scarlet absolutely did not want Karina to be the villain. But she still needed to get to the root cause of Karina's unease and pinpoint how both the paintings and the money had simply evaporated into thin air.

She dared to ask, "What other project was that money allocated to?"

Karina's gaze narrowed. "It was a personal cause, Miss Drake."

"Please understand, Mrs. Vandenberg, that vagueness doesn't help."

Karina hitched her chin and said, "And if I told you it was none of your business, Miss Drake?"

"That would imply you have something to hide, Mrs. Vandenberg." Scarlet stared the woman down.

Sam drew up short. "This has gone far enough."

Michael stood as well. He reached for the back of Scarlet's chair once again.

She said, "I'm asking a simple question."

"Scarlet, come on," Sam coaxed, trying to reason with her. "The insurance company paid the claim. The FBI closed the case. There's no authoritative governance for—"

"No, there isn't," Scarlet concurred. "Not since the statute of limitations ran out on the time to prosecute. Even though lying about the disappearance of your personal property and collecting from your insurance carrier is considered a felony. Punishable by incarceration. This isn't a criminal investigation. However, there's still a small window for the insurance company to file a civil suit and win compensatory damages. Fabrications on your part will only cause you more trouble down the line. Therefore, I highly recommend that you're honest with me."

"And if I tell you exactly where that money went, Miss Drake, will that be the end of this? Will you stop badgering me and my family?"

"I'm not trying to badger—"

"I'm asking *you* a question, Miss Drake."

"It would be incredibly helpful to know where the money went so that I can report back to my client and we can wrap this up."

"It's not a crime to spend the payout," Sam contended.

"It is if that payout came from a fraudulent claim," Scarlet corrected.

"But it didn't," Michael insisted.

"I understand your natural compulsion to protect her," Scarlet said to both men. "But if she's covering something up—"

"She's not covering anything up," Sam insisted in an edgy voice.

"Then it shouldn't be so difficult to ascertain where the money went." Scarlet's gaze snapped back to Karina. "It's a simple ques—"

"A gambling debt!" Karina blurted.

Looking just as shocked and devastated by her abrupt confession as Michael and Sam.

SIXTEEN

"It was a gambling debt, okay?" Karina repeated. "A very large one, Miss Drake."

Sam sank back into his chair. Michael's brow crooked.

Karina shook her head. Let out a heavy breath.

Scarlet's stomach plummeted. But she asked, "You couldn't have just told me that from the onset?"

"No one knew," Karina said. "Aside from Mitcham. I didn't want my sons to find out."

"Mother—"

Karina lifted a hand to cut Sam off. She explained, "I developed a vile and evil addiction not long after that artwork was stolen. I started drinking in the afternoons. Sipping vodka with my Valium. Call it cliché if you must, Miss Drake, but you have no idea, I'm sure, what it's like to be a waitress living in a horrific neighborhood and doing everything you possibly can to raise a son. Only to fall in love with a man of Mitcham Vandenberg's caliber. He moved me and Sam out here. To a completely different world in so many ways. There were expectations to meet. There were people to convince that I truly did love my husband, and that I wasn't just after his money. There was pressure, Miss Drake, to *fit in*."

Scarlet asked, "You feared you were falling short?"

"Miserably."

"I'm not calling you cliché," Scarlet told her. "And you're right, I don't understand what you went through. I can comprehend it in my mind, but I can't fully relate to it."

"I did everything I could think of," Karina continued as she toyed with her napkin between her finger and thumb. "I was willing to do anything to prove I was genuine, to be the kind of wife Mitcham deserved, to live up to the image and reputation of his first wife." Her gaze lifted from the table and landed on Michael. "I know it was a painful situation for you. It all happened so fast."

"Yes, it did." Michael sat again with the rest of them. The air in the solarium shifted from tense to dismal.

Karina told him, "I worked in a café close to Mount Sinai. Your father would come in mid-afternoon. He'd order coffee but he never drank it. He'd stare out the window toward the hospital, not saying a word. With his frequent visits always around the same time of day, we reached a point where he didn't even have to ask for the coffee. I just brought it to him. He didn't have to speak at all, and I could tell he preferred that. He'd just gaze outside, lost in his thoughts. It was perfectly evident to see that he was distraught. Tormented."

"My mother got ill suddenly," Michael said. "Died quickly."

Karina nodded. "After a couple of weeks, I noticed a change in him. The tear in his eye as he stared out the window. Just one. It'd pop up on the rim and he'd whisk it away before it fell. Then his entire demeanor would change. His jaw would clench and his fists would ball on the table, next to his untouched coffee. He'd take a few deep breaths, and then he was composed again. On the outside, at least."

Scarlet stared at the woman, seeing Karina's turmoil much as Karina had witnessed, become wrapped up in, the turmoil of the stranger in her café.

Karina's eyes misted as she said, "I didn't know who he was, but I could tell he was a strong, prideful man. From the way he dressed to the way his shoulders were always squared, no matter the hell playing out in his mind. In his life. I didn't doubt that he felt out of control of this situation that I knew nothing about and it tore him up." She paused a moment, sniffled, then told them, "It tore me up, too. I didn't even know him, but I was heartbroken for him."

"That was very compassionate of you," Scarlet said in a soft voice.

Karina dabbed the corners of her eyes with her napkin. "I wondered when he'd stop coming in, but every day he continued to show up. After a month or so, he appeared a little less wrecked. Not quite so angry. He started drinking his coffee. Glancing around the café, I guess really seeing it for the first time. Really seeing me for the first time. One day, he smiled. Not a full one. Just enough to express gratitude that I'd respected his space, his privacy. That I'd been there for him, in a sense."

"I appreciate that," Michael said.

"I liked his quiet strength, his commanding presence, in the obvious face of tragedy," Karina explained. "I didn't speculate about what he did for a living or who he was. I was curious, of course. But mostly I was interested in what had brought him in that very first day and why he kept coming back."

"So you eventually asked him," Scarlet ventured.

"No. He was the one to start the conversation. I was about to take my break before a double shift started and he asked if I'd sit with him. He wanted to buy me a coffee. And a slice of pie." She grinned, albeit shakily. "He said I looked like I could use more than one slice. I was rail thin back then, and I'm sure he could tell I couldn't afford to splurge on dessert."

Scarlet did not miss the shame that crossed the other woman's beautifully made-up face. The shame of being poor, of being a struggling single mother, of living in the hellish neighborhood she'd mentioned, had clearly been emotional baggage she'd brought to the Hamptons. Had not fully rid herself of even fourteen years later.

Scarlet found that intriguing. Karina was a humble woman. One with secrets, certainly. But she'd been fighting her demons since she set foot in this house. That resonated within Scarlet, because she'd witnessed Karina's son battling his own mental monsters in a home he was supposed to have shared with his wife and child.

Scarlet's gaze shifted to Sam, who sat stiffly. Perhaps he hadn't known all of these things about his mother. The shame. The difficulties she'd confronted when moving here. The addictions.

Getting back to that, Scarlet asked, "How did you hide the gambling debt from your husband?"

Karina sipped her mimosa, then said, "I took out a private loan. Not with a bank," she pointedly added.

"Ah. One of *those* types of loans."

"Yes. All very shady-like, but also confidential."

"Mother." Sam sighed. "Why didn't you tell me? Why didn't you come to me for the money?"

"Sam." She shook her head again. "I never wanted you to know any of this. Of course I wouldn't want you to know. Nor could I ever have asked you for help."

He started to speak, but Scarlet asked Karina, "What did you use as collateral?" She didn't want Karina getting sidetracked and drawing this out to be something more painful than it already was.

"The Vandenberg name, of course."

That would go far, no doubt.

"But you said Mitcham knows," Scarlet recalled.

Karina went back to fidgeting with her napkin. "I told him about the loan after he handed me the check. The initial debt wouldn't have made a solid dent in the settlement money, but the substantial interest on the loan tipped the scales."

"Jesus," Sam muttered. And resumed his pacing.

Scarlet's heart went out to him. To Karina, too, for having to reveal this dark truth to her own son. To both of them, really.

Michael draped an arm around Scarlet's shoulders and asked, "Does that cover all the bases?"

Not wholly. But Scarlet felt she'd done enough damage for the day. She didn't want to destroy this woman in Michael's and Sam's eyes.

She said to Karina, "I appreciate your candor. I know this hasn't been easy for you, and I apologize for that. Please understand that I'm just doing my job. It's nothing personal."

Karina gave her a serious look. "It's not?" Her gaze flitted from Scarlet, to Michael, and then to Sam.

"I've had to question them as well," Scarlet said. "I haven't been happy about it, but this is what I do. I have a responsibility to my client."

"And you're clearly quite talented in your field. I'm sure you were much easier on me than you would have been under different circumstances."

Scarlet's stomach twisted. Now her loyalty was divided. Because it was true. Scarlet would have driven harder from the onset were she not interviewing the mother of the two men she was sleeping with.

But that was another issue to obsess over when all was said and done. When this case was closed, how exactly could she continue her relationship with Michael and Sam? How could she ever return to this house, after the confession she'd forced from Karina, in front of her family?

And for God's sake, that might not even be a consideration. Because she'd pissed off Sam by being so invasive. By pushing his mother until she'd cracked.

Would he be able to forgive her?

Another concern was how this affected Michael. He appeared quite troubled by the revelation and how it'd come about. Because he hadn't been so welcoming of his stepmother from the get-go? He hadn't given her much of a chance to prove herself worthy of his father's affection and replacing the matriarch of this estate?

Possibly. And now he knew the story of how Karina and Mitcham had fallen in love. The impediments she'd encountered because she'd followed her heart.

It couldn't have been easy walking through these doors the first time. Scarlet actually could empathize with the woman since she'd felt a similar challenge when she'd sat down to a lovely brunch in the home of a family who had invited her in—and then she'd finagled a bombshell that had left Michael, and especially Sam reeling.

Scarlet got to her feet, and Karina did the same. Scarlet shook her hand and said, "I truly am sorry I had to put you on the spot. I hope you'll—" Scarlet let out a sharp breath. "I have no right to ask for your forgiveness or your understanding. Just please know that I wish I was meeting you all under a different scenario."

"I can accept that," Karina graciously allowed.

Over her shoulder, Scarlet asked Michael, "How can I get back to the airport? Should I call a car?"

"Of course not. We'll take the helicopter."

"Would it be all right if I stepped into the restroom first?" she asked.

"Out the double doors and to the right."

She left Michael and Sam with Karina, knowing they'd need a few private minutes with her. From the look on Michael's face, Scarlet suspected he had an apology to make. And then there was Sam. . . .

Scarlet had no idea how that interaction between son and

mother would play out. In all honesty, that was Sam and Karina's business.

So Scarlet wasn't surprised when Michael joined her in the hallway without his stepbrother.

She said, "You don't have to accompany me back to the city. I'm sure you have other things to take care of."

"I am going back with you." He kissed her forehead. "And I want you to stay the night at my apartment. I think it's important that you do."

She stared up at him. "After what I just did?"

"Your job? Scarlet, I knew you wouldn't be satisfied unless you had a chance to speak with Karina. Am I happy that she actually did have something to hide? Hell, no. But on the other hand . . . This is the first time she's opened up about her struggles here in this house, in this town. And I'd never heard the story of how she and my father fell in love. My guess is that he never wanted her to discuss it with me, because he wasn't able to bring himself to talk to me about it. Make no mistake, I heard every word she said. It—"

Michael let out a low growl as sheer agony flashed in his smoky eyes.

He said, "I thought of her as someone who'd taken advantage of a distressing situation. Turns out, all she did was pour the man coffee and let him work out his troubles and the pain inflicted in his head while she quietly stood by, obviously providing some sort of reassuring or comforting presence to a man who was wrecked. Now I have my own debt to pay. I owe her my gratitude."

Scarlet wound her arms around his neck and held on as he tightly embraced her.

"I feel horrible for upsetting Karina," she told him. "I wish she wasn't someone I'd suspected of wrongdoing."

"I know. And I appreciate that."

Scarlet buried her face in the crook of his neck, trying to get her bearings, compose herself. It took a while and Michael didn't rush her in any way. Eventually, she released him and stepped away. "What about Sam?" she asked. "He has to be livid with me. Not to mention shredded by now knowing what his mother has been silently going through all this time."

"They're talking. At the moment, he's mostly concerned that she's okay. That she realizes this doesn't make her a bad person in mine or Sam's eyes. She's a victim of circumstance, Scarlet. I respect that she's held her head high no matter the roadblocks and setbacks."

"I'm glad something good came out of all of this," Scarlet told him. "Karina doesn't have to carry the secret around her sons and you see her in a better light. I believe she truly loves your father. And in so many ways, everything she does is to protect him. That's valiant, even if she did periodically stumble."

"I can't dispute any of that. I can, however, admit guilt in not making it easy for her when she first came to live with us."

"I don't think she'd want you to harbor any guilt, Michael. She clearly saw the big picture from the beginning. She just wasn't fully equipped to deal with it all, so she turned to vices in order to cope. She's not the first, or the last. Sam and I did the same."

Michael's expression darkened. "Such as?"

"I'll explain some other time. What I'm saying is that Karina obviously isn't proud of her secret behavior and that's understandable."

"Yes." Michael studied Scarlet for several seconds, then said, "Thank you for caring about the people under this roof. Even my father. I could see you were affected by Karina's story, by the fact that my father actually was emotionally devastated over my mother's illness and death."

"As were you. I'm sorry he never talked to you about it."

"Pride can be a pain in the ass sometimes."

"I suppose so." She hugged him again. "I would like to spend the night in your apartment. See where you live. Just . . . be with you. And Sam." She gave Michael a hopeful look.

His brow furrowed. "I'd like that, too, but no guarantees, sweetheart. He's not just disturbed by Karina's admission; he's mad as hell at you for pushing her to make it."

"I don't doubt that. And I won't press him about anything. I'll just be there for him."

"Sam can be a bit of a hothead when warranted."

"If he needs to yell at me, then let him yell at me. I don't perform my investigations without grasping the fact that repercussions are a huge possibility. I wouldn't be surprised if Sam wanted to have words with me, and I think he deserves the opportunity."

"Fine. We'll all go back to Manhattan together, if he consents."

Scarlet flattened her palm against Michael's corrugated abs and said, "I hate that I've upset everyone, but I'm grateful you understand why I had to come here." She stretched on tiptoe and swept her lips over his.

"Maybe it was time this all unraveled."

She knew he was being optimistic. Knew Sam wouldn't feel the same. Was certain of it when she saw him stalk from the solarium, catch sight of her and Michael, and scowl.

"Sam." Scarlet moved away from Michael. "I really am sorry."

"Let's go," was all he said. And he marched down the marbled corridor.

Their luggage had already been stored in the helicopter since they'd all packed up before brunch. The tension inside the cabin was grueling. Scarlet sat in one of the chairs across from the sofa, which Michael and Sam occupied. She glanced at one man and then the other. Michael appeared deep in thought. Sam glowered. Perhaps not at her, just in general.

Either way, Scarlet's insides remained knotted.

She desperately wanted to sit between the two men. Feel their heat and smell their cologne. Revel in their closeness. Cover Sam's hand with hers and do exactly as Karina had done with Mitcham—be a silent supporter.

She couldn't quite bring herself to move, though. It'd be audacious and presumptuous on her part. And gut instinct told her that it was much too soon for that.

Thus, the trip into the city was a strained one. When they touched down, a hint of panic crept in on Scarlet.

Sam slung the strap of his bag over his broad shoulder and headed toward the limo awaiting them.

Scarlet gripped Michael's arm and whispered, "You didn't say anything to him about going to your apartment."

"You need to be the one to ask him."

She gaped.

Michael said, "This is mostly between the two of you. Just don't forget that his temper might flare."

"I'm not afraid of his temper," Scarlet said. "He'd never hurt me. But I hurt him."

"Yes."

She cringed inwardly. "I'd love to say that wasn't my intention, but I knew going into this that it comes with the territory. The possibility existed."

Damn it.

They all climbed into the limo, with Scarlet in the middle. She turned to Sam and said, "Michael would like to talk. And so would I. Will you go to his apartment with us?"

"I have a flight to catch, Scarlet. There's a birthday party I'm supposed to be at tonight."

She shot a look over her shoulder at Michael. His chin hitched, telling her to press on.

Returning her attention to Sam, she tried to engage him once more. "I won't lie that I was hoping for a piece to the puzzle when

I spoke with your mother. But I most certainly was not hoping to reveal something you'd find disconcerting. You or Michael."

"She fought a battle she told no one about, Scarlet," Sam said. "At least, not until she'd started gambling and had dug a huge hole for herself. She kept it all inside, covered it all up."

"Yes," Scarlet said. "She's been carrying around a lot of guilt and shame and the fear and reality of not being accepted. The inadequate feelings didn't just go away once she had a ring on her finger, and chances are very good that's because Mitcham had married her so quickly, she had a not-so-savory background, and she had to compete with Lindsay Vandenberg's ghost."

"Scarlet," Sam hissed.

"What?" she insisted. "I can't say that out loud? After all, Sam, I had to compete with Cassidy's ghost until you caved to what you were feeling for me."

"Yes. I know." He stared out the window.

Michael, ever the voice of reason, suggested, "Maybe we all need a drink and a few minutes to process."

Scarlet crossed her arms over her chest. She contritely said, "I have trouble letting things like this go. I stew over them. I apologize, but you have to realize that this is who I am."

"No one's putting the blame on you, Scarlet," Michael told her. "It's not an ideal situation, no question about it. But let's face facts. All three of us knew what we were getting into when we started this affair. It's been no secret that you're looking for answers to solve a crime. Neither Sam nor I have those answers. Karina doesn't, either. My father won't have anything new to impart since his wife made her confession. I get that you still feel there's an avenue to pursue, and while Sam and I would prefer you close the vein, we can't be upset with you for keeping your investigative options open."

Sam's head whipped around and he said, "He's right. But, goddamn it. I *am* pissed."

She nodded. "I think you have the right to be. I put your mother on the stand. I made her admit something I'm sure she never wanted her sons to know." Scarlet looked at Michael. "She's held herself accountable for her actions. She told her husband about her addictions. About the trouble she'd gotten herself into. Frankly, I admire that. I like Karina. Does it mean I'm done with my work?" She groaned. "I want to say yes. With every fiber of my being. I swear it."

Sam radiated disgruntlement. Scarlet couldn't begrudge him that. They rode the remainder of the way in silence. Traveled to the Tribeca district of Manhattan. They took the elevator up to the top of Michael's apartment building. Scarlet admired the stylish décor and the panoramic skyline views, a nice distraction from her inner turmoil.

Silvery moonlight filtered in through the unadorned windows. A few lamps were set on a dim up-glow in the corners. The entire atmosphere was shadowy and seductive. As Scarlet gazed out of the tall glass panes, Michael stole behind her.

"What can I pour you?"

"Nothing at the moment, thanks." She turned to him and pressed her mouth to his. Their lips parted a breath later and she kissed him with a mea culpa riding the wave of desire.

When they pulled away, Michael said, "Sam's going to have a different perspective."

She went to him as he stood by the gas fireplace that he'd flipped on. Splaying her hands over his pecs, she said, "Be angry with me all you want, as much as you need."

"Until it's out of my system?" he asked in a low, husky voice.

"If that's possible."

"I warned you once about carte blanche."

"And I let you take it."

"Scarlet." His jaw set. His cerulean eyes deepened in color.

"I hurt you," she told him. "I feel horrible about that. But I know you won't retaliate. You won't hurt me."

"I'll try not to." He took her hand and led her to a desk set at an angle in the corner. He jerked the chair away and positioned her in front of the smoky glass top. He shoved her skirt up to her waist with no prelude. Whisked her sweater over her head. Guided her to bend over the smooth surface. From behind her, Scarlet heard the unfastening of his belt and the gliding of his zipper down its track on his dress pants.

He hooked an arm at the crook of her leg and lifted her thigh, so that her knee rested on the desk. His hand slid along her inner thigh to her apex. He stroked her folds, then her clit. Until she was wet and ready for him. Then he thrust into her from behind.

Hard and fast.

His palm flattened against the middle of her back so that she was pinioned to the glass top. His other hand was still between her legs and he massaged the swollen knot of nerves while he plunged into her. Drove quickly and forcefully.

Scarlet's breath was labored, erratic. Sam pushed deep into her, aggressively, the way Michael tended to do. It was exhilarating. His pumps were filled with angst and lust. An erotic, powerful combination. One that heightened her arousal.

From the opposite side of the desk, Michael watched. He was hard and wanting her, too. But Sam had his frustration, his irritation, his passion, to take out on her first.

His cock stroked feverishly and he kept his hand at her back, kept her in place so that she couldn't move. Just had to take what he gave her.

And that was a sensational feeling. Succumbing to him. Absorbing his emotions, his dark need.

"Yes," she whispered as he pushed her higher. "Fuck me. Come inside me."

His rugged features were stormy. But as furious as he was, his desire for her seemed to be overriding everything else. Because he could have simply taken what he'd wanted from her and been done with her. He wasn't just reaching for his own release, though. He clearly needed to spark hers as well.

He thrust wildly, stroking wickedly until Scarlet's raspy moans echoed around them.

"Make her come," Michael insisted, his tone tight as he watched his stepbrother thrust into her.

"Yes," Scarlet pleaded.

Sam's pumps were short and rapid. Two fingers massaged her clit. Scarlet continued to gaze at him over her shoulder, caught in the hunger, the urgency, exuding from him. He could be mad as hell at her, but she could see he easily got fully, completely caught up in her.

"Scarlet," he murmured. His expression softened. He removed his hand from her back and instead leaned over her. He kissed her. Sweetly, yet fiercely. And she fell apart for him, the climax flowing through her, making her shudder.

Sam broke the kiss and pressed his forehead to her temple. "Yes," he whispered. "Oh, fuck, yes."

She felt the tremors in his legs. Felt him drain himself inside her. Felt the anger lessen.

And very acutely felt their emotional bond strengthening.

He forgives me.

SEVENTEEN

Sam was caged by the fiery sensations Scarlet evoked and the brutal reality that he could fall for this woman.

The fury he'd experienced when she'd pushed his mother to finally put a voice to the abyss she'd been immersed in since starting a relationship with Mitcham had given way to the intensity of Sam's feelings for Scarlet and the way she'd accepted his anger and literally sapped it from him.

His chest heaved against her back and his cock was still buried inside her. He couldn't move just yet. Needed to feel her skin on his, needed to keep the physical connection with her.

Being pissed off at her had intensified his desire for her. But there was more to it than that. She'd wanted to steal his rage and he'd needed her to do it. Because even though Sam hated the hell his mother had lived in her mind, Sam knew that she had turned to Mitcham and had received his support—and kept his love. That was all that mattered. That Karina and Mitcham were still solid as a couple.

Sam had to let the morning's confrontation be a bygone, and Scarlet had helped him to do that.

He kissed her cheek, then planted his hands on the desk and

pushed himself up. He withdrew from Scarlet and swept her into his arms.

To Michael, he said, "How about a shower? Might relax us all."

"Good idea," his stepbrother concurred.

Scarlet wrapped her arms around Sam's neck and snuggled close to him. She didn't say anything and that was fine with him. Having her near him was what was most important to him, he now realized. Sam had been damn close to bypassing this visit to Michael's apartment and flying back to Montana. As it was, he'd have to make it up to Layton for missing his birthday party. But Sam had recognized that blowing off Michael and Scarlet because he was irritated wasn't the right way to go.

Michael had been spot-on earlier. What was happening with the three of them couldn't be swept under the rug. Sam couldn't walk away from it any more than Michael.

But that didn't mean it was suddenly an easy-to-remedy situation. There were tenuous nuances and complicated logistics to consider, not to mention the fact that Scarlet had crossed a line at the estate that Mitcham would deem traitorous.

No, neither Sam nor Michael required his approval in this stage of their lives. But they'd become a family regardless of the difficult dynamic that came with the second marriage. Now, when Sam's mother told her husband that she'd spilled all to Scarlet and the boys . . . There just might be hell to pay in the form of Mitcham Vandenberg.

Sam carried Scarlet upstairs to Michael's room and passed through to the enormous bathroom. Michael turned the rain showerhead on and stripped off his clothes as Sam set Scarlet on her feet and divested her of her skirt, shoes, and lingerie. Then he got naked.

Scarlet's hands skimmed over his chest as she stared up at him and said, "I'm sor—"

He pressed a finger to her lips. "Don't apologize. You never once misrepresented who you are and what you do. What you're trying to accomplish when it comes to this case. Michael and I willingly let you question us. My mother consented to the brunch, even knowing why you were there. For all we know, maybe she subconsciously wanted to crack. She's kept a lot bottled up and this might have been an outlet she needed."

Gently brushing his finger from her mouth, Scarlet asked, "Then you do forgive me?"

"Without doubt."

"Sam." She clasped the sides of his neck with her hands, went on tiptoe, and kissed him.

He slipped his arms around her waist and pulled her to him, feeling her hard nipples and satiny skin—and getting worked up all over again. He knew Michael was wanting her, too.

So Sam reluctantly ended the kiss and guided Scarlet into the shower. Michael followed. The water cascaded over all three of them. Scarlet closed her eyes and tipped her head back to drench her hair and face. Sam gave her a washcloth and she scrubbed away her light makeup. The men lathered their hands with soap, and with Michael at her front and Sam at her back they left suds over every inch of her.

Her ass ground against Sam's erection. Her fingers coiled into Michael's biceps. Michael kissed her as Sam palmed her breasts and caressed them before rolling and pinching her nipples with the aid of water and soap as lubricants. Michael's hand slipped between her legs to rub her clit.

Sam whispered in her ear, "Do you want us both again?"

"Oh, God, yes," she vehemently said.

Michael shifted and grabbed her hips. He lifted her up and she wound her legs around him. From behind her, Sam cupped her ass cheeks. Michael eased into her first. Then Sam's cockhead pressed into the small hole in her cleft and she let out an erotic cry.

Her head fell back against Sam's shoulder, her eyes closed. He kissed and nipped her neck as Michael's tongue flitted over her nipples.

Scarlet's arm stretched upward and her fingers tangled in Sam's wet hair and Michael's with her other hand. The men moved slowly inside her, in unison. Doubling her arousal. And their own.

As much as Sam loved being buried in her pussy, it felt incredible to fuck her ass. She was so damn tight. But the water had slickened his cock and he carefully pumped into her.

Scarlet moaned softly. Then said, "There is absolutely nothing better than feeling you both at the same time."

"And this is better than it's ever been with anyone else," Michael said.

"Yes," Sam added.

"I was hoping you'd both think that."

Michael kissed her. Then Sam. They picked up the pace, their hips bucking, their breathing accelerating.

"Yes," she murmured. "Just like that." She writhed between them. "It's too much to hold on to, but so, so perfect." Her body tensed. She squeezed tight. And then she cried out again as she came.

Sam's excitement spiked and he exploded inside her, a mere second before Michael did.

"Oh!" Scarlet's body jerked and she clenched firmly. "That's so amazing. You both coming inside me, filling me. Oh, God. I don't know if I can ever get enough of you."

A similar sentiment lodged in Sam's brain. His gaze locked with Michael's. And Sam was certain it was a reality his stepbrother shared.

Michael returned to the estate two days later. He sauntered into the art gallery where he'd been informed Karina was currently located. He was a little shocked to learn that tidbit, since she'd boycotted the room following the theft and he'd figured she'd be even less inclined to visit following the "big reveal" at brunch.

She was standing toward the end of the gallery, staring in the general direction of where the van Gogh had hung.

Michael cleared his throat so he didn't startle her. It took a few seconds for her to drag her gaze away and turn to face him. She pulled in a deep breath and then gave him a fragile smile.

Michael's gut wrenched. Guilt was one thing to contend with. Feeling like a colossal asshole was something altogether different.

He kissed her lightly on the cheek and told her, "I came to apologize."

She frowned, looking perplexed. "You have absolutely nothing to apologize for, Michael. This is a mess I created for myself."

"Don't put this all on you, Karina. We all contributed to the problem."

"No. These were my struggles and I should have been more transparent from the beginning, at least with your father. But the truth is . . . I saw how losing your mother affected him. It cut deep, Michael. And I know he hid that from you. That's who he is. He internalizes and calls upon his own strength, not someone else's, to pull through. I respect and admire that about him."

"But not everyone is that way, Karina. *You* don't have to be that way. He wouldn't have expected it from you. My mother immediately went to him when she was diagnosed with ovarian cancer and you can be damn sure he did everything in his power to try to save her. The best doctors, the best treatments, *everything*."

"I know." She swallowed down a lump of emotion as tears built in her eyes. "I didn't want to be an additional burden. I just wanted to be with him. And the added benefit was that Sam finally had a safe place to live, an extraordinary world to grow up in. One I could never give him on my own. I'm eternally grateful for all the things your father has done for us. I didn't want to heap one more thing on him. But I did."

She walked past Michael. But he stopped her in her tracks as he said, "Sam and I certainly clashed with my father on a regular basis, but he never expected either of us to be flawless. He didn't gloat when we tried something new and failed at it. He didn't hold it against us. Just told us to try harder, do better. Yes, it was frustrating, but . . . he always made a good point. And when we did something to make him proud, he let us know. He never demanded absolute perfection from us—or from you, either, Karina."

"I feel as though he deserves it from me," she asserted.

"Christ, you're still taking on so much. He loves you, Karina," Michael imploringly said.

"And I love him. I would do anything for him. Anything and everything. I would go to any length; do you understand that?"

"Yes. You'd go so far as to harbor anything that might seem the tiniest bit displeasing or distressing to the family. But you're forgetting that you *are* a part of this family, Karina. No matter what. We're *all* a part of this family. That's not going to change."

She raised a hand to splay across his cheek. "Thank you for coming. It means a lot to me, Michael." Her hand slipped away and she continued out of the room.

He found it disheartening that she put so much pressure on herself. Knew he hadn't helped the situation. And Michael could clearly see that all of this weighed heavily on his stepmother's mind. Even years later.

She'd made the transition seem easy, but Michael had never looked close enough to gauge whether that was actually true. He'd just assumed. Because he hadn't wanted to be bothered with her emotions when he was so bogged down by his own. And so angry with his father for abruptly moving on.

Fuck.

If his father just would have expressed some of his feelings, shared some of his pain with Michael, come home more often than once or twice a week during that pivotal time of their lives, maybe the initial adjustment period following his marriage to Karina would have been a smoother one for everyone concerned.

But Mitcham had kept it all to himself. So had Karina.

Now it was biting them all in the asses, including Sam.

Michael left the gallery and found his father in his study. The conversation they were about to have was a long time coming. That was if he could engage Mitcham.

Michael's father glanced up from his laptop at the interruption. He said, "We just saw you on Sunday. This is a surprise."

"I came to apologize to Karina for the tough spot I helped to put her in."

Mitcham sat back in his large executive chair. "She knew Scarlet was an insurance fraud investigator looking into the art theft. I gave her an out—told her to take the plane to Paris for the weekend. She said no."

"I'm thinking that maybe she was in need of getting it off her shoulders."

"Could be."

Michael took a seat in front of his father's massive mahogany desk and said, "I'm not just talking about apologizing about the tough spot I put Karina in this past weekend. I'm talking about all of it. Dating back to the first time you brought her here."

"You weren't exactly welcoming."

"And you weren't exactly forthcoming." Michael stared his father down. "You could have told me more about how the two of you met. You could have said she was more than just a waitress—that she was someone who'd stood by you when you'd needed it most and that there was something about her that made you open up to her. Something that made it okay for you to talk to her about my mother and everything you felt about her illness, your inability to save her, and your love for her."

Mitcham pushed to his feet. He raked a hand through his thick hair and began to pace.

He didn't speak for a spell and Michael didn't press him. He recalled what Karina had said about that single tear sitting on the rim of Mitcham's eye—his father's eye.

Michael had never seen this man demonstrate emotion to that degree. Even at the funeral. He'd been impassive, a pillar of strength, perpetuating the image everyone had of Mitcham Vandenberg—powerful and in control.

But he'd had no control over cancer. No control over losing his wife and the mother of his child. No control over how it gutted him.

Michael understood his father's living hell now. Because of the admission Scarlet had coaxed from Karina. He said, "I wasn't ready for you to bring another woman into this house. Not so soon. But I feel differently about that today. I'm glad you met Karina. I'm glad you fell in love again and that she's so devoted to you. So much so that all she's ever wanted from the time she moved in was to please you and to prove that what the two of you have is real."

Mitcham drew up short and speared Michael with a tormented look. "I didn't think of the challenges she'd face. Your mother was a New York socialite. There was nothing about marrying me or living in the Hamptons that evoked insecurity or a sense of inferiority. She handled it all beautifully, gracefully. Karina did as well—on the outside. I had no idea how she was beating herself up on the inside, feeling as though she'd never measure up or be good enough."

Michael nodded. "I feel bad for her. I really do."

"That's not what she wants, Michael." Standing behind his chair and clasping the top of it, Mitcham said, "She doesn't want anyone's pity. Doesn't deserve it, either. Yes, she fell into a trap and it led to desperate feelings and actions. And she tried to solve her problems on her own. I give her credit for that. Would I prefer she simply come to me with whatever's troubling her? Of course. I love her. I want her to be happy. But I also recognize that she's willing to do whatever she has to in order to stand on her own two feet.

She was secretly making jewelry and selling it online in order to make the payments on her loan until the check came. She didn't ask me for the money."

Michael's brow furrowed. "That was a huge loan amount. How could she possibly—"

"She's very successful. But no one knows. She has an LLC set up with a DBA name."

"Why?"

"Michael, her friends don't work. They're 'ladies who lunch.' Their husbands neither expect nor want them to have careers. It would be one more thing for Karina to feel like a misfit over if she actually said she had a job."

"Mother didn't work," Michael mused.

"And that was fine by me."

"But you don't mind that Karina has her own enterprise?"

His father grinned. "Not at all. It makes her happy. Again, Michael . . . that's all I care about."

"Right." He got to his feet. "Well, this has all been very enlightening. I only wish you could have met Scarlet under different circumstances."

"Me, too. Though . . . one does have to appreciate her tenacity."

"Indeed."

Mitcham tapped his index finger against his chin and asked, "What exactly does this woman mean to you?"

"She fascinates me," Michael said without hesitation. "In every way."

"Hmm. And what does she mean to Sam?"

"Fascinates him, too."

"Interesting." Mitcham took his seat.

Michael said, "I don't expect you to understand except . . . You loved two women within the same year. Probably still do. So it's not exactly a foreign concept."

His father's head snapped back. *"Love?"*

Michael shrugged. "I'm not knowledgeable enough to qualify whether or not that's what I'm feeling—or Sam. All I know is that we both want to continue seeing her."

Mitcham's gaze drifted to the large windows and he watched the snow fall for a few quiet moments. Then he returned his attention to Michael and said, "I'm not a fan of her accusing this family of a crime."

"No one is. But you can't dispute that it's commendable she takes her job and her responsibilities seriously. She's a woman with principles and convictions. I find that admirable. And sexy."

With a soft chuckle, Mitcham said, "I can see that about you. Perhaps now that we're off her radar screen for committing a felony we can try another brunch."

Michael fought a cringe. He had no idea if the Vandenbergs were off Scarlet's radar. So he nonchalantly said, "We'll see how that goes."

"All right. Well. I have work to finish."

"Of course." Michael left the office, not having much more to say. It'd been his first real heart-to-heart with his father. They could probably both use a little time to digest it all.

So Michael returned to Manhattan.

And contemplated what his and Sam's next move with Scarlet might be.

EIGHTEEN

"You are *not* going to believe what I've discovered."

Bayli's blatant dismay filled Scarlet with dread. "You found Sam's father?" she guessed.

"Oh, I found more than that."

Scarlet sighed. "Oh, God. Please don't say that. All I want is the man's name."

"Then brace yourself. I've just ripped the lid off a can of squirming worms."

"Fuck." She tossed the mail she'd been sifting through onto her desk. "Tell me Sam's not about to become a suspect again."

"Uh, no. Pretty sure not. I've got nothing on that guy. Clean as a whistle. Michael, too, at this point."

"And Karina Vandenberg . . . ?"

"Yeah . . . not so much."

Scarlet cringed. She'd put Bayli on speakerphone and would have started walking her office with anxiety except that her feet were somehow cemented to the floor.

"May as well just yank the Band-Aid in one fell swoop. I've already ground the woman under my heel in front of her sons. Let's see how much more damage I can do."

"Hey, this isn't *your* fault, Scarlet," Bayli contended. "Karina Reed Vandenberg has plenty of skeletons in her closet. And apparently, she's been incredibly good at keeping them locked away."

"I can't imagine what's so hush-hush about this from her side of the story. Sam said his dad bailed and possibly changed his name. He didn't want to have any connection to a kid and a woman who might try to tap him for child support. So that really should be that."

"Should be. . . ." Bayli paused before saying, "If you're not sitting at the moment, you might want to."

"Bayli!" Scarlet wailed. *Now* how much was she about to torture Michael and Sam—and their family?

"Just take a deep breath. Or ten."

Scarlet plopped down on her sofa and inhaled. Exhaled. Repeated. Then she said, "Okay, spill."

"All right. So, first things first. I got my hands on some yearbooks from Karina's high school alma mater. She was a cheerleader, very popular, voted 'Most Likely to Rock the World.' And there were plenty of photos with her and the same guy. Total modern-day James Dean ringer. *Rebel Without a Cause* to the extreme."

"Explains Sam's rugged good looks."

"For sure. Dad was quite easy on the eyes."

"Was?"

"Well, there's no telling what a life of crime has done to the man."

"So he's still alive?"

"Unless he's recently been shanked in prison." There was some rustling of papers on the other end of the line; then Bayli added, "Wyatt Hill—real name, not changed following Karina's pregnancy stick displaying a plus sign—is currently incarcerated in Florence, Arizona."

"Something tells me I'm going to regret asking this, but what's he in for?"

"This time? Money laundering and bribery."

"And the last time?"

Bayli's tone dripped sarcasm as she said, "Money laundering and bribery. And the time before that and the time before that."

"What the fuck?" Scarlet was on her feet and circling the den.

"He has a law degree, if you can believe that. He's some sort of *Better Call Saul* shyster."

"So it's drug money he's laundering."

"That's what the convictions claim."

"Nice. And now I know about it. How do I keep this from Sam?"

"That's the warning I issued when you asked me to find him." Bayli had the good grace not to hammer her point in further. But she did say, "There's a bit more to the story. Think you can handle it?"

Scarlet's eyes rolled. "Of course there is. On a scale of one to ten, how much worse does it get?"

"Solid ten. Maybe an eleven, depending on whose shoes you're standing in."

With a groan, Scarlet said, "Better lay it on me. You know I can't stand being left in the dark."

"I'd prefer this one wasn't something I'd uncovered. But the truth is, I didn't dig for it. It fell in my lap."

"That's ominous."

"Oh, sweetie, it's worse than that."

Scarlet dropped into her chair behind her desk. "I'm all ears. Go ahead . . . ruin my day."

"*Year* is more like." Bayli took a deep breath, then blurted, "So Sam Reed has a brother! Biological. And . . . his twin."

"Oh, fuck, no!" Scarlet's palm slammed onto the blotter before her.

"Fuck, yes. Here's what happened." A hint of excitement tinged Bayli's tone, because she was an intrigue junkie as much as

Scarlet was. "I called the hospital in Camden, Colorado, where Sam was born. Told the clerk we were getting married and needed a copy of his birth certificate because he'd lost it in our last move. She enthusiastically declared that they now have the capability to scan the certificates and send via email."

"How very new millennium," Scarlet said in a dry tone.

"Be nice. She was quite proud. In a town of three thousand and one, it's apparently a big deal to connect to the digital world."

"You got me on that one."

"Okay, well, as thrilled as she was, she clearly lacked attention to detail. She sent me the wrong birth certificate. It was for a Reed . . . Just not the one we were searching for."

"I don't believe it."

"I checked all the facts. Dylan Reed was born on the same day as Sam, about five minutes afterward. Mother: Karina Reed. No father listed."

Scarlet stared up at the ceiling, her head spinning. She asked, "Is there a more *holy shit I can't believe it* word in the English dictionary than *fuck*?"

"Not that I'm aware of. Now," Bayli continued, all conspiratorial-like, "I contacted Karina's landlady in good ole Camden, Colorado, and told her the same story I told the clerk, but that I was also interested in secretly getting in touch with Sam's long-lost brother, Dylan, as a surprise for my betrothed and she informed me that Dylan had been put up for adoption just a few days after he was born."

"Sam has no idea he exists?" Scarlet's stomach plummeted. "He has no idea he has a twin brother?"

"It's entirely possible that, metaphysically, he knows. I've read some crazy stuff about how twins separated at birth lived for years or decades with that sense of missing something until they're reunited. Or living with that feeling forever if they never meet up with each other."

"Difference is that now I *really* know. No speculation or metaphysical sense of the ambiguous, but actual fact."

"Set in stone. Not a great position for you to be in," Bayli agreed. "I do not envy you."

"*I* don't envy me."

"So," Bayli tentatively ventured, "what are you going to do?"

"Tell Sam?" Scarlet let out a long breath. "I mean, what the hell else am I going to do? It's not like I can keep it a secret now that I'm in on it. But . . . goddamn. How much is this going to send him over the edge?"

"Not just because you're the one to drop the bomb on him, but because you went snooping in the first place. Well, technically, *I* went snooping," Bayli amended. "But it was your directive."

"I take complete responsibility, no doubt there." *Why, oh, why do I have to be so damn inquisitive?*

"Look," Bayli said, "I can see where this might create an uncomfortable situation with you and Sam. Maybe even ultimately you, Sam, and Michael. But the bottom line, Scarlet, is that you were hired to find out everything you could about that missing art collection. That includes finding out about the people closest to that collection. It's all part and parcel."

"Not morally justifiable when I'm sleeping with the man whose past I had you investigate."

"How I came by the information is my cross to bear," Bayli assured her.

"But it still all comes down to me asking you to pry into Sam's life. Karina's, too. And now I have to figure out how I'm going to break the news to him."

"I get the pickle you're in. If there's anything I can do—"

"You did exactly as I asked, Bayli, and I appreciate all your hard work and resourcefulness."

Scarlet drummed her nails on the leather blotter as she considered this new twist. Bayli tried to soothe her nerves, but eventually

Scarlet let her friend off the hook for hand-holding and disconnected the call.

Only to place another one.

She needed to make a trip to the Arizona State Prison in Florence. To do that in an expeditious manner, she had to contact a
specialist in her grandmother's network to ensure Scarlet could
circumvent the sixty-day application process for an out-of-state facility. Her background check was already on-file with numerous
agencies, so she hoped to be on a plane the next day.

"Now that's some damn fine jumping," Sam said as Layton Travers
slid from his daddy's saddle, the one Sam had restored.

"Sucking up because you missed my birthday party?"

Sam ruffled the teen's shaggy brown hair. "Not sucking up.
Your form has always been good—DNA, I'm guessing. But it's
pushing exceptional and I want you to keep at it. How you carry
yourself on that horse when he's jumping isn't just about improving your score in competitions, it's critical in avoiding injuries, and
I'm not just talking about you." Sam ran a hand over the bay Mor-
gan's neck and added, "Raider's a champion. We want to keep him
in tip-top shape."

"Yes, sir."

Sam's expression softened and he said, "I am sorry I missed
your party. Some unexpected business came up and I needed to be
in New York with my family."

"I understand. And Mom told me about all the work you put
into my gift. It's the best, Sam."

"Glad you're enjoying it. Now, Miss Hadley's finishing up
with Jason, and then I want her to spend some more time with
you. All right?"

"Absolutely." The kid beamed. "She's real pretty."

"And just a tiny bit too old for you," Sam said with a chuckle.
By about twenty years.

"So maybe *you* should ask her out," Layton suggested. "She doesn't know anyone in town."

Sam hedged, fighting the grin. "Well, see, I sort of have my hands full with someone else."

Layton's brow crooked. "Anyone I know?"

"No. And it's really none of your business. So go join Miss Hadley. And no flirting."

"Now you're just plain takin' the fun out of this."

"Smart alec."

Layton climbed back onto the horse and trotted off. Sam headed to the stables to make the rounds.

He'd inadvertently left his cell in Win's office after making some calls and had then gotten caught up in a conversation with Jeanette Hadley before they'd gone over to the indoor arena together for training. So Sam had forgotten about the phone. He retrieved it from the stable manager and noted a couple of missed calls from Scarlet.

When he got to the house, he gave her a ring, but it went to voice mail. He'd had a number of things on his to-do list when he'd returned from their weekend on the East Coast, not to mention he'd had a hell of a lot of emotions to wade through, but he was itching to speak with her.

There were plenty of mixed feelings tearing him in different directions. He'd never responded so strongly to a woman other than Cassidy. Physically, sure. He'd had his fair share of mutual attractions. But what he'd experienced with Cassidy and now with Scarlet went well beyond attraction.

Scarlet was gentle with Rudy, deeply affected by his mistreatment, and Sam could easily surmise she'd be kind and compassionate to the horses in his care, too. She was also bold and daring. Intelligent and sexy as hell. All in all, everything Sam would have been looking for in a woman if he'd been looking.

Funny how that happened sometimes. When you were purposely

searching for that special someone, it was tough to find exactly what you wanted. But when it was the last thing on your mind, it showed up on your doorstep. Or at least, attempted to, if not hindered by a snowstorm and highway-hazard elk.

Sam would contend that having Scarlet all to himself had been incredible, but sharing her with Michael, the two of them bringing her even more pleasure . . . well, that had been downright mind-blowing.

Even the angry sex had rocked. Not just because of the intensity between him and Scarlet but also because Michael had been watching. Had been turned on by what Sam was doing to her—and how she'd responded.

Scarlet had wanted Sam to take her like that. He'd felt it deep in his bones. She'd wanted to soak up all of his fury, all of his emotions. And there was a part of him that wanted to strip away everything that haunted her as well. Not just through sex but also by being a stable, steady presence for her. Solid as oak. Someone who wouldn't leave her. Because he knew that was her biggest fear.

And that made her current case all the more tormenting for her, since she'd had to go to a dark place to get the information she'd needed from Sam's mother. In doing so, Scarlet had risked both Sam's and Michael's affection.

Sam recognized that quite clearly. It didn't make the situation easier, though. It was still convoluted. But at the heart of it, there seemed to be something the threesome needed that they could only get from one another. Michael had rejected any sort of emotional commitment from the time Sam had met him, and that was all wrapped around the loss of his mother and the strain between him and his dad.

Karina and Sam joining the fold had only added to Michael's strife. Thankfully, Sam had been able to break through some of Michael's defenses and become a friend, a confidant, a brother to him. That connection had strengthened the first time they'd set their sights on the same woman, long before Misty and Pembroke. It'd been a pre-Princeton summer fling they'd had with a reality TV star who'd rented a beach house in the Hamptons not too far from the mansion. A spontaneous hookup during a party that had led to many more steamy nights.

The three-way affair, however, had fizzled before summer had even come to an end. But it'd given Sam and Michael a taste of the alternative lifestyle. And they'd both enjoyed the indulgence.

Sam hadn't expected that he and his stepbrother would ever get emotionally entangled in a ménage, but that was clearly happening with Scarlet. Which set off a few alarms in the back of Sam's head. Mostly related to what he and Michael had discussed about logistics. Geography could be a real bitch sometimes.

But Sam was going to take a leap of faith and rely on the tried and true *where there's a will, there's a way* adage.

And dialed Scarlet again.

NINETEEN

Scarlet had been on the visitors' side of prisons and correctional facilities before. Yet she'd never been quite so nervous as when Wyatt Hill entered with a guard.

Even if Bayli hadn't scanned and emailed the yearbook photos of him, Scarlet would have pegged him instantly as Sam's father. Wyatt was a mammoth of a man, all brawn and earthy good looks.

Incarceration and the criminal lifestyle had nothing on this guy. Sure, he was a bit weathered around the eyes and mouth, but he'd be an easy pick-out in a lineup, with unforgettable chiseled features and bright blue eyes.

Wyatt slid into the seat on the other side of the glass partition and lifted the phone. Scarlet pressed her own receiver to her ear.

"Mr. Hill, my name is Scarlet Drake. I'm an independent insurance fraud investigator."

His gaze narrowed on her. "You're not from my lawyer's office?" he asked with a deep Southern drawl.

"No, sir."

"Then what the fuck makes you think I want to speak with you?"

She inhaled sharply. The nerves were clearly justified. After a long, though somewhat discreet, exhale, she said, "I'm looking into the disappearance of an art collection from the Vandenberg estate in the Hamptons."

"And that has *what* to do with me?"

Scarlet's gaze met his as she said, "It belonged to Karina Reed. Your high school sweetheart. The mother of your two sons, Sam and Dylan. Your twins."

His jaw clenched, the way Sam's did when he was tense. "You can go fuck yourself, lady. I don't know what the hell you're talking about." Wyatt slammed down the receiver, then shoved back his chair and jerked his chin at the guard, indicating he was done.

Scarlet hung up and heaved a sigh.

That went oh, so well.

She gathered her belongings and returned to her rental car, then drove back to Phoenix to catch her flight home. On the plane, she stewed over the brief interaction with Hill and wondered if she should have stayed and tried again, but in all honesty, Scarlet wasn't entirely sure what she hoped to gain from engaging him in conversation.

Her interest in the man was predicated on his relationship to Sam—well, lack thereof, but Wyatt was Sam's birth father. And the father of Sam's brother. So naturally, Scarlet wanted to pick the man's brain about his romance with Karina, why he'd bailed, and whether or not he'd ever been in contact with Dylan. If he'd ever considered reaching out to Sam.

Scarlet had learned from Bayli that an absentee parent could be like a black hole. There might be curiosity to explore it, but chances were very good you'd just get sucked into an inescapable abyss.

Bayli had had *what if?* moments while growing up, all centered on finding her dad. Who was he, why had he split before she was even born, why had he told her mother he loved her when it clearly wasn't true?

And what if Bayli were to locate him?

She'd wanted to on a few occasions, Scarlet knew. Particularly when her mother required a series of heart surgeries—and the bills had started to pile up. Bayli had been a kid then and she'd needed not only some financial support from her father but emotional support as well.

But he'd left them both. Willingly. Consciously. So Bayli had finally decided to write him off, as her dad had done with her and her mother.

Had Dylan done the same, or had he searched for his birth parents? Had he found Wyatt?

As the plane touched down at SFO, Scarlet once again reached that mental question when it came to all of her internal queries on this particular subject: Did it matter? If Dylan had somehow tracked down Wyatt or vice versa, did it matter? Did it make any difference in Sam's life?

Not that Scarlet could see.

So she'd come to another dead end.

She'd learned who Sam's father was and that Sam had a brother. The rest remained a void.

Well, except for the fact that she was privy to something Sam was not.

Guilt ate at her as she left the terminal, retrieved her car, and drove back to River Cross. Her gran was off on her own wild adventure for a new book, so the house was empty and quiet. Scarlet took a shower and slipped into a nightgown and robe. She was mentally exhausted. Conversely wound up, though.

She snatched her cell from the nightstand, slid between the sheets, and hit the speed-dial number for Michael.

"I was just thinking of you," he said as he connected the call.

Scarlet's spirits didn't fully lift. Though Michael's words were exhilarating, her dark cloud loomed.

She said, "I wish I was simply calling to tell you that I miss you."

Michael was silent a moment, then asked, "Why does this sound like a Dear John call?"

She laughed softly, despite her tension and melancholy. "That's not it at all. In fact, it could actually be the other way around."

"Not likely," he quietly, though vehemently, told her.

"You say that now. . . ." Scarlet's heart hurt. Her very soul felt weighted down, sinking lower and lower.

"Hey, sweetheart," Michael said in a concerned tone. "What is it? What's wrong?"

"What's wrong is . . . me, Michael. *I'm* wrong."

"About?"

Scarlet sighed dejectedly. "It's not so much an *about* scenario. It's more like a compulsion. A sickness, really."

"Okay, now you're worrying me."

"Sorry. It's just . . ." Sheer agony lanced through her. "I have this insatiable need to know *everything* when it comes to investigations. I can't help myself. Sometimes I don't have to delve too deep. Sometimes I do. Whatever the job entails, I do it. But this time . . . I went too far. I looked into something I had no business looking into. Well, aside from voracious curiosity."

Michael didn't say anything for a few moments. Scarlet's tension mounted.

Finally, he asked, "What exactly were you looking into?"

"Sam's past," she admitted, not willing to keep this from Michael because she needed his advice. His help.

"Why, Scarlet?" Michael inquired. "What bearing does that have on anything? On the case?"

"I don't know. I'm not so sure it was about the case. Sam told me he has no idea who his father is, not even a name. And I just . . . I couldn't let that go. I had to find out. I couldn't stop myself."

Christ, what a horrific confession to make.

But then again, Karina Vandenberg had bared her soul in front of her sons. That had taken some courage. So here was Scarlet, womaning up, so to speak.

She said, "I'm not particularly proud that I can't let well enough alone, that I have to collect as much information as I possibly can until either I'm facing a brick wall that can't be breached or I've broken through that wall."

"And somehow Sam's dad's identity was crucial to your plight?"

Michael's tone was level, not accusatory. So Scarlet didn't retreat. Rather, she told him, "It was mostly important to me since Sam is important to me. I want to know him the way I'm getting to know you. I've met your parents. Or at least, I've met your father and stepmother, and I've read about your biological mother. I can at least connect dots on your side. On Sam's side, there was an anomaly. A variable I couldn't define."

"You're doing a hell of a lot of veiled apologizing, Scarlet."

"To the wrong person, granted. But I called you because I want your advice."

"It's simple and you know it. No mystery here. You have to tell Sam what you've learned."

She honestly hadn't expected Michael to tell her anything different. She wasn't a fool. And this wasn't rocket science.

What it was for Scarlet was a complicated matter of the heart.

When she'd tasked Bayli with unearthing Sam's dad's name, she'd been fueled by inquisitiveness, sure, but it'd mostly been related to the art theft. Then the dam had broken at the Vandenberg estate and Scarlet had witnessed Karina's vulnerability. Scarlet figured that at that point she should have called off Bayli's hunt. But Scarlet had been caught up in Sam's anger and then fixated on where the shock wave of a weekend had left the three of them.

Now she had *this* shock wave to ride out.

Michael said, "Sweetheart, you're not one to hold back the truth. You need to tell him."

"We've been playing phone tag, but you're right."

"Just don't do it tonight."

"Michael! You just said—"

"I know what I just said. But you'll only get his voice mail. I spoke with him earlier about some things the three of us are going to have to figure out. He mentioned he was flying out to Texas tonight. There's a show Andalusian for sale that he wants to look at before the Great Southwest Winter Series starts in February. I don't know what the hell any of that means. But he's on a plane right now."

"Damn it," she mumbled. Because the guilt was just going to keep on munching away at her. She did latch on to a diversionary topic, though. "So what did the two of you discuss that actually involves the three of us?"

"Mainly, when we're going to see one another again. And secondarily . . . the seemingly serious nature of our involvement."

"Seemingly?"

"Well," he said before taking a sip of what she figured was probably brandy or scotch this late in the evening. "I can tell you how I feel and I can tell you how Sam feels, but neither of us is being presumptuous when it comes to your feelings."

Scarlet could use a drink herself. But she didn't leave the bed. She earnestly told Michael, "I'm hating my very lonely bedroom right now."

"Think we're all on the same page there."

"Then I've got to get things straightened out with Sam. I'll give him some time to wrap up his business before I drop another bomb on him."

"Call me if you need me."

"I need you."

He let out a low growl. "Why don't we meet in Montana for

the weekend? You can tell Sam everything you've discovered. Much better to do it in person."

"Excellent idea. Though as a sidebar, my understanding is that you're not a fan of the country."

"I'll survive. It's worth the sacrifice."

"Great. I'll check in with Sam and see how he feels about it. If he'll even be around."

"Let me know the outcome. Now I've got some more work to do."

"And I need sleep."

Neither disconnected the call. That made her toes curl.

"Hang up, Michael."

"Yeah."

Obviously, there were things he wanted to say to her. But he was putting it all on the back burner until they were with Sam. The sensible way to go. It was just difficult for her to not instigate the conversation. Because Scarlet had a lot to say, too.

A few quiet seconds ticked by before he simply told her, "Sweet dreams, Scarlet."

"Thank you. Good night." She forced herself to tap the end button.

Scarlet returned the phone to the nightstand and switched off the light. She settled in the bed and closed her eyes, wondering how her discussion with Sam would go when she told him she knew who his deadbeat dad was and that Sam had a brother. She was relieved Michael would be there with them, not just for her sake but for Sam's as well. A little moral support never hurt. And Scarlet's news wasn't going to be easy to accept.

Nor was her prying.

Sam was back at the ranch Thursday evening. He'd been on the fence about the Andalusian but not the black Arabian when he'd caught sight of it—and had immediately made an offer. The horse would be delivered early next week; a nice addition to Sam's show team.

He was feeling quite pleased with his latest acquisition and whistling a tune when his cell rang.

Sam grinned. It was Scarlet.

"Well, hello there, darlin'," he said as he bent down to scratch Rudy behind the ears and then went to the fridge for a beer. "'Bout time we reached each other."

"Crazy week. And I hear you were in Texas looking at a horse."

"Bought one, actually." He popped the top off the bottle and settled at the kitchen island. "So you spoke with Michael?"

"Last night. He suggested a date. In Montana."

"I like his thinkin'."

"Me, too."

"So plan on it. I've got a few things to take care of around here over the weekend, but my evenings are free."

"You're getting ready for a competition?" she asked.

"Yes, we are."

"That'll be exciting to see all that goes into the preparation. I'm fascinated by what you do. And I didn't get a chance to meet your horses."

"They're not all mine. I board for some folks. But I'd love to give you the grand tour, since we didn't get to it the last time you were here. Not that I minded what we were doing instead."

"I wouldn't change a thing, even if I could. And maybe we can get Michael to take a look around as well. Get him into the stables or arena."

Sam chuckled. "Don't go countin' on it. Although . . . you might provide just the right motivation to sway him."

"I'll be sure to put extra effort into it."

Sam heard the mischief in her voice and it turned him on. Hell, everything about the woman turned him on. Even when she was several states away.

He took a long drink from his beer, then asked, "What are you up to this evening?"

"I just left dinner with Jewel, Rogen, and Vin. Nice night. I'm on my way home now, with some asshole tailgater trying to push me down the road."

"Pull over and let him go around you."

"I think he's too close to me for that." Panic suddenly edged her tone.

Sam tensed, his gut clenching. "Scarlet—"

"Shit! He just put his high beams on and they're glaring in my rearview mirror!"

Sam set his beer aside and got to his feet. "Scarlet, for God's sake, pull over."

"I'm just looking for a sp—" She screamed. "He slammed into me!"

"Scarlet!" Sam's heart leapt into his throat.

She screamed again.

Sam could hear metal mangling and glass shattering as Scarlet cried out in terror.

And he was helpless to do anything about it.

"Son of a bitch!" he yelled. "Scarlet! Talk to me!"

"I—uh . . . Oh, God." Her voice was strained, her breathing jagged.

No!

Fury and fear ripped through Sam. "Scarlet! Say something!"

In the background Sam heard another voice. "This is OnStar. What's your emergency?"

"I'm upside-down," Scarlet croaked out. "And I'm stuck."

Sam listened, his pulse hammering in his head, as Scarlet apparently attempted to free herself from the seat belt. He gripped his cell so tightly it was a wonder he didn't crush the device. His other hand balled at his side. Horror clawed at him.

He didn't say anything, not wanting to impede the emergency

call, but Jesus Christ! He didn't know how badly hurt she was. Where she was. How difficult it was going to be for someone to get to her.

Sam paced the kitchen as the dispatcher contacted 911 and relayed the accident details to them and Scarlet's location pinpointed from their GPS capability.

"I'm going to pass out from all the blood rushing to my head if I can't get out of this belt," she said.

"Just hold on, darlin'." Sam's eyes squeezed shut briefly. This was the absolute worst torture. Reliving the nightmare. Not being able to do anything to save Scarlet just like with Cassidy. "Can you still hear me?"

"You're on speaker on my cell," she said on a broken breath.

A heartbeat later Sam heard sirens wail. "Thank God! Someone's on their way."

"Yes. I can see the lights."

"How hurt are you?" Sam asked, trying to keep his anxiety from echoing over the phone.

"I'm bleeding," she said, her voice weak and raspy. "My forehead. And the shoulder harness pulled too tight when the belt locked up. It dug into the side of my neck. Other than that, I think I'm okay."

"All right. Just try to stay calm." He said that as much for himself as for her.

"I'm a little worried," she shakily confessed. "There's a lot of blood. It's running into my hair. My bangs are soaked."

There were more voices in the background, a bit of commotion. The sound of a door opening was a monumental relief to Sam. Scarlet explained to the first responder that she was stuck. Sam stayed on the call as they talked her through how they were going to get her out and then went about extracting her from the belt and the vehicle. Then there was silence.

Sam was ready to jump out of his skin. He waited for what

seemed like an eternity, pacing and trying not to picture Scarlet cut up and covered in blood. It was an agonizing wait before someone came on the line.

"This is an EMT," he told Sam. "We're taking Miss Drake to the hospital. I'm going to have to disconnect you."

"Yes, of course. Just . . . tell her I'm on my way."

"Will do."

The EMT dropped off. Sam immediately called Michael.

"Calling about—"

"Scarlet's been in an accident," Sam instantly interjected. "She's on the way to the hospital in River Cross right now. I'm going to California."

"I'll pick you up in Kalispell," Michael told him, alarm in his voice.

"It'll take you four hours to get here in your Lear, Michael."

"Yes, but do you really think you're going to get a flight to San Francisco out of that airport at this time of night? And nonstop? Not likely. It'll take you just as long if not longer than if I pick you up. And if there's a municipal airport in River Cross we can land there and save the time it'd take to drive from the city."

"Good point." But what the fuck was he going to do for four hours to keep from going crazy over Scarlet?

"Look, just hang in there, all right? I know you're rattled."

"I was on the phone with her when someone ran her off the road. I'm guessing he took off, because he didn't help her."

"Shit." Michael's tone was razor sharp. "How bad is it?"

"She rolled the vehicle and was hanging upside down for a while. Belt jammed. Or her fingers were too shaky to release the latch. She's bleeding, but she was conscious."

"Goddamn it, that must have been a bitch for you to go through."

"Without there being a fucking thing I could do for her!"

His nerves were shot to shit and his panic didn't abate.

"Have a drink and take a few deep breaths," Michael told him. "I've got to make all the arrangements. I'll call you from the air."

"Fine."

"Sam . . ."

"I'll be okay. Just get a move on it. I don't want to waste time."

"Neither do I."

Sam hung up. Bypassed his beer and poured a stiff drink instead. Prayed like hell Scarlet would be all right—and that she'd call him as soon as she could.

TWENTY

Michael was worried about Scarlet, but he was equally concerned about Sam, whose knee was bouncing up and down as he sat across from Michael. The Lear was too small for effective pacing, especially for a man Sam's size. So Michael knew the confinement was as torturous for his stepbrother as not being with Scarlet when she was injured.

Sam said, "Her friend Jewel called me from Scarlet's cell while she was getting stitched up and looked over. I let her know I contacted you and we're flying out there. Jewel said Scarlet's shaken up, but they didn't think anything was broken. She has a concussion, so she's being kept at the hospital overnight. We'll arrive right around the time visiting hours start in the morning."

"We should probably try to get a few hours' sleep, then," Michael suggested.

Sam glared at him.

"Right." Michael sighed. "Not likely until we've seen Scarlet."

"I hope the police have nailed the asshole who rammed her. I'm guessing it was a drunk driver."

"Chances are good."

Michael stared out the window, into the dark night, and stewed.

He very much wanted to kick the shit out of whoever did this to Scarlet. And while he was trying to keep a level head and project some calm so Sam didn't get further agitated, Michael's insides were twisted and his rage simmered just below the surface.

He was anxious to see Scarlet but trying damn hard not to amp Sam's rage and worry. Making it feel like the longest fucking trek across country for Michael.

He considered discussing the news Scarlet had already shared with him, but he didn't know if she'd broached the subject with Sam yet or if she'd still intended to tell him about his dad and twin brother in person. And besides, talking about it would only heap more strife on Sam at the moment.

And because Michael knew from experience how wrecked Sam had been following the car accident he and Cassidy had been in, he didn't want to torment Sam.

So to pass the time, Michael did a little mindless work that would be easy to toss aside if Sam decided he needed to bend his ear. But Sam was currently keeping his thoughts and angst to himself.

When they finally landed at the small community airport in River Cross, the sun was already up. The tension both Michael and Sam felt didn't ease even as they drove a rented SUV that was waiting for them to the hospital. Sam called Scarlet's cell and she answered. Sam put her on speaker.

Michael asked her, "How are you feeling, sweetheart?"

"Like I've been mowed over by a steamroller. But mostly, my head is throbbing, despite the pain meds."

Sam winced. Michael continued to strive for an even keel. No easy feat. He said, "We're almost to the hospital, according to our GPS. You're still there?"

"Yes. I just got word that I'm cleared for discharge this morning. Jewel brought me clothes, so I should be ready to get the hell out of here before they serve me any sort of breakfast slop."

Michael chuckled. "Nice to know your feisty spirit is still intact."

Sam said, "We'll get you settled at your house and I'll make something to eat. Is your grandmother home? We're not going to throw her for a loop that we're both here?"

"She's still on a research trip. And she'd be impressed you both came running. . . ." Scarlet paused, then added, "*I'm* impressed. Grateful. Comforted. All that mushy stuff."

"Mushy's fine, darlin'," Sam assured her. "I'm a bit torn up and Michael is ready to spit nails."

"Hey, I've been perfectly cool," Michael insisted through clenched teeth because he was still worked up.

Sam snorted. "There's murder in your eyes and your jaw hasn't loosened since Kalispell. Probably not since New York."

Michael tried to school his features to not be so stony. He hadn't realized he'd been wearing his emotions on his face—thought he was doing a much better job of dealing with the situation.

Well, it wasn't much of a surprise, really. He was upset about Scarlet. Couldn't wait to see her. And was so damn glad she wasn't worse off.

Was alive.

"I've got some paperwork to sign," she told them. "So I'll see you when you get here. Room two-sixteen."

"We'll be there in ten," Sam said before hanging up.

"I'm impressed as well," Jewel mused with a knowing look on her pretty face and a twinkle in her sapphire eyes. "Clearly, they couldn't get here fast enough. And when I spoke with Sam last night, he was severely on edge. Those two are deeply concerned about your health and well-being. Very into you, girlfriend."

Scarlet nodded, despite the pounding in her head, above her right eye where there'd been a huge gash to stitch closed. She said, "I'm so glad they came. I just want to be in their arms right now.

Especially Sam. That must have been pure hell for him to be on the line when I crashed. I mean, how horrific to relive that epic disaster in his life, having absolutely no control over what was happening to me, no ability to save me. Or even have the chance to try."

"I imagine he hasn't had a moment of peace since your Range Rover flipped. And won't until he sees for himself that you're okay. Well, relatively speaking. You are a little ghostly."

"Thanks for washing most of the blood out of my hair with the towel. Now I need some makeup. One of the police officers who responded to the call retrieved my stuff from my car and brought it all by. Josh Lofton from high school. Remember him? Anyway, there's makeup in my purse. Oh, and I told Josh I caught the first three letters of the license plate as it whizzed by. White SUV. Maybe an Explorer."

Jewel's brow lifted.

"What?" Scarlet asked. "Am I too scatterbrained? All over the place?"

"Not so much. Well, yeah, a little. It just makes my mind reel that you're in some terrifying situation and yet it doesn't escape you to collect clues along the way."

"Well, I am a trained professional."

"True." Jewel shrugged. "Anyway, hopefully Josh will come up with some answers as to who our hit-and-run a-hole is."

"Fingers crossed." Scarlet used her cosmetics to cover up some of the paleness to her skin, though there wasn't much she could do to chase away the tumult in her eyes. Not just because her nerves were still jangled over her ordeal but also because she was so worried about Sam.

Who basically barreled through the door moments later.

He very gingerly clasped Scarlet's biceps and stared intently at her, as though needing to ensure it was really her, that she'd survived. Then he carefully hugged her.

While she was sore from the rollover, she wished like hell he wouldn't be so tentative. But that was how Sam was. Soft voice, tender touch for the bruised and battered. The sweetest of sweet.

And it was hugely comforting to be in his arms. She closed her eyes and just gave herself over to his quiet strength and the feeling of being engulfed by him. She let him hold her for as long as he needed.

Across the room, she heard Michael introduce himself to Jewel. That seemed to bring Sam around and he reluctantly released Scarlet so that Michael could have his turn with her. She walked into his embrace.

As he stroked her hair, he whispered, "You scared the hell out of us."

"Not intentional. I'm so sorry."

"I know." He kissed her temple.

"I'd apologize about you having to drop everything and come all this way, but I'm so happy to see you. I needed to see you both."

Admittedly, her own sentiment caught her off-guard. Scarlet had been full throttle since her parents' deaths. She'd flirted with danger every chance she got. But there was something about being on the phone with Sam when the accident happened and Michael being all the way across the country that caused her to think far beyond herself. She really had scared them. Because they cared about her. Because they were the type of men who'd want to protect her—and her lifestyle actually did put her in crosshairs from time to time.

Glancing over her shoulder, she told Sam, "I wasn't being reckless last night. It was a two-lane road and there wasn't much space to pull off to the side."

"I believe you."

"I wouldn't purposely make you worry about me," she said.

"You were just driving home from dinner," Jewel reminded her. "It wasn't your fault."

"Right." Scarlet untangled herself from Michael and tried to gain a little composure. She dabbed at the corners of her eyes with a tissue, then said, "I appreciate everyone's concern."

"You should definitely take it easy today," Jewel told her. "Feet up. Let these guys look after you. And of course, if you need anything from me, do not hesitate to call."

"I won't. I'll be good," Scarlet promised, her heart aching over having terrified everyone.

Jewel told the men it was good to meet them and then departed. Sam was collecting Scarlet's belongings when Josh walked in.

She said to Sam and Michael, "This is Officer Lofton. He and I go way back. He was on the scene last night."

They all shook. Josh told her, "You cracked the case for us, Scarlet. We have your hit-and-run driver, thanks to the information you provided. He thought he'd pull a Houdini by ditching the vehicle he used to smash into you. It was a rental. Only had it for the day, which led us to the airport here in town, but the SFPD got involved as well and detained him at San Francisco International. They were able to connect with TSA in time so that someone checking IDs and boarding passes could tip them off when our perp went through security for a red-eye flight. Naturally, he claims he's not the Dylan Reed we're all looking for, but the guy's got a rap sheet a mile—"

"Dylan *Reed*?" Scarlet, Sam, and Michael all said in shocked unison.

Scarlet's gaze snapped to Michael, who gave her a pointed look, appearing as though he wanted to rip someone's head off. Sam's brother's head, to be exact.

Her gaze shifted to Sam. His eyes darkened.

"My father?" he ventured aloud. "Did he and my mother secretly marry all those years ago and she never told me Reed isn't her maiden name? Or is this just some bizarre coincidence?"

Scarlet did not take Sam Reed for being the type to buy into coincidences of this caliber. So her moment of reckoning was upon her.

"It's not your father," she quietly said. "No coincidence, either. It's your brother, Sam. Dylan Reed is your brother. Your twin, in fact."

Sam's mouth worked as though he had something to say, but no words came out.

Scarlet rushed on. "I was going to tell you. This weekend. In Montana." She shot Michael a look and he nodded in confirmation to back her up.

Sam's brow furrowed as his eyes landed on Michael. "You knew about this?"

"Scarlet was upset over discovering your long-lost family members and she confided in me. Asked for my advice."

"Discovering?" Sam said the word with a hint of accusation.

Scarlet wouldn't lie. "Yes, I snooped. Or, rather, I had Bay do it. See, I had this insatiable need to gather every piece of this puzzle, because I'm coming up with nada in solving the art theft. But it was more than that. I wanted to know more about you, Sam. And what I learned was that your father is a criminal serving time in Arizona. Your brother's been incarcerated as well."

"And likely will be again," Josh chimed in, "if it's proven he's our culprit. Leaving the scene of the crime is a serious offense."

"Add in deadly conduct," Michael said in a surly tone. "He intentionally ran Scarlet off the road."

"Wait." Sam raised his hand to stop the litany. "First things first. *Why* would he run Scarlet off the road on purpose?"

"Oh, that." She let out a long stream of air. "Best guess is that he took the directive from his father. His name is Wyatt Hill. I went to see him in prison. Very brief visit. Pretty much told me to fuck off when I mentioned the art theft."

Sam stared at her. His Adam's apple rose and fell slowly as

he processed all of this. Then he said, "You think my dad and my brother were in on the heist?"

"I didn't have a strong gauge of the situation going into it," she confessed. "I just wanted to talk to Wyatt. Read the barometer where he and Karina were concerned."

Sam rubbed his nape in obvious consternation. "And you struck a nerve. Because you're on to something?"

"Could be. Dylan's move says a hell of a lot, don't you think?"

Sam's eyes remained stormy. "My twin brother could have killed you."

"Don't go on a guilt trip," she urged. "You didn't even know he existed until five minutes ago, and his actions aren't your responsibility, even if they involve me."

Michael stepped closer and he gripped Sam's shoulder. "Man, what happened to Scarlet isn't for you to take on emotionally."

Sam's jaw clenched.

Scarlet said, "There are consequences to my grilling people, Sam. I get in their business and sometimes they push back."

"When they've got something to hide," he ground out.

"That's usually the way it works," she agreed.

"Fuck!" His hands fisted and he appeared as though he wanted to slam them into the wall.

Michael said, "We don't have anything conclusive here. Why don't we all bring this down a notch? Get Scarlet home so she can rest. And eat."

"I am currently commiserating with migraine sufferers the world over," she said.

"Jesus." Sam's angst clearly multiplied. "Yes, let's go."

She turned to Josh. "Anything else you need from me right now?"

"You didn't get a glance at the driver, so no. But you have been a huge help. I hope you're feeling better soon."

She gave her old friend a quick hug. "Thanks for following up on my lead."

"Thanks for providing it."

Scarlet left the hospital with Michael and Sam. She directed them to the house she shared with her gran. Michael set her up in the living room with pillows and a blanket on the sofa. Built a fire. Sam went into the kitchen and it wasn't long before mouthwatering scents wafted from that direction.

Her stomach growled. Michael chuckled.

"Hey," she playfully snapped, "I live a very active life. I require sustenance."

He leaned in from his perch on the edge of the sturdy coffee table and kissed her. "I'm just teasing you."

"I know." She smiled.

"Ah, finally. I've been waiting for that."

With a shrug, she said, "I brought this on myself. But I do appreciate that you and Sam are here. How do you think he's doing?"

"We'll get the answer to that when breakfast is ready. If it's just eggs and sausage, I'd say he's dealing. If it's a massive feast to rival brunch at the Dorchester, then he's really fucked up in the head. And in the heart."

She sniffed the air and frowned. "I smell vanilla-laced French toast."

"Damn."

Now Scarlet's stomach churned—and not from hunger. "I can't believe how twisted this has all become."

"I feel the same." He swept away strands of hair from her cheek. "I want to know what the hell happened to that art collection and why there are so many layers to penetrate."

She eyed him quizzically. "You told me the night we met that you didn't give a rip about what happened to the paintings."

Michael grimaced. "That was a self-serving response. I didn't give Karina the full benefit of the doubt back then. I didn't want to believe that she really loved my father. That it was all real."

"But you believe her now?"

"I can see where her complications are legit. I can say my ambivalence toward her didn't help the situation. And it's evident my father honestly feels as strongly for her as she does for him. I suspect it's not the same as his relationship with my mother. A few weeks ago I didn't fully grasp that concept. But the way everything's unfolding with you, me, and Sam . . . I have a better acceptance of how things fell into place."

Scarlet nodded. Then said, "I need to go back to New York. Speak with Karina again."

"You're in no condition to travel, sweetheart."

She really couldn't dispute that. Nor could she shut down her mind as it whirled with more questions. "Sam told Jewel when she phoned him that you were picking him up in your Learjet. It'll be a quicker flight than commercial back to New York, with no airport tedium. I can survive that."

"Scarlet—"

"You don't think Sam's going to have a million questions himself?" She pinned Michael with a serious look. "Questions I can't answer. Only Karina can."

Michael stood. He paced in front of the fireplace with his hands on his waist. "The guy's getting the shit kicked out of him these days."

"Yes. And I feel wretched about that. I want to be there with him when he gets the full story. You should be there, too. It's obvious you both provide support for each other. He's going to need it."

"Sam can take care of himself." Scarlet's gaze flashed to the mountain of a man standing in the archway that led to the kitchen. Sam's arms were crossed over his chest. His expression was impassive. Yet he added, "Doesn't mean I don't want the company."

Scarlet drew in an unsteady breath and asked, "Including me?"

"Including you. Breakfast is ready." He returned to the kitchen.

Scarlet exchanged a look with Michael. He said, "Guess we're going to New York."

TWENTY-ONE

Sam had never really considered his mother a keeper of secrets, but she was certainly racking them up.

He wasn't sure how he felt about this latest one. Without doubt, she had every right to make a decision to keep a child or give him away. And Sam could wholeheartedly comprehend the difficulty with being a young, financially strapped single parent of two newborns. He knew his mother hadn't had much of a familial support group—Sam's grandparents had pretty much carved Karina out of their lives when she'd come home pregnant her senior year of high school. She'd told Sam that they couldn't have the "devil's mistress" living under their roof and kicked her out.

Sam knew very little about George and Sally Reed. Only that they'd never changed their minds about having contact with their daughter. Or him. Perhaps that life lesson was why he'd never sought out the identity of his father. The guy had blown town. Didn't want to have anything to do with Sam or Karina. In Sam's opinion that meant they shouldn't want to have anything to do with him either. If being part of a family wasn't what Wyatt Hill wanted, then it was best not to have the man pretending otherwise.

But Sam had already reconciled that situation in his head.

What troubled him now was that he had a brother. Yet as he spared a glance at Michael, sitting in one of the single seats facing the sofa in the back of the plane where Sam and Scarlet were settled, Sam knew that Dylan might be his blood relative, but he wasn't a true brother. The asshole had gone after Scarlet because she'd confronted Wyatt in prison.

Scarlet had broken it all down for Sam and Michael during the flight. She'd ID'd herself to Wyatt and had told him she was an insurance-fraud investigator. All Wyatt had to do after he walked out on her visit was place a call to Dylan to look her up, track her down, and run her off the road.

Again, it wasn't the *how?* that chipped away at Sam. It was the *why?*

What were those two up to . . . and was his mother involved? Had she been in contact with Wyatt over the years? Dylan, too? Did she know that Wyatt would likely have an electronic Rolodex filled with the names of shady characters who would lend her money for her gambling debt? Was that how she'd found someone to bankroll her addiction?

Tension seized Sam. His shoulders were squared, every muscle pulled taut.

But it wasn't just the speculation over what his father and brother might be up to that had Sam disconcerted. It was that Scarlet was involved.

He covered her hands with one of his as they lay in her lap and told her, "I'm the one who has to apologize now."

"No," she quickly said. "Not at all."

"Scarlet, what happened to you is—"

"Not your fault by any stretch of the imagination." She glanced at Michael. "Yours, either." Returning her attention to Sam, she said, "No one invited me into this investigation. I willingly—and enthusiastically—took on the assignment. Therefore, I have to accept the potential hazards inherent to it. I don't carry a weapon and practice Krav Maga for nothing. This actually can be a very dangerous business. That's a reality I'm fully aware of and assent to. I'm responsible for my own actions, Sam. I chose to travel this path."

Sam scowled, his frustration burning brighter because he couldn't pace or otherwise work off some of his angst.

Michael said, "She does make a good point. I'm not saying I fully agree with it—I get where you're coming from, Sam, why you're so upset."

"You're upset, too," Sam contended, wanting Michael to stop feeling as though he had to be the levelheaded voice of reason when it was so obvious that he was as tormented by what had happened to Scarlet—by how much worse that car accident could have been—as Sam. "You don't have to play it cool with me. Or with her."

Michael reached for his drink and sipped.

Scarlet said, "Let's not stay mired in my accident. We need to move forward in order to figure out what the hell is really going on."

Sam draped his arm around her and coaxed her closer so that she snuggled against him and put her head on his shoulder. "You should rest."

"Not a bad idea," she agreed. "My doctor said I could fly this soon after the concussion, but that it'd be best if I tried to sleep the whole way. And I am exhausted." Her eyelids dipped.

Sam's gaze flitted to Michael. They stared at each other a few moments, no more words necessary. They were both pissed about Scarlet's rollover. Upset because she was injured and it had all started with missing artwork at their family's estate.

Naturally, Sam was doubly disturbed, since it was his father and brother who'd done the most damage. And Sam was also deeply concerned about how his mother fit into all of this.

It was a grueling position for Sam to be in. His feelings for

Scarlet had intensified from the first time they'd made love. When he'd been on the other end of the call as her vehicle had flipped, he'd realized that he was intricately entwined with this woman, feared for her life, would have been wrecked all over again if anything more serious had happened to her. And at the hands of his family?

His gut coiled. What a fucking disaster this was. All of his internal strife and his inability to do anything about it at the moment made the flight seem like an insanely long one, despite the fact that he derived a small measure of comfort from Scarlet's soft, steady breathing as she slept.

Though Sam's restlessness increased during the helicopter ride to the estate. As did his tension. He was getting sucker punched around every corner and wondered what else was in store for him.

At the mansion, the trio found Karina in one of the living rooms. Hearing them approach, she glanced up from a magazine she was perusing and gasped.

"Miss Drake," she said as she set aside the magazine and got to her feet. "Dear Lord, what happened to you?"

Sam bit back a growl, the constant reminder of Scarlet's rollover eating away at his soul like a vicious piranha. She had a bandage on her forehead, a bruise on one cheek, and a long angry-red slash across her neck and collarbone from the seat belt digging into her skin when she'd been suspended in air. And she was deathly white, even though she'd obviously tried to add color to her face with makeup.

Basically, she was a fucking mess that made him want to strangle someone.

Michael spoke in a tight voice. "Hit-and-run. She could have been killed."

"I'll be fine," Scarlet interjected, her tone steady and professional. "But we have more questions for you, Karina."

Sam's hand was at the small of Scarlet's back and he felt her rigidity, sensed the undercurrent of irritation she clearly tried to contain.

"I've told you everything I could," Sam's mother insisted.

"*Could?*" Scarlet baited. "But not all that you know."

"Mother," Sam said, his own agitation close to the boiling point. "We know about Wyatt Hill. We know about Dylan Reed. My twin brother is the one who caused Scarlet's accident."

"I—oh, my God. I—" Karina's jaw slackened and her eyes widened. Her hand pressed to her chest, over her heart.

"Enough of the secrets," Sam quietly demanded, doing his best not to lose it completely.

Scarlet said, "I went to see Wyatt in prison. A couple of nights later, I was hanging upside down in a ditch."

Karina's other hand covered her mouth. Tears sprang to her eyes.

Sam's gut wrenched again, his chest pulling tight. He was already in an emotional hell because of Scarlet's injuries. Now he was faced with the turmoil of his mother's reaction to him finding out about his dad and brother—from someone other than her. And her apparent horror over the danger Scarlet had been in.

It took all the willpower Sam possessed to not press his mother, not rush her. Instead, he forced himself to let her process the implication of what Scarlet had said.

Michael was equally frustrated, shifting from foot to foot and looking as though he was biting his tongue so he didn't jump into the fray.

But they both knew this was Scarlet's investigation. She was the one who needed to get to the bottom of this, and justifiably so. Sam didn't want to say anything that would have his mother running off to her room, Mitcham intervening, or some other inciting incident leaving them all hanging. This had to be resolved. *Now.*

"Honestly, Karina," Scarlet said, her dropping the polite

"Mrs. Vandenberg" label speaking volumes. "I need to know exactly what's going on. What you're involved in. What your connection is to Wyatt and Dylan, because they didn't just come after me for popping into the prison unexpectedly. I specifically mentioned the art theft to Wyatt. And then *this* happened." She swept a hand in the air, close to her neck and face. "That tells me loud and clear that I was getting much too close to a truth they wanted to keep covered up. And the only trigger was the reference to the missing collection. That means we've all come full circle."

Sam's heart constricted further as his mother's eyes squeezed shut and tears leaked out of the sides.

"Jesus!" he hissed, unable to control himself a moment longer. "You know something, don't you? You know what this is all about and—"

"And you didn't put a stop to it when you had the chance," Michael quietly blasted. "You could have told Scarlet everything the last time she was here and she wouldn't have gotten hurt."

Karina's eyes flew open. "I never intended that!" Through her tears, she said, "I had no idea they'd harm her. I would *never* condone that." Her gaze bored into Sam. "You have to believe me. I wouldn't put *anyone* in danger, especially someone you care for!"

"Yet Scarlet *is* in danger!" he roared. "Why? *Why* did they go after her?"

"Sam." It was a simple warning from Michael. If they amped up this confrontation, they might not get the answers they so desperately needed.

Scarlet was the one to proceed, more calmly. Deceptively calm, because Sam detected the underlying steeliness to her tone.

She said, "I think I have it all pieced together. It was a scam from the beginning. Karina actually did know who Mitcham was when he came into her diner. Somehow, through whatever research or reconnaissance she did, she learned his wife was ill and in the hospital. Using Mitcham's grief against him, she got close to him. At some point, it was 'love'—for him, anyway. And then she found the perfect way to steal eighteen million dollars from him. For herself and for Wyatt and Dylan."

"Scarlet!" Sam thundered. Not at her. But in general. Because goddamn it, her conjecture was precisely what he was suddenly thinking. Yet . . . it just couldn't be. "There *has* to be another explanation."

"It's a fantastically plotted-out crime," Scarlet continued, undeterred by Sam's outburst. "More spectacular than anything I've ever dealt with before." She pinned Sam's mother with a hard look. "That was the plan all along, right? To collect the insurance money, have Wyatt launder it or otherwise disperse it into offshore accounts so that it wasn't traceable if anyone started to dig too deep into the theft, even after the FBI closed the case?"

"And once the statute of limitations ran out," Michael added, "you all could take eighteen mil and disappear." Michael swallowed hard. Started to circle the room looking as tormented as Sam felt, because Michael had just recently developed a soft spot for Karina. He'd doubted her integrity initially, had gradually warmed to her, but after she'd fessed up to the addictions and the difficulties in fitting in here, he'd succumbed to guilt and empathy. And now he felt as though he'd been played the fool.

It was easy to jump to that conclusion. Sam experienced the same angst. Though it was magnified a thousand times over because this was his mother they were talking about. And because Sam still couldn't fully accept that she'd planned this all along.

He stepped toward her, grabbed her by the shoulders, and stared into her eyes. "Is Scarlet right?" he demanded much more forcefully this time. "Was this all a scam?"

Her lids fluttered closed again. Her breathing turned choppy.

"Mother," he urged. "Is this true?"

Her eyes snapped open. She glared at him. "No!" She shook loose of his hold on her and moved away. "Absolutely not. I love

Mitcham." She rushed over to Michael, clasped his forearms in her hands, and insisted in a breathless tone, "I love your father. Never, ever doubt that. I was deeply moved by his pain. I was drawn into something with him that I hadn't imagined possible. Unconditional love, soul-deep love. We have that and I'm so, so blessed. Everything I told you last weekend about how we met and fell in love is the truth. I swear it."

She released him and returned to where Scarlet and Sam stood. She laid a hand against Scarlet's upper arm and said, "I am truly sorry you got caught in the middle of this. I'm positively horrified that you were hurt. And for it to have been a potentially deadly car accident that Sam had to live through again—"

More tears fell as Karina turned to him. Sam's insides were a mess. He felt gutted, shredded to the core. His stepbrother was reeling from the possibility of his father being duped when Mitcham had so freely given his affection to Karina. Scarlet sported wounds indirectly inflicted by Sam's mother. And Sam . . .

He was a man raised on principle, honor, and loyalty.

All of that was being challenged today, pushed to the limits.

Then there was the matter of his mother fisting his shirt and staring up at him, imploringly, while fat drops rolled down her flushed cheeks. The agony in her eyes killed him.

She said, "I can explain all of this. I know it's too late to apologize for it, but I can assure you that this was no sort of setup. Not in the way you all are thinking."

When Sam swallowed, it felt like razor blades slicing his throat. "This had better be the truth, Mother. Tell us the honest-to-God truth."

"Yes. I will." She sucked in a sharp breath. Spared a glance over her shoulder at Scarlet and said, "You're right in that I had a hand in this. And that I did work with Wyatt and Dylan to steal the collection."

"Mother!" Sam exploded.

Her head whipped back to him. She rushed on, saying in a quavering voice, "It wasn't for personal gain, Sam. I promise. I had to do it. I had no choice. Wyatt and Dylan came to me." She relinquished her hold on Sam and turned once again to Michael. "I had to do what they demanded. I couldn't let your father suffer any sort of humiliation because of me."

"Oh, my God." This from Scarlet. A low, sympathetic whisper.

Sam eyed her. "What?"

Scarlet shook her head. Said, "It's not that she had *no* other choice. Your mother's back was to the wall."

"Yes," Karina fervidly contended. "Wyatt didn't want to have anything to do with me when he found out I was pregnant. He vanished. I had to give up Dylan. I just couldn't manage two babies. Not financially. Physically. Emotionally. And I'm so sorry about that. But I did what I thought was right for all of us. I truly believed Dylan would have a better life with different parents. I was wrong."

"Because he has his father's genes," Scarlet surmised.

"Yes." Karina nodded. "Clearly, that apple didn't fall too far from the tree. And when he was old enough, curiously enough, he went looking for Wyatt. When he found him, they started down the path of father-son criminal activity. And when Wyatt saw my picture in the paper with Mitcham at a society event . . . he and Dylan hatched a plan."

"They extorted that money from you," Scarlet deduced, her entire demeanor softening. "They threatened you."

Karina sank into a chair. Pulled in a few breaths. Sam handed over tissues and his mother dabbed at her eyes. She said, "I didn't have a gambling debt. I don't gamble at all. There was no loan to repay. But everything else I told you last weekend really is the truth. I had a terrible time adjusting to the Hamptons. And all I wanted was to be perfect for Mitcham, because I felt he deserved it. I feel that way even today. He's been so good to me.

And to Sam. I love him with all my heart. I just couldn't have him caught up in my drama. I didn't want him to know about my past."

"It has to be more than that," Michael said, leveling Karina with a look.

The color drained from her face, her complexion turning stark. "Yes."

Sam said, "They really did threaten you."

"No." Her gaze locked with Sam's and she told him, "They threatened *you*."

Scarlet gasped. Stepped closer to Sam. An innate response, even though the man could certainly take care of himself. And there was no imminent danger at the moment.

Karina said, "Wyatt showed up at a charity luncheon one day, after I'd married Mitcham. He stood in the periphery so that I'd know he was there. He didn't approach me. Then I caught sight of him at a gallery opening. Followed by a concert in the park. I knew I had to confront him. But I also knew that if he'd suddenly reappeared in my life after making a huge statement about not wanting to be in it by leaving Colorado, then he wanted something from me."

"You didn't tell my father about the sightings because you'd have to reveal that you have a second son? That you gave him up?" Michael was the one to make the observation.

"That's correct," Karina said. "It wasn't quite a year before you and Sam turned twenty-four. Mitcham had just given me the art collection."

She mangled the tissue in her hands. Took a few moments to compose herself as best as possible. No one else spoke.

Finally, Karina told them, "When Wyatt came at me, telling me he'd let all of New York society and my friends in the Hamptons know what 'trash' I was for 'giving it up' in the backseat of his car when we were eighteen, getting pregnant, and then putting one of my children up for adoption . . . All I could think of was how it'd tarnish Mitcham's reputation and undermine the strides I'd made in proving I was sincerely in love with him. That I could be a part of his life and the community. Not just be some outsider, some waitress from a diner that he'd brought home to the Hamptons." She shook her head miserably. Added, "I asked that he not tell anyone I was a waitress but instead let them know I was a docent at a gallery . . . say we met there. Otherwise, I feared we'd be doomed from the lies I'd crafted to fit in. Mitcham didn't feel that way, but I begged for his acquiescence."

Scarlet heard again in Karina's voice the guilt and shame. And it tugged at her heartstrings. Sam's as well, she had no doubt.

He knelt alongside the chair his mother sat in and covered her hand with his. "How'd it all spiral out of control?"

Hitching her chin, Karina said, "I refused to be victimized." Then her gaze dropped, as did her tone. "At first."

"You would have told Mitcham everything at that point— before Wyatt could do it," Scarlet guessed.

"I figured that would neutralize the situation with Wyatt. And I believed enough in my relationship with my husband that I felt I could tell him about my past. More so than what I'd ever said, which was just that I'd met someone, we'd gotten carried away, and I had Sam."

"But there was a game-changer," Scarlet ventured.

"Yes." Karina sighed. "Wyatt threatened Sam's life. I'm a mother, Miss Drake," she said as her gaze lifted to meet Scarlet's. "I couldn't have that. Wyatt wanted twenty million. I told him I could get him eighteen."

Scarlet frowned. "Why didn't you go to the police or the FBI with this from the onset?"

"I just couldn't."

"They would have provided protection," Scarlet told her. "Mitcham would have—"

"It was more than that, Miss Drake."

"You didn't want any of your self-perceived dirty laundry aired," Scarlet said. "I get that. But—"

"It wasn't just about Sam," Karina hissed out. "Or me." Her gaze shifted. "Wyatt threatened Michael's life, too."

Scarlet shot him a look. He appeared on the verge of erupting with his own fury.

Karina continued. "He accused me of neglecting one son, not loving Dylan enough to keep him. And now I had a new son. One he was willing to take away from me—along with Sam."

"Son of a bitch!" Sam jerked upward, towering over Scarlet and Karina.

"Jesus," Scarlet mumbled. "Didn't see that one coming."

"Believe me, Miss Drake, if I'd really thought I could turn my back or go to the FBI and we would have all come out of this unscathed, that's precisely what I would have done. But it all got so convoluted. And I couldn't discount Wyatt's threats. I'd witnessed his temper and his wrath before. I've been on the receiving end of it, as a matter of fact."

More shame visibly tormented her. She couldn't look at Sam. Or Michael. Her gaze remained on Scarlet.

Karina said, "It's the reason my parents kicked me out of their house when they found out I was pregnant."

"The 'devil's mistress'?" Sam offered.

"Yes," his mother said, her focus still on Scarlet. "They didn't call me that because of some religious affinity. They believed it because they knew the damage Wyatt was capable of and I kept going back to him. Refused to tell the police he'd beaten me. My parents had no choice but to shut the door on me. Tough love and all that. It was tearing them up to see me with Wyatt. I was eighteen and could do what I pleased. They were correct in their assessment that I was going to continually choose Wyatt over them. I was young and foolish, absurdly so. But I had this incredibly sunny disposition—it was all going to work out. *It'd be all right. . . . I'd show them. . . .* That sort of thing. Then Wyatt disappeared."

Sam seethed. Scarlet desperately wanted to comfort him, but she couldn't make a move toward him or do anything that might derail Karina's confession.

Karina told them, "My parents had given me some money when they'd thrown me out and I moved us to New York. I knew it'd be expensive, but I also knew there'd be more job opportunities here. Longer shifts I could work to earn extra money and accommodate a babysitter. I also had some theatrical aspirations and performed in small playhouses from time to time. Those stints came with paychecks. I got by. Not well, but we always had a roof over our heads and food on the table, even if it was just ramen and a couple slices of bread sometimes."

Scarlet's heart wrenched. She'd had no idea Sam's upbringing had been quite so bleak. Apparently, Michael hadn't either.

Across the room, he muttered, "Fuck."

Sam said, "Get over it. I survived."

"Yeah." Michael's expression turned intense. Remorseful, even. "And I lived here, with limos and country club memberships and Sunday brunch."

"And no college tuition or a trust fund until you're forty," Sam pointed out, "so you weren't exactly Bill Gates from the get-go. You had to make that happen."

The two men stared at each other. Scarlet sensed their camaraderie, their solid connection with each other that had nothing to do with blood and everything to do with the fact that they'd chosen to be friends when thrown together. That they'd bonded at a difficult time in their lives. And that bond clearly could not be broken.

Scarlet found a measure of relief in that, particularly because everything was unraveling in this house.

She asked Karina, "It was your idea to stage the theft?"

"It was the only thing I could think of. The only way to get the money without having to explain anything to Mitcham, without having to reveal my past to him or his friends. His son. And of course, I couldn't allow Michael and Sam to be in any sort of danger. You yourself have suffered Wyatt's cruelty. I didn't doubt for a second that he'd go through with his plan to terrorize my new family."

"Yes, I can attest to his diligence."

"Mitcham told me when he gifted me with the collection that it was mine. Hang the pieces where I wanted, exchange anything that didn't suit me, whatever. It was all mine. He took out the policy but said that if anything ever happened to the paintings— he was thinking in terms of a fire, mostly—I'd have the funds to replace them. So in my mind, I really did consider the collection mine to do with as I pleased. Having it 'stolen' wasn't what pleased me, but I didn't feel I had an alternative. I worked with Wyatt to get the paintings out of the house. In the exact fashion you detailed, Miss Drake."

Damn. At the moment, it was hideously painful to be right.

Karina said, "I made sure no one was in this wing when they boxed up the paintings. Mitcham filed the claim and you know the rest of the story."

"Not entirely," Scarlet told her. "I don't know where that collection is and the curiosity has been driving me mad."

"In a warehouse," Karina said on a heavy sigh. "Perfectly safe and sound."

"Tucked away until the statutes run out," Sam added.

"Yes," his mother said. More tears spilled as she told Scarlet, "I may not be an ethical person in your eyes, but I've always been a good mother and wife. I can't let someone hurt my family if there's something I can do about it. Yes, I was willing to lie, cheat, and steal to protect them. I'm sorry to say that I would do it all over again. Because it was worth trying to keep Wyatt and Dylan away from us and to safeguard Mitcham's reputation, his image. I did struggle; I still do. I never thought it was fair for him to take on the burden of my insecurities. He's given me and Sam so much. I felt I owed him."

"You never owed me anything."

At Mitcham's deep, distinguished voice, Scarlet's whirled toward the archway. Not a smooth move on her part, because that spot above her right eye started to throb again. She winced from the pain and Michael was instantly by her side.

"You need to sit down," he insisted, and helped her to the sofa.

Karina was on her feet in the next instant, but she didn't go to her husband. She poured a glass of water for Scarlet and handed it over.

Gingerly lowering herself to the cushion next to Scarlet, she said, "I am so sorry you got caught in the cross fire. I never dreamed things would go this far." She sniffled, then added, "I thought it was over. I put Wyatt and Dylan behind me. Focused all my energy on being a wife, being a volunteer in the community, being someone respectable. Not so . . . shady. And I've worked hard, for my own company. I'm making back the insurance money. I've had every intention of returning it. Unfortunately, it takes quite a bit of time to earn that sort of cash, even when business is booming."

"I'll pay it back," Sam told her.

"No," she was quick to say. "It's my debt. I'm sure the insurance carrier will set up some sort of payment plan after I make a good-faith installment."

"I'll look into it when I notify them," Scarlet assured her.

"*I'll* take care of the restitution," Mitcham said.

"It's not your responsibility," Karina maintained.

"You're my wife."

They stared at each other across the room.

Scarlet knew she wasn't helping to ease the tension when she said, "I have to report all of this, Karina. And it'll make the papers, have no doubt. It's eighteen million dollars' worth of artwork we're talking about."

Karina dragged her gaze from her husband and nodded at Scarlet. "Yes, I understand. And I'll do whatever's asked of me. If there's any criminal recourse at this point, past the statute of limitations, community service, whatever . . . I will do anything to make up for this." Her attention returned to Mitcham. "I never meant to hurt you. Everything I did was for the direct opposite result. I made a huge mistake. I can't apologize enough, but please know that I did it because I love this family. Because I love *you*."

"We'll talk," was all Mitcham Vandenberg said. He held his hand out and Karina went to him.

At the archway, she turned back to Scarlet, Sam, and Michael. "I really am so very sorry."

More tears fell as Karina left with her husband.

For once in her life, Scarlet did not want to be a fly on the wall. Lord only knew how *that* discussion would go.

Besides, she had her own cross to bear. A heavy, painful one.

Gazing at Michael and Sam, she said, "I have to turn her in."

"Yes." Michael eased onto the seat next to her and put an arm around her shoulders.

Sam stared down at her, understanding in his sky-blue eyes.

Still . . . Scarlet felt shredded to the core. She'd cracked the case—and this family. She'd revealed Sam's mother as the villain. Not an intentional one, because Scarlet considered Karina a victim of circumstance. But Karina Reed Vandenberg had, indeed, committed a crime.

It was in Scarlet's nature to want to see justice served. Yet she could also empathize with Karina, could wholly fathom her motive. Could accept she was a woman who would go to any length to protect the people she loved. And perhaps she really had saved this family six years ago. Unfortunately, she'd torn it apart today.

With Scarlet's help.

The backs of her eyes burned. Emotion swelled in her throat. How did relationships bounce back from something like this? Karina's or Scarlet's?

Scarlet was going to hand over Sam and Michael's mother as the mastermind of the theft. She'd be committing romance homicide. Had no choice but to do so.

Michael told her, "You look wiped out. Let's get you to my apartment so you can rest."

She didn't currently have the wherewithal to protest or provide another suggestion. She certainly wasn't in any shape to wait around JFK for a flight home.

So Scarlet let Michael help her up. The trio left the mansion just as silently as they'd entered, each of them engrossed in their own dismal thoughts.

Scarlet mostly fearing that the end for the threesome was very, very close at hand . . .

TWENTY-TWO

This time, it was Michael's shoulder Scarlet slept against. She hadn't thought she could curb all of her rampant ruminations and concerns in order to rest, but she was mentally and physically fatigued and was out almost immediately. She woke briefly when the helicopter landed and they filed into the limo. Then she cozied up next to Michael once more and dozed all the way to his apartment.

Sam cooked them a late dinner and awkward silence ensued. Scarlet only picked at her food, her stomach too twisted in knots to take on the mahi-mahi Sam had prepared. Both men quietly urged her to eat, though they knew the reason for her lack of appetite. While they cleared the table, Scarlet poured herself a glass of scotch and sipped as she stood at the tall windows, gazing out at the glittery Manhattan skyline.

Eventually, Michael joined her. He slid his arms around her waist from behind and said, "Sam and I both know you're in a bad position."

"It's a rock and a hard place of epic proportions," she corrected. Then sipped.

"It's not your doing, Scarlet. You're not the one who committed the crime."

She cringed. "But I am the one who brought it to light. In front of all of you. I hurt your stepmother and your father. I hurt you and Sam." She wiggled out of Michael's embrace and turned to face him. "I damaged your family."

"No." His hands gingerly cupped her face. "Wyatt Hill and Dylan Reed damaged our family."

Scarlet's gaze narrowed. "You don't blame Karina?"

He blew out a soft breath. "It's complicated. I don't condone her actions. Of course not. But I can respect how fiercely she tried to protect everyone. She was resourceful and even courageous in fending off her adversaries. In truth, I'm mostly relieved that this didn't turn out to be a case of her insinuating herself into my father's life with the intention of robbing him. I still believe that she's deeply in love with him and that everything she did was because of that love. And to keep any threat away from her son. And me. Now it's all over."

"Hardly," Scarlet scoffed. She stepped away from Michael, out of his reach. Drained her cocktail. The liquid burning down her throat was actually a welcome sensation to the pain and uncertainty slicing through her. She set the glass aside and said, "I will forever be known as the woman who turned Sam's mother in. Your stepmother. Mitcham Vandenberg's wife. Sam's not going to forgive me this time. I'm not even sure you'll be able to forgive me. And, Christ, your father . . . that man will gladly squash me like a bug the first chance he gets."

Her heart hurt. This really was the beginning of the end.

But Michael didn't exacerbate her worries. Instead, he gently gripped her upper arms and stared deep into her eyes. "Sweetheart, you did what you had to do by investigating and pressing Karina until she confessed all. And it was the right thing to do. Not to mention, I'm fairly sure she can breathe easier now that her darkest deed has been revealed and she no longer has to fear discovery. In fact, chances are damn good she's glad to be free of all the secrecy."

Michael pulled Scarlet to him and held her tight. Tears stung her eyes and she wanted to give in to them and have a really good cry. But she still had work to do.

"I need to talk to Sam," she said. "Doesn't have to be alone. In actuality, I'd prefer it if you were with me."

"He's in the den."

Michael released her and followed her through the apartment. They found Sam sprawled in an oversized leather chair, scotch in hand. He was staring out the windows as Scarlet had done when Michael had comforted her. Her hand slid over Sam's shoulder as she rounded the chair.

"Mind if I sit?" she asked.

"No."

She eased into his lap. Bold of her, but she needed to be close to him. And he didn't balk.

He did, however, inquire, "Make your phone call?"

"Not yet. It can wait until the morning. Give Karina some time to adjust. Talk to Mitcham. Figure out how she's going to pay back the money if she chooses to do it on her own, or if she'll let him help her."

"He won't turn his back on her," Michael said. "Money's not the issue. What'll be most difficult for him to digest is that she didn't immediately turn to him when Wyatt first showed up. That she would take on something this huge by herself. He'll understand why she felt it was necessary, but he'll still be upset about it. That's one thing I noted when it came to my mother's cancer. They went through it together and he wouldn't have had it any other way. He was the one with the connections to get her the best care and he wouldn't leave it in anyone else's hands, not even hers."

"Karina was too vulnerable from the beginning," Scarlet mused. "Too conflicted by her past and her bleak present to deal with an attack of this magnitude. Yet she did her best. And I can appreciate that. Makes it all the more excruciating to hand her over to the insurance company." Scarlet's fingertips grazed Sam's furrowed brow. "I'm not really sure how I'm going to bring myself to do it."

"You have no choice," Sam said. Not at all accusatory. He simply stated a fact.

Tears welled in her eyes and crested the rims.

Sam whisked them away, saying, "Don't cry. This isn't your fault. You didn't create this problem; you solved it."

"Yet *I* feel villainous," she admitted. "For what I've done to all of you."

"Scarlet." Sam gathered her close, holding her to him. His warm breath teased strands of her hair at her temple as he told her, "No one's blaming you for anything."

"It changes everything between the three of us."

"No."

She pulled slightly away and she stared into his glowing eyes. "I—"

"It changes nothing, Scarlet," he said with conviction.

Her pulse hitched. She gazed at him a few seconds more, then turned to Michael.

He gave a half grin. "Told you."

"You'll really forgive me?" she asked.

"Nothing to forgive," Michael said. "Again . . . this wasn't your doing."

Her attention returned to Sam. "And you?"

"He's right." Sam kissed her softly and added, "I've been to hell, remember? And what did I learn?"

She stared quizzically at him.

He said, "You can come back. That's what I learned."

Her fingers swept through his hair. She gave a shaky smile. "You are the real deal, Sam Reed." She kissed him. Then she looked over at Michael again. "And you are so much more than a silver-tongued devil."

"Shh," he said as he pressed a finger to his lips. "Don't tell anyone."

Scarlet laughed quietly. "That's one secret I'll keep, if you insist."

"Better for business."

"Ah, yes," she teased. "The Wolf of Wall Street."

Michael leaned in and whisked his lips over hers, murmuring, "A much better image to perpetuate outside these walls."

He straightened.

Scarlet gazed into Sam's eyes and said, "And my huntsman?"

"Happy to be all manly for you, darlin'."

Her toes curled. "Then why don't you take me to the bedroom?"

"To sleep," Michael insisted. "You need to take it easy, sweetheart. Your body can't be feeling all that refreshed."

"I'm sore as hell," she confessed. "And I need more ibuprofen for my head."

Michael carefully lifted her into his arms. "Bed it is."

She glanced back at Sam. "And you'll join us?"

He hauled himself up. Kissed her, then said, "Yes."

Scarlet had no delusions that all was well. That they were cured of all that ailed them.

Because she still had that damn phone call to make in the morning.

Scarlet slept soundly enough, nestled between Michael and Sam. The second day following her accident was pretty much equivalent to the two-day pain of a really hard workout. Her neck ached, her head still throbbed, and her legs were toast. She limped to the bathroom and soaked in the tub while Michael and Sam went about their business. Eventually, she smelled food, her stomach grumbled, and she finished up and joined the men at the breakfast table.

THE BILLIONAIRES: THE STEPBROTHERS 279

Michael's apartment was opulent, with endless black marble and modern artwork and sculptures. Panoramic views.

Scarlet literally dragged out the meal as long as possible, dreading the task that lay ahead.

She was in no particular hurry to destroy Karina's reputation. Or taint the rest of the family's.

It kind of surprised Scarlet that Michael hadn't made a plea for her to turn a blind eye to all she'd learned. After all, it wasn't the FBI she was reporting to. And Michael had been so sensitive from the get-go about anyone poking around in family business. Then she recalled what he'd told her that night in the near-impossible-to-locate club. That her ethics would be his undoing.

An interesting premonition to have come true.

Sam wasn't making any appeals to her, either. That perplexed Scarlet in that Sam was incredibly protective and his emotions ran deep. He had to be reeling from the recent events. From knowing all the lies his mother had told and the secrets she'd kept.

Conversely, he was a straight shooter and stalwart. So Scarlet really couldn't imagine him asking her to bend the truth or make blatant omissions—not even for his mother's sake. Apparently, he wouldn't put Scarlet in that position any more than Michael would.

In addition, she surmised that both men likely felt it was all best left in Mitcham's care. He was Karina's husband. It appeared he intended to stand by her, so probably the greatest defense she could have in surviving all of this was for him to help her through.

That did not free Michael and Sam from their own guilt. Scarlet could see that quite clearly, could sense it as the grave undertone permeated the apartment. Karina had taken it upon herself to protect her children. Her household. And Scarlet suspected two strong men such as Michael and Sam would have sympathy for Karina for that ever having to be the case. That she had to go to such drastic measures to thwart whatever Wyatt might have planned for the family.

All of this left Scarlet with even more extreme difficulty in phoning her client. She watched the snow fall on New York City as she tapped the business card for her contact at the insurance agency against her fingertips. Her cell was on an end table not far away. She just couldn't bring herself to reach for it.

The do-gooder was flailing miserably.

Maybe it'd be better if Michael and Sam had put some pressure on her to not rat out Karina. That might have compelled Scarlet to spring into action. To pull the whole "justice will prevail" card on them.

But no.

As best as she could tell at the moment, they accepted her current stance.

Scarlet let out a long-suffering sigh. *Right now* they accepted her stance. But when the shit really hit the fan . . . ? This was no petty crime they were talking about here. No misdemeanor that only warranted a slap on the hand. Insurance fraud, particularly of this magnitude, was a felony. Plain and simple. Whether the statute of limitations for prosecution had run out or not.

The Hamptons "ladies who lunch" would no doubt be deleting Karina Vandenberg from their contact lists. She'd become a social pariah. One of her biggest fears come to life.

"Fuck," Scarlet mumbled.

"Not until you're fully healed," Sam whispered in her ear.

She laughed softly, despite her dismay and melancholy. "Wrong context. But it's nice to see you still have your sense of humor."

"Hanging on by a thread," he admitted. He shoved his hands into the front pockets of his Levi's and heaved a sigh.

Scarlet studied him, thinking he was so damn hunky and

sweet . . . and probably all messed up on the inside over the recent state of affairs.

"You have a visitor, sweetheart." This from Michael as he came up behind her.

Scarlet turned. And gasped.

"Mr. Vandenberg." She gazed up at the imposing man, her stomach knotting at the sight of him.

"May I speak with you alone, Miss Drake?"

She swallowed hard. Said, "Certainly." She'd contended all along that in order to do her job she had to take her lumps.

But neither Michael nor Sam made a move to leave her side.

Mitcham's dark brow rose.

Scarlet ventured, "I suppose they're thinking that whatever you have to say to me you can say to them."

"I'm thinking we don't need to rack up more secrets," Sam said.

Mitcham gave a slow nod. "Fair enough." To Scarlet, he said, "I came because it's nearly one o'clock and you have yet to alert the insurance company of my fraudulent claim. Why is that?"

Scarlet's head started to pound again. She told him, "Seems I'm suffering my own moral dilemma. Making that call will hurt Michael and Sam. I know it's inevitable, but I'm not looking forward to it."

"They don't appear to be trying to coerce you differently," Mitcham pointed out.

"No. They're much more stand-up than that."

Mitcham's jaw briefly clenched. He said, "I'm not here to coerce you, either. Both Karina and I deduced you'd have a difficult time following through when there could be an impact on Michael's and Sam's lives or reputations."

She nodded.

"You care that much about them?" Mitcham asked.

"I wouldn't still be here if I didn't. I achieved what I set out to do," she reminded him. "I gathered the information I needed and I discerned who the culprits were. Case closed, right?"

"Hmm." He crossed his arms over his massive chest and said, "You don't concur with your own statement. Your own rationale."

"Hard to do when you're . . . in love." She gave Mitcham a pointed look, because Scarlet was pretty sure that he was a man who'd do whatever he had to for Karina no matter the trouble she'd gotten herself into.

Michael snickered. "Don't anyone say anything about me not being loveable."

Sam gave a half snort.

Scarlet said, "Don't get all cocky on me, Michael."

"No promises, sweetheart." He leaned in and kissed her cheek. Murmured, "For the record, the feeling's mutual."

He stepped away.

Scarlet's heart flipped. Her gaze slid to Sam. He wore a deathly serious look that made tears prickle the backs of her eyes.

"I couldn't get to you fast enough when you were in that accident," he said. "Makes me want to keep you by my side twenty-four-seven so nothing will ever happen to you again."

She sucked in a sharp breath.

"And yeah," he added. "Feelin's mutual."

Mitcham handed over the handkerchief from his impeccably tailored navy-colored suit as fat drops rolled down her cheeks. She told him, "I know what I have to do, but I also wanted to give you and Karina a little more time."

"We appreciate that. And I suspected as much. So did she." He inhaled deeply. Exhaled slowly. "Which is why she turned herself in."

Scarlet's eyes popped. *"What?"*

"She wanted to do it first thing this morning, so that you wouldn't have to. Out of respect for Michael and Sam . . . and the fact that my wife genuinely likes you. But then she feared if she was too hasty it might cause problems for you. So she waited. We heard nothing from the insurance agency, and that was when she decided it had to be done. I'm here right now so that you know and can make your own calls. Explain you were detained. Whatever. Bottom line is that Karina didn't want you to be the one to break the news that Sam's mother, Michael's stepmother, committed a crime."

Scarlet sank into a chair. Not just because her legs were so sore, but holy hell, she hadn't seen this coming. And maybe it didn't exonerate her completely—since she'd wholeheartedly gone after the Vandenbergs when it came to this case. But Karina had just spared her a world of hurt. She'd made a huge sacrifice for Scarlet.

"I owe her for that one."

"You don't," Mitcham assured her. "We owe you our gratitude for giving us some time to work through how we're going to make amends. Talk to my legal and PR teams. Figure out what direction we'll take when it comes to Wyatt Hill and Dylan Reed. We want to go directly to the FBI. Be completely transparent. Hopefully keep Wyatt in prison and make damn sure Dylan doesn't get away with what he did to you, Miss Drake."

She lifted her head from where she'd been staring at the handkerchief in her lap. Told him, "That's commendable. Thank you, Mr. Vandenberg."

He gave a slight nod and said, "You might want to think about calling me Mitcham."

She let out a semi-hysterical laugh. "And he has a sense of humor." She wiped away the last of her tears and said, "Please call me Scarlet, Mitcham."

"Of course." His attention shifted to Michael. He said, "I know we've had our differences. I never explained this before, but one of the reasons I made it so that you didn't have access to your trust fund, or you to yours, Sam," he said as he acknowledged his stepson, "is because I wanted you to build your own lives. No rules, no boundaries. But I also wanted to ensure that those fortunes were never sacrificed for the wrong causes. Handsome young men with access to family money can unwittingly invite false affection into their lives. I've been lucky. I've had two great loves. I wanted both of you to find someone who possesses as much scruples as she does beauty. Someone who will love you for what you've achieved. For who you are as a person, not for your last name. Someone worthy of you."

"Would it have killed you to tell us that when we were sixteen?" Michael quipped.

Mitcham shrugged a broad shoulder. "I'm not so sure you would have grasped the concept back then. But today . . . well. I'm not going to lie and say I fully understand what's going on with the three of you or how it's all going to pan out, but I can't dispute that you do seem to work as a cohesive unit. And that's what matters most."

Scarlet stood. "Sorry it's so unconventional. But make no mistake. I do love your sons. And it has nothing to do with money or status. Well . . . there is the matter of a puppy, but that's another story."

Sam smirked.

Scarlet said, "I don't want to crush this family. I want it to thrive. And if there's anything I can do to help Karina, I'll do it. I knows she's earnest about paying her debt to the insurance company and society, and I'm behind her one hundred percent."

"She'll be pleased to hear that. Now," Mitcham said. "I have to get back to her. She's put on a brave face, as always, but now that I know the full extent of her struggles, I want to make sure she's no longer battling them alone."

He turned to go.

Michael called out, "Dad . . . !"

Mitcham glanced over his shoulder.

Michael grinned. And simply said, "Thank you."

Mitcham nodded once more. Then left.

Scarlet had no doubt that Michael's note of gratitude was for Mitcham finally coming around and expressing himself. Not keeping all of his thoughts and emotions to himself for Michael to guess at.

She hugged him tight. "It's crazy to say this because of what Karina faces, but this family is taking a positive turn in the right direction."

"You do have a way of finding the upside."

She released him and walked into Sam's embrace. "I meant what I said," she told him. "I'll do whatever I can to help her in this situation."

"I know. But remember . . . it's not your burden or your fault, darlin'."

"I just want this all to work out."

"Me and Michael, too. Don't doubt that." Sam pulled away and stared her in the eyes. "I do love you."

She smiled. Kissed him.

Michael joined them. "Goes for me, too."

"Because it would torture you so to say the actual words," she jested.

He laughed. "Fine. I love you, Scarlet Drake."

"Hmm." She kissed him.

He let out a hearty laugh. "Now who's the pain in the ass?"

She wrapped her arms around his neck and said, "I love you, too, Michael Vandenberg."

"Now, about our weekend in Montana?" Sam prompted.

Scarlet told them, "I'm all in."

Michael grunted. "Really, Montana? Why don't we just stay here in the city?"

"Because Sam has work to do. Competitions to prepare for. And I want to watch."

"Figures."

"Stop grumbling," she chided Michael as she untangled herself from him. "We've spent plenty of time in New York. It's only fair to make the rounds."

"If it's what you want," he conceded, albeit reluctantly. "I'll have my assistant arrange everything."

"Aw, look at you," Scarlet teased as she gazed into his smoky eyes, "compromising."

He tapped the tip of her nose with his finger and told her, "Don't make me regret this."

"Brother," Sam said, "you have a lot to learn about women."

"Particularly how willing this one is to reward you for good behavior." Scarlet's lips glided over Michael's. Then she nipped at the corner of his mouth. "So play nice."

"Only for you."

"That's all I'm asking."

"Well," Sam said, pleased. "Montana it is."

EPILOGUE

Three months later . . .

"Girlfriend," Jewel said with a lilt in her tone, "you have that ménage à trois glow going on."

Scarlet grinned mischievously. "You would recognize it. You both see it in the mirror every day." She nudged Bayli with her shoulder.

"Loving every minute of it," Bayli concurred.

This beautiful spring evening, they were on the patio of Bristol's in River Cross. The restaurant was Christian and Rory's flagship establishment and a favorite of locals and tourists to the wine country alike. An apropos spot for a celebratory dinner that was about to start with a champagne toast.

Michael had secured a deal with Christian and Rory to open rooftop restaurants in his major department stores, and Bayli and Rory were plotting how they'd incorporate the creation of the eateries and grand openings into their food/travel show.

Jewel would be contributing wine to Michael's extensive list from the Catalano winery and—in the future—from hers, Rogen's, and Vin's vineyard. Rogen's family, the Angelinis, would offer their finest cognacs.

Scarlet loved how intertwined they were all becoming. She'd learned how fulfilling it was to be tangled in her two lovers' lives, and having their friends around them enhanced the overall experience, helping to seal some of the cracks and crevices split wide open by the deaths of her parents.

The girls joined their men and Sam handed Scarlet a crystal flute.

Michael told the group, "To new friends and partnerships, both professional and"—he stole a glance toward Scarlet and Sam—"personal." He winked. And Scarlet's heart soared.

They all raised their glasses and said in unison, *"Salut!"*

The first two books in the
sexy new billionaire ménage
Lovers' Triangle series by
CALISTA FOX

THE BILLIONAIRES
Available April 2017

THE BILLIONAIRES:
THE BOSSES
Available September 2017

 St. Martin's Griffin

"There's HOT.
And then there's
CALISTA FOX."
—Erin Quinn,
New York Times Bestselling Author

READ THE ENTIRE
BURNED DEEP TRILOGY

AVAILABLE WHERE BOOKS ARE SOLD

 St. Martin's Griffin